DEADLY CONFRONTATION

The toadies surged forward. One gorilla grabbed Sten from behind, but Sten wriggled an arm free and swung a fist up and back, thumb extended.

With a howl, both hands over his right eye, the tough dropped Sten. Sten spun, his foot breaking the bully's neck.

"Get him, you clots!" the Foreman thundered.

Sten dropped his right hand limply. Curled his fingers. A crystal knife appeared. Cold. Comforting.

The man with the steel bar reached Sten first, swinging, but Sten stepped inside the swing and cut his throat.

The blademan feinted once as Sten spun, then lunged for Sten's stomach. Sten overhanded a block, and the man's arm thudded to the deck.

The Foreman turned and ran, but Sten caught up with him just before the shift-room . . .

STEN

ALLAN COLE
and CHRIS BUNCH

A Del Rey Book

BALLANTINE BOOKS • NEW YORK

A Del Rey Book
Published by Ballantine Books

Library of Congress Catalog Card Number: 82-90501

ISBN 0-345-28503-4

Manufactured in the United States of America

First Edition: September 1982

Cover art by Ralph Brillhart

DEDICATED TO
Jason and Alissa
and
the late Robert Willey

BOOK ONE

VULCAN

CHAPTER ONE

DEATH CAME QUIETLY to The Row.

The suit stank. The Tech inside it stared out through the scratched port at the pipe that looped around the outside of the recreation dome and muttered a string of curses that would've peeled a deep-space trader.

What he wanted more than anything was a tall cool narcobeer to kill the hangover drumrolls in his head. The one thing he didn't want, he knew, was to be hanging outside Vulcan, staring at a one-centimeter alloy pipe that wouldn't hook up.

He clamped his waldos on the flange, set the torque rating by feel, and tried another round of obscenities, this time including his supervisor and all the stinking Migs enjoying themselves one meter and a world away from him.

Done. He retracted the waldos and slammed the suit's tiny drive unit into life. Not only was his supervisor a clot who was an exjoyboy, but he was also going to get stuck for the first six rounds. The Tech shut down his ground-zeroed brain and rocketed numbly for the lock.

Of course, he'd missed the proper torque setting. If the pipe hadn't been carrying fluorine, under high pressure, the error wouldn't have made any difference.

The overstressed fitting cracked, and raw fluorine gradually ate its way through, for several shifts spraying harmlessly into space. But, as the fracture widened, the spray boiled directly against the outer skin of The Row, through the insulation and, eventually, the inner skin.

At first the hole was pin-size. The initial pressure drop inside the dome wasn't even enough to kick over the monitors high overhead in The Row's roof control capsule.

The Row could've been a red-light district on any of a million pioneer planets—Company joygirls and boys picked their way through the Mig crowds, looking for the Migrant-Unskilled who still had some credits left on his card.

Long rows of gambling computers hooted enticements at the passing workers and emitted little machine chuckles when another mark was suckered into a game.

The Row was the Company-provided recreational center, set up with the Migs' "best interests" at heart. "A partying Mig is a happy Mig," a Company psychologist had once said. He didn't add—or need to—that a partying Mig was also one who was spending credits, and generally into the red. Each loss meant hours added to the worker's contract.

Which was why, in spite of the music and the laughter, The Row felt grim and gray.

Two beefy Sociopatrolmen lounged outside The Row's entrance. The older patrolman nodded at three boisterous Migs as they weaved from one bibshop to another, then turned to his partner. "If ya gonna twitch every time somebody looks at ya, bud, pretty soon one of these Migs is gonna wanna know what you'll do if they get *real* rowdy."

The new probationary touched his stun rod. "And I'd like to show them."

The older man sighed, then stared off down the corridor. "Oh-oh. Trouble."

His partner nearly jumped out of his uniform. "Where? Where?"

The older man pointed. Stepping off the slideway and heading for The Row was Amos Sten. The other man started to laugh at the short, middle-aged Mig, and then noticed the muscles hunching Amos' neck. And the size of his wrists and hammer fists.

Then the senior patrolman sighed in relief and leaned back against the I-beam.

"It's okay, kid. He's got his family with him."

A tired-looking woman and two children hurried off the slideway to Amos.

"What the hell," the young man said, "that midget don't look so tough to me."

"You don't know Amos. If you did, you would've soaked your jock—specially if Amos was on the prowl for a little fight to cheer him up some."

The four Migs each touched small white rectangles against a pickup and Vulcan's central computer logged the movement of MIG STEN, AMOS; MIG STEN, FREED; MIG-DEPENDENT STEN, AHD; MIG-DEPENDENT STEN, JOHS into The Row.

As the Sten family passed the two patrolmen, the older man smiled and tipped Amos a nod. His partner just glared. Amos ignored them and hustled his family toward the livee entrance.

"Mig likes to fight, huh? That ain't whatcha call Company-approved social mannerisms."

"Son, we busted the head of every Mig who beefed one on The Row, there'd be a labor shortage."

"Maybe we ought to take him down some."

"You think you're the man who could do it?"

The young patrolman nodded. "Why not? Catch him back of a narco joint and thump him some."

The older man smiled, and touched a long and livid scar on his right arm. "It's been tried. By some better. But maybe I'm wrong. Maybe you're the one who can do something. But you best remember. Amos isn't any old Mig."

"What's so different about him?"

The patrolman suddenly tired of his new partner and the whole conversation. "Where he comes from, they eat little boys like you for breakfast."

The young man bristled and started to glower. Then he remembered that even without the potgut his senior still had about twenty kilos and fifteen years on him. He spun and turned the glower on an old lady who was weaving happily out of The Row. She looked at him, gummed a grin and spat neatly between the probationary's legs, onto the deck. "Clot Migs!"

Amos slid his card through the livee's pickup, and the computer automatically added an hour to Amos' work contract. The four of them walked into the lobby, and Amos looked around.

"Don't see the boy."

"Karl said school had him on an extra shift," his wife, Freed, reminded him.

Amos shrugged.

"He ain't missin' much. Guy down the line was here last offshift. Says the first show's some clot about how some Exec falls for a joygirl an' takes her to live in The Eye with him."

Music blared from inside the theater.

"C'mon, dad, let's go."

Amos followed his family into the showroom.

Sten hurriedly tapped computer keys, then hit the JOB INPUT tab. The screen blared, then went gray-blank. Sten winced. He'd never finish in time to meet his family. The school's ancient computer system just wasn't up to the number of students carded in for his class shift.

Sten glanced around the room. No one was watching. He hit BASIC FUNCTION, then a quick sequence of keys. Sten had found a way to tap into one reasoning bank of the central computer. Against school procedure, for sure. But Sten, like any other seventeen-year-old, was willing to let tomorrow's hassles hassle tomorrow.

With the patch complete, he fed in his task card. And groaned, as his assignment swam up onto the screen. It was a cybrolathe exercise, making L-beams.

It would take forever to make the welds, and he figured that the mandated technique, obsolete even by the school's standards, created a stressline three microns off the joining.

Then Sten grinned. He was already In Violation . . .

He drew two alloy-steel bars on the screen with his lightpen, then altered the input function to JOB PROGRAM. Then he switched the pen's function to WELD. A few quick motions, and somewhere on Vulcan, two metal bars were nailed together.

Or maybe it was a computer-only exercise.

Sten waited in agony as the computer screen blanked. Finally the computer lit up and scrolled PROJECT COMPLETED SATISFACTORILY. He was finished. Sten's fingers flashed as he cut out of the illegal patch, plugged back into the school's computer, which was just beginning to flicker wearily back into WAITING PROGRAM, input the PROJECT COMPLETED SATISFACTORILY from his terminal's memory, shut down, and then he was up and running for the door.

"Frankly, gentlemen," Baron Thoresen said, "I care less about the R and D program's conflicting with some imagined ethical rule of the Empire than our own Company's health."

It had started as a routine meeting of the Company's board of directors, those half dozen beings who controlled almost a billion lives. Then old Lester had so very casually asked his question.

Thoresen stood suddenly and began pacing up and down. The huge director's bulk held the board's attention as much as his rumbling voice and authority.

"If that sounds unpatriotic, I'm sorry. I'm a businessman, not a diplomat. Like my grandfather before me, all I believe in is our Company."

Only one man was unmoved. Lester. Trust an old thief, the Baron thought. He's already made his, so now he can afford to be ethical.

"Very impressive," Lester said. "But we—the board of directors—didn't ask about your dedication. We asked about your expenditures on Bravo Project. You have refused to tell us the nature of your experimentation, and yet you keep returning for additional funding. I merely inquired, since if there were any military possibility we might secure an assistance grant from one or another of the Imperial foundations."

The Baron looked at Lester thoughtfully but unworried. Thoresen was, after all, the man with the cards But he knew better than to give the crafty old infighter the least opening. And Thoresen knew better than to try threats. Lester was too scarred to know the meaning of fear.

"I appreciate your input. And your concern about the necessary expenditures. However, this project is too important to our future to risk a leak."

"Do I sense distrust?" Lester asked.

"Not of you, gentlemen. Don't be absurd. But if our competition learned of Bravo Project's goal, not even my close ties with the Emperor would keep them from stealing it—and ruining us."

"Even if it did leak," another board member tried, "there would still be an option. We could possibly affect their supplies of AM_2."

"Using your close, personal ties with the Emperor, of course," Lester put in smoothly.

The Baron smiled thinly.

"Even I would not presume that much on friendship. AM_2 is the energy on which the Empire and the Emperor thrive. No one else."

Silence. Even from Lester. The ghost of the Eternal Emperor closed the conversation. The Baron glanced around, then deliberately dropped his voice to a dry, boring level.

"With no further comments, I'll mark the increased funding as approved. Now, to a simpler matter. We're fortunate in that our maintenance expenditures on Vulcan's port facilities have dropped by a full fifteen percent. This includes not only internal mooring facilities, but the presealed container facility. But I'm still not satisfied. It would be far better if . . ."

*   *   *

Amos' eyes flickered open as the livee ended and the lights came up. As near as he could gather, the Exec and his joygirl, after they'd moved to The Eye, had gone off to some pioneer planet and been attacked by something or other.

He yawned. Amos didn't think much of livees, but a quiet nap came in handy every now and then.

Ahd nudged him. "That's what I wanna be when I grow up. An Exec."

Amos stirred and woke up all the way. "Why is that, boy?"

" 'Cause they get adventures and money and medals and . . . and . . . and all my friends wanna be Execs, too."

"You just get rid of that notion right now," Freed snapped. "Our kind don't mix with Execs."

The boy hung his head. Amos patted him. "It ain't that you're not good enough, son. Hell, any Sten is worth six of those cl—"

"Amos!"

"Sorry. People." Then Amos caught himself. "The hell. Callin' Execs clots ain't talkin' dirty. That's what they is. Anyway, Ahd, those Execs ain't heroes. They're the worst. They'd kill a person to meet a quota. And then cheat his family outa the death benefits. You becomin' an Exec wouldn't make me and your ma—or you—proud."

Then it was his little girl's turn.

"I wanna be a joygirl," she announced.

Amos buried his grin as he watched Freed jump about a meter and a half. He decided he'd let her handle that one.

Pressure finally split the pipe, and the escaping gas forced it directly against the hole it had punched through into The Row.

The first to die was an old Mig, who was leaning against the curving outer wall of the dome a few centimeters from the sudden hole in the skin. By the time he'd seen the fluorine burn away flesh and ribcage, leaving the pulsing redness of his lungs, he was already dead.

In The Row's control capsule, a group of bored Techs watched a carded-out Mig try to wheedle a joygirl into a reduced-rate party. One Tech offered odds. With no takers. Joygirls don't give bargains.

The pressure finally dropped below the danger threshold and alarms flared. No one flinched. Breakdowns and alarms were an every-shift occurrence on Vulcan.

The Chief Tech strolled casually over to the main computer. He tapped a few keys, silencing the *bong-bong-bong* and flashing lights of the alarms.

"Now, let's see what the glitch is."

His answer scrolled up swiftly on a monitor screen.

"Hmm. This is a little dicey. Take a look."

His assistant peered over the Tech's shoulder.

"Some kind of chemical leak into the dome. I'll narrow it some." The Tech tapped more computer keys, cutting a bit deeper into the information banks.

AIRLOSS INDICATED; PRESENCE OF CONTAMINANT; POTENTIAL LIFE JEOPARDY; REDLINE ALARM.

The Chief Tech finally reacted with something other than boredom.

"Plinking Maintenance and their damned pipe leaks. They think we've got nothing better to do than clean up after them. I've got a mind to input a report that'll singe every hair off their hairless—"

"Uh . . . sir?"

"Don't interfere with my tantrums. Whaddaya want?"

"Don't you think this should be repaired? In a hurry?"

"Yeah. Figure out where—half these damned sensors are broke or else somebody's poured beer in them. If I had a credit for every time . . ."

His voice trailed off as he traced the leak. Finally he narrowed the computer search down, pipe by pipe.

"Clot. We'll have to suit up to get to it. Runs over to that lab dome—*oh!*"

The diagram he was scrolling froze, and red letters began flashing over it: ANY INCIDENT CONNECTED TO BRAVO PROJECT TO BE ROUTED INSTANTLY TO THORESEN.

His assistant puzzled. "But why does it—" He stopped, realizing the Chief Tech was ignoring him.

"Clotting Execs. Make you check with them anytime you gotta take a . . ." He tapped for the registry, found Thoresen's code, hit the input button, and settled back to wait.

The Baron shook the hands of each of his fellow board members as they filed out. Asking about the health of their families. Mentioning dinner. Or commenting on the aptness of someone's suggestions. Until Lester.

"I appreciate your presence, Lester, more than you can imagine. Your wisdom is definitely a guiding influence on the course of—"

"Pretty good duck-and-away on my question, Thoresen. Couldn't do it better myself."

"But I was not avoiding anything, my good man. I was only—"

"Of course you were only. Save the stroking for these fools. You and I understand our positions more clearly."

"Stroking?"

"Forget it." Lester started past, then turned. "Of course you know this isn't personal, Thoresen. Like you, I have only the best interests of *our* Company at heart."

The Baron nodded. "I wouldn't expect anything else of you."

Thoresen watched the old man as he hobbled out. And decided that old thieves get foolish. What could be more personal than power?

He turned toward the source of a discreet buzz and pointed. Six shelves of what appeared to be antique books dropped away, allowing access to a computer panel.

He took three unhurried steps and touched the RESPONSE button. The Chief Tech floated into view. "We have a problem, sir, here in Rec Twenty-six."

The Baron nodded. "Report."

The Chief Tech punched keys, the screen split and the details of the leak into The Row scrolled down one side. The Baron took it in instantly. The computer projected that the deadly gas would fill the rec dome in fifteen minutes.

"Why don't you fix it, Technician?"

"Because the clotting computer keeps spitting 'Bravo Project, Bravo Project' at me," the Chief Tech snarled. "All I need is a go from you and I'll have this thing fixed in no time flat and no skin off anybody's—I'll have it fixed."

The Baron thought a moment.

"There's no approach to that leak by now except through the Bravo Project lab? Can't you just put a vacuum maintenance Tech out?"

"Not a chance. The pipe's so badly warped we'll have to chop it off at the source. Yessir. We'll have to get into the lab."

"Then I can't help you."

The Chief Tech froze.

"But—that leak won't stop at Rec Twenty-six. Clotting fluorine'll combine, and then eat anything except a glass wall."

"Then dump Twenty-six."

"But we've got almost fourteen hundred people—"

"You have your orders."

The Chief Tech stared at Thoresen. Suddenly nodded and keyed off.

The Baron sighed. He made a mental note to have Personnel up recruiting for the new unskilled-labor quotient. Then rolled the event around, to make sure he wasn't missing anything.

There was a security problem. The Chief Tech and, of course, his assistants. He could transfer the men, or, more simply— Thoresen wiped the problem out of his mind. His dinner menu was flashing on the screen.

The Chief Tech whistled tunelessly and slowly tapped a fingernail on the screen. His assistant hovered nearby.

"Uh, don't we have to . . ."

The Chief Tech looked at him, then decided not to say anything. He turned away from the terminal, and swiftly unlocked the bright red EMERGENCY PROCEDURES INPUT control panel.

Sten pyloned off an outraged Tech and hurtled down the corridor toward The Row's entrance, fumbling for his card. The young Sociopatrolman blocked his entrance.

"I saw that, boy."

"Saw what?"

"What you did to that Tech. Don't you know about your betters?"

"Gee, sir, he was slipping. Somebody must have spilled something on the slideway. I guess it's a long way to see what exactly happened. Especially for an older man. Sir." He looked innocent.

The younger patrolman brought an arm back, but his partner caught his wrist. "Don't bother. That's Sten's boy."

"We still oughta . . . oh, go ahead, Mig. Go on in."

"Thank you, sir."

Sten stepped up to the gate and held his card to the pickup.

"Keep going like you are, boy, and you know what'll happen?"

Sten waited.

"You'll run away. To the Delinqs. And then we'll go huntin' you. You know what happens when we rat those Delinqs out? We brainburn 'em."

The patrolman grinned.

"They're real cute, then. Sometimes they let us have the girls for a few shifts . . . before they put them out on the slideways."

. Hydraulics screamed suddenly, and the dome seal-off doors crashed across the entrance. Sten fell back out of the way, going down.

He looked at the two patrolmen. Started to say something . . . then followed their eyes to the flashing red lights over the entrance:

ENTRANCE SEALED . . . EMERGENCY . . . EMERGENCY . . .

He slowly picked himself up. "My parents," Sten said numbly. "They're inside!"

And then he was battering at the solid steel doors until the older patrolman pulled him away.

Explosive bolts fired around six of the dome panels. The tiny *snaps* were lost in the typhoon roar of air blasting out into space.

Almost in slow motion, the escaping hurricane caught the shanty cubicles of The Row, and the people in them, and spat them through the holes into blackness.

And then the sudden wind died.

What remained of buildings, furniture, and the stuff of life drifted in the cold gleam of the faraway sun. Along with the dry, shattered husks of 1,385 human beings.

Inside the empty dome that had been The Row, the Chief Tech stared out the port of the control capsule. His assistant got up from his board, walked over and put his hand on the Tech's arm.

"Come on. They were only Migs."

The Chief Tech took a deep breath.

"Yeah. You're right. That's all they were."

CHAPTER TWO

IMAGINE VULCAN.

A junkyard, hanging in blackness and glare. Its center a collection of barrels, mushrooms, tubes, and blocks stacked haphazardly by an idiot child.

Imagine the artificial world of Vulcan, the megabillion-credit heart of the Company. The ultimate null-environment machine shop and factory world.

The Company's oreships streamed endlessly toward Vulcan with raw materials. Refining, manufacture, sub- and in many cases final assembly of products was completed, and the Company's freighters delivered to half the galaxy. To an empire founded on a mercantile enterprise, the monstrous vertical trust was completely acceptable.

Six hundred years before, Thoresen's grandfather had been encouraged by the Eternal Emperor to build Vulcan. His encouragement included a special C-class tankerload of Antimatter$_2$, the energy source that had opened the galaxy to man.

Work began with the construction of the eighty-by-sixteen-kilometer tapered cylinder that was to house the administrative and support systems for the new world.

Drive mechanisms moved that core through twenty light-years, to position it in a dead but mineral-rich system.

Complete factories, so many enormous barrels, had been prefabricated in still other systems and then plugged into the core world. With them went the myriad life-support systems, from living quarters to hydroponics to recreational facilities.

The computer projections made the then unnamed artificial world seem impressive: a looming ultraefficient colossus for the most efficient exploitation of workers and materials. What the computer never allowed for was man.

Over the years, it frequently was simpler to shut down a factory unit after product-completion rather than to rebuild it. Other, newer factories, barracks, and support domes were jammed into place as needed. In a world where gravity was controlled by McLean generators, up and down were matters of convenience only. In two hundred years, Vulcan resembled a metal sculpture that might have been titled *Junk in Search of a Welder*.

Eventually, atop the catch-as-catch-can collection of metal The Eye was mounted—Company headquarters linked to the original cylinder core. The sixteen-kilometer-wide mushroom was, in Sten's time, only two hundred years old, added after the Company centralized.

Below The Eye was the cargo loading area, generally reserved for the Company's own ships. Independent traders docked offworld and were forced to accept the additional costs of cargo and passenger transfer by Company space-lighter.

Under the dock was the visitors' dome. A normal, wide-open port, except that every credit spent by a trader or one of his crew went directly into the Company's accounts.

The visitors' dome was as far South as offworlders were permitted. The Company very definitely didn't want anyone else dealing with—or even meeting—their workers.

Vague rumors floated around the galaxy about Vulcan. But there had never been an Imperial Rights Commission for Vulcan. Because the Company produced.

The enormous juggernaut delivered exactly what the

Empire needed for centuries. And the Company's internal security had kept its sector very quiet.

The Eternal Emperor was grateful. So grateful that he had named Thoresen's grandfather to the nobility. And the Company ground on.

Any juggernaut will continue to roll strictly on inertia, whether it is the Persian Empire or General Motors of the ancients, or the sprawling Conglomerate of more recent history. For a while. If anyone noticed in Sten's time that the Company hadn't pioneered any manufacturing techniques in a hundred years, or that innovation or invention was discouraged by the Company's personnel department, it hadn't been brought to the Baron's attention.

Even if anyone had been brave enough or foolish enough to do so, it wasn't necessary. Baron Thoresen was haunted by the fact that what his grandfather created was slowly crumbling beneath him. He blamed it on his father, a cowering toady who had allowed bureaucrats to supplant the engineers. But even if the third Thoresen had been a man of imagination, it still would probably have been impossible to bring under control the many-headed monster the elder Thoresens had created.

The Baron had grown up with the raw courage and fascination for blood-combat—physical or social—of his grandfather, but none of the old man's innate honesty. When his father suddenly disappeared offworld—never to be seen again—there was no question that the young man would head the Company's board of directors.

Now, he was determined to revitalize what his grandfather had begun. But not by turning the Company upside down and shaking it out. Thoresen wanted much more than that. He was obsessed with the idea of a kendo masterstroke.

Bravo Project.

And now it was only a few years from fruition.

Under the Baron was his board, and the lesser Executives. Living and working entirely in The Eye, they were held to the Company not only by iron-clad contracts and high pay but that sweetest of all perks—almost unlimited power.

Under the Execs were the Technicians—highly skilled, well-treated specialists. Their contracts ran for five to ten years.

When his contract expired, a Tech could return home a rich man, to set up his own business—with the Company, of course, holding exclusive distribution rights to any new products he might have developed—or to retire.

For the Exec or Tech, Vulcan was very close to an industrial heaven.

For the Migs, it was hell.

It's significant that the winner of the Company's Name-Our-Planet contest, a bright Migrant-Unskilled worker, had used the prize money to buy out his contract and passage out as far from Vulcan as possible.

Fellahin, oakie, wetback—there will always be wandering laborers to perform scutwork. But just as the Egyptian fellah would marvel at the mechanical ingenuity of the Joads, so the twentieth-century assembly-line grunt would be awed by the likes of Amos Sten.

For Amos, one world could never be enough. Doing whatever it took for a full belly, a liter of gutbuster, and a ticket offworld, he was the man to fix your omni, get your obsolete harvester to working, or hump your new bot up six flights of stairs.

And then move on.

His wife, Freed, was a backwater farm-world kid with the same lust to see what the next planetfall brought. Eventually, they guessed, they'd find a world to settle on. One where there weren't too many people, and a man and a woman wouldn't have to sweat for someone else's business. Until they found it, though, any place was better than what they'd already seen.

Until Vulcan.

The recruiter's pitch sounded ideal.

Twenty-five thousand credits a year for him. Plus endless bonuses for a man of his talents. Even a contract for ten thousand a year for Freed. And a chance to work on the galaxy's most advanced tools.

And the recruiter hadn't lied.

Amos' mill was far more sophisticated than any machine he'd ever seen. Three billets of three different metals were fed into the machine. They were simultaneously milled and electronically bonded. Allowable tolerances for that bearing—it took Amos ten years to find out what he was building—was to one millionth of a millimeter, plus or minus one thousand millionth.

And Amos' title was master machinist.

But he only had one job—to sweep up burrs the mill spun out of its waste orifices that the dump tubes missed. Everything else was automatic, regulated by a computer half a world away.

The salaries weren't a lie either. But the recruiter hadn't mentioned that a set of coveralls cost a hundred credits, soymeat ten a portion, or the rent on their three barracks rooms was one thousand credits a month.

The time-to-expiration date on their contracts got further away, while Amos and Freed tried to figure a way out. And there were the children. Unplanned, but welcome. Children were encouraged by the Company. The next generation's labor pool, without the expense of recruiting and transportation.

Amos and Freed fought the Company's conditioning processes. But it was hard to explain what open skies and walking an unknown road meant to someone who grew up with curving gray domes and slideways.

Freed, after a long running battle with Amos, had extended her contract six months for a wall-size muraliv of a snowy landscape on a frontier world.

Almost eight months passed before the snow stopped drifting down on that lonely cluster of domes, and the door, with the warm, cheery fire behind it, stopped swinging open to greet the returning worker.

The mural meant more to Amos and Freed than it did to Sten. Even though young Karl didn't have the slightest idea of what it was like to live without a wall in near-touching distance, he'd already learned that the only goal in his life, no matter what it took, was to get off Vulcan.

CHAPTER THREE

"YOU GOTTA REMEMBER, boy, a bear's how you look at him."

"Dad, what's a bear?"

"You know. Like the Imperial Guard uses to scout with. You saw one in that viddie."

"Oh, yeah. It looks like the Counselor."

"A little—only it's a mite hairier and not so dumb. Anyway, when you're in a scoutcar, looking down at that bear, he don't look so bad. But when that bear's standing over you . . ."

"I don't understand."

"That bear's like Vulcan. If you was up The Eye, it'd probably look pretty good. But when you're a Mig, down here . . ."

Amos Sten nodded and poured himself another half liter of narcobeer.

"All you got to remember in a bear fight, Karl, is you don't *ever* want to be second. Most of all, you don't want to get caught by that bear in the first place."

That was a lesson Sten had already learned. Through Elmore. Elmore was an old Mig who had the solo apartment at the end of the corridor. But most of the off-shift time Elmore was in the children's play area telling stories.

They were the never true, always wonderful part of the

21

oral tradition that industrial peasants from a thousand worlds had brought to Vulcan, making their own underground tradition.

The Drop Settling of Ardmore. The Ghost Ship of Capella. The Farmer Who Became King.

And Vulcan's own legends. *The Delinqs Who Saved the Company.* The eerie, whispered stories of the warehouses and factory domes that were generations-unused by humans . . . but still had something living and moving in them.

Sten's favorite was the one Elmore told least often—about how, one day, things would change. How someone would come from another world, and lead the Migs up, into The Eye. A day of reckoning when the air cycling system would spew the blood of the Execs. The best was the last, when Elmore said slowly that the man who would lead the Migs would be a Mig himself.

The corridor's parents never minded Elmore. He kept the kids out of their hair, and, very grateful, they all chipped in to card Elmore some kind of present every Founder's Day. If any of them knew most of Elmore's stories were anti-Company, they never said anything. Nor would they have cared.

The end was inevitable. Some kid talked around the wrong person. Like the Counselor.

One off-shift, Elmore didn't return. Everyone wondered what had happened. But the topic became boring, and everyone forgot.

Not Sten. He saw Elmore again, on The Row. The man was a shambling hulk, stumbling behind a streetcleaning machine. He paused beside Sten and looked down at the boy.

Elmore's mouth opened, and he tried to speak. But his tongue lolled helplessly, and his speech was guttural moans. The machine whistled, and Elmore obediently turned and stumbled away after it. The word crawled out of Sten's mind: brainburn.

He told his father about what he'd seen. Amos grimaced. "That's the secret you gotta learn, boy. You got to zig when they zag."

"What'd I tell you about zigging, son?"

"I couldn't, pa. There were four of them, and they was all bigger than me."

"Too bad, boy. But there's gonna be a lot of things bigger than you come along. How you gonna handle this one?"

Sten thought for a minute.

"They won't look nigh as big from the back, would they, dad?"

"That's a terrible thought, Karl. Terrible. Especially since it's true."

Sten got up.

"Where you headed?"

"I'm . . . gonna go play."

"Naw. First you're gonna let that black eye go away. And let people forget."

Two weeks later, one of the four boys was shinnying up a rope in exercise period when it broke and dropped him twenty feet to the steel deck.

Three days after that, two more of the group were exploring an unfinished corridor. It was probably just their bad luck to be standing under a wallslab when the fasteners broke. After the boys were released from the hospital, the Counselor reprimanded their parents.

The leader of Sten's attackers was just as unfortunate. Out after curfew, he was jumped from behind and battered into unconsciousness. After an investigation, the Counselor said it had probably been a Delinq—a member of one of the wild gangs that roamed the abandoned sectors of Vulcan, one step ahead of brainburn.

Despite the explanations, Sten was left pretty much alone after that.

"Karl. Gotta have a word with you."

"Uh . . . yeah, dad?"

"Me and the other folks been to a meeting with the Counselor."

"Oh."

"You wonderin' what he wanted?"

"Yeah. Oh, yeah. Sure I am."

"Don't have any idea, do you?"

"Nossir."

"Didn't think you did. Seems that some Mig's kid went and invented something. Some kinda spray. You don't know anything about that, do you, boy?"

"Nossir."

"Uh-huh. This spray smells just like . . . well, like when the sewage recycler blew up down on Corridor Eighteen—forty-five. Remember that?"

"Yessir."

"Kinda quiet tonight, aren't we? Anyway. So somebody went and sprayed this on the Counselor and four of those aides he's got. Sprayed on their pants where they sit down. Is that a laugh you're hidin'?"

"Nossir."

"Didn't think so. The Counselor wanted all of us parents to find out who's got themselves a antisocial kid and turn him in."

"What're you gonna do, dad?"

"Already done it. Dropped by the microfiles. Your ma talked to the librarian, while I sort of looked at who's been reading books on chemistry."

"Oh."

"Yeah. Oh. Unfortunately, I went and forgot to give them records back."

Sten didn't say anything.

"My pa told me once—before you go setting a man's foot on fire, you best make sure there's at least six other people with torches in their tool kits. You follow what I mean?"

"Yessir."

"Thought you might."

* * *

One of the best times was what Sten always thought of as the Off-shift Xypaca.

Xypacas were incredibly nasty little carnivores that had been discovered on some hellworld by the Company's probeships. Nobody knew why the crew had brought back specimens of the psychopathic little reptiles. But they did.

Measuring barely twenty centimeters in height, the Xypaca had a willingness to use its claws and teeth on anything up to a hundred times its own height. One of Sten's teachers, originally from Prime World, said Xypacas looked like minityrannosaurs, whatever they were.

If the Xypaca hated almost everything equally, it had a special hard place in what passed for its heart for its own species. Except during the brief breeding cycle, the Xypaca loved nothing more than tearing its fellow Xypaca apart. Which made them ideal pit-fighting animals.

Amos had just been rewarded by the Company for figuring out his mill would run an extra thousand hours between servicing if the clearing exhaust didn't exit just above the computer's cooling intake. With great ceremony, they knocked a full year off of Amos' contract.

Amos, always one for the grand parlay, used that year's credit to buy a Xypaca.

Sten hated the reptile from the first moment, when a lightninglike snap of its jaws almost took off his little finger.

So Amos explained it to him. "I ain't real fond of that critter either. I don't like the way it looks, the way it smells or the way it eats. But it's gonna be our ticket off of Vulcan."

His spiel was convincing. Amos planned to fight his Xypaca in small-time preliminary fights only, betting light. "We win small—a month off the contract here, a week there. But sooner or later it'll be our ticket out of here." Even Sten's mother was convinced there was something to this latest of Amos' dreams.

And Sten, by fifteen, wanted off Vulcan more than anything else he could imagine. So he fed the Xypaca cheerfully, lived with its rank smell, and tried not to yell too loudly when he was a little slow in getting his hand out of its cage after feeding.

And it seemed, for a while, as if Amos' big plan was going to work. Until the night the Counselor showed up at the fights, held in an unused corridor a few rows away.

Sten was carrying the Xypaca's cage into the arena, following Amos.

From across the ring, the Counselor spotted them and hurried around. "Well, Amos," he said heartily, "didn't know you were a Xy-man."

Amos nodded warily.

The Counselor inspected the hissing brute under Sten's arm. "Looks like a fine animal you've got there, Amos. What say we pitch it against mine in the first match?"

Sten looked across the ring and saw the obese, oversized Xypaca one of the Counselor's toadies was handling. "Dad," he said. "We can't. It'll—"

The Counselor frowned at Sten.

"You letting your boy decide what you do now, Amos?"

Amos shook his head.

"Well then. We'll show them we're the best sportsmen of all. Show the other corridors that we're so bored with the lizards they've got that we'd rather fight our own, right?"

He waited. Amos took several deep breaths. "I guess you haven't decided about the transfers over to the wire mill yet, have you, sir?" he finally asked.

The Counselor smiled. "Exactly."

Even Sten knew that handling the mile-long coils of white-hot metal was the deadliest job on Amos' shift.

"We—me and my boy—we'd be proud to fight your Xy, Mister Counselor."

"Fine, fine," the Counselor said. "Let's give them a real good show."

He hurried back around the makeshift ring.

"Dad," Sten managed, "his Xy—it's twice the size of ours. We don't stand a chance."

Amos nodded. "Sure looks that way, don't it? But you remember what I told you, time back, about not handling

things the way people expect you to? Well—you take my
card. Nip on out to that soystand, and buy all you can
hide under your tunic."

Sten grabbed his father's card and wriggled off through
the crowd.

The Counselor was too busy bragging to his cronies
about what his Xy would do to notice Sten shoving strands
of raw soy into the large Xypaca's cage.

After a few moments of haggling, bragging, and bet-
placing, the Xy cages were brought into the ring, tipped
over, and quickly opened.

The Counselor's thoroughly glutted Xypaca stumbled
from his cage, yawned once, and curled up to go to sleep.
By the time he was jolted awake, Amos' Xypaca had him
half digested.

There was a dead silence around the ring. Amos looked
as humble as he knew how. "Yessir. You were right, sir.
We showed them we're sure the best sportsmen, didn't we.
Sir?"

The Counselor said nothing. Just turned and pushed his
way through the crowd.

After that, Amos couldn't get a fight for his Xypaca in
any match at any odds. Nobody mourned that much when
the Xypaca died—along with all the others—after a month
or two. Lack of necessary trace elements, somebody said.

By that time, Amos was already busy figuring out another scheme to get himself and his family off Vulcan.

He was still scheming when Thoresen dumped the air
on The Row.

CHAPTER FOUR

THE BARON'S WORDS rolled and bounced around the high-roofed tube junction. Sten could pick out an occasional phrase:

"Brave souls . . . Vulcan pioneers . . . died for the good of the Company . . . names not to be forgotten . . . our thirty million citizens will always remember . . ."

Sten still felt numb.

A citizen, coming off shift, elbowed his way through the crowd of about fifty mourning Migs, scowling. Then he realized what was going on. He pulled what he hoped was a sorrowful look in his face and ducked down a tube opening.

Sten didn't notice.

He was staring up at the roof, at the many-times-magnified picture of the Baron projected on the ceiling. The man stood in his garden, wearing the flowing robes that Execs put on for ceremonial occasions.

The Baron had carefully picked his clothes for the funeral ceremony. He thought the Migs would be impressed and touched by his concern. To Sten he was nothing more than a beefier, more hypocritical version of the Counselor.

Sten had made it through the first week . . . survived the shock. Still, his mind kept fingering the loss, like an amputee who can ghost-feel a limb he no longer owns.

Sten had holed up in the apartment for most of the time. At intervals the delivery flap had clicked and every now and then he'd walked over and eaten something from the pneumatiqued trays of food.

Sten had even been duly grateful to the Company for leaving him alone. He didn't realize until years later that the Company was just following the procedure outlined in "Industrial Accidents (Fatal), Treatment of Surviving Relatives of."

From the quickly vidded expressions of sympathy from Amos' and Freed's supervisors and the children's teachers to the Sympathy Wake Credits good at the nearest rec center, the process of channeling the grief of the bereaved was all very well calculated. Especially the isolation—the last thing the Company wanted was a mourning relative haunting the corridors, reminding people just how thin was the margin between life and death in their artificial, profit-run world.

The Baron's booming words suddenly were nothing but noise to Sten. He turned away. Someone fell in beside him. Sten turned his head, and then froze. It was the Counselor.

"Moving ceremony," the man said. "Touching. Quite touching."

He motioned Sten toward a slideway bibshop and into a chair. The Counselor pushed his card into a slot and punched. The server spat two drinks. The Counselor took a sip of his drink and rolled it around his mouth. Sten just stared at the container before him.

"I realize your sorrow, young Sten," the Counselor said. "But all things grow from ashes."

He took something from his pocket and put it in front of Sten. It was a placard, with KARL STEN, 03857-CON19-2-MIG-UNSK across the top. Sten wondered when they'd snapped the picture of him on the card's face.

"I knew that your great concern was, after the inevitable mourning period, what would happen to you next. After all, you have no job. No credits, no means of support. And so forth."

He paused and sipped his drink.

"We have examined your record and decided that you deserve special treatment." The Counselor smiled and tapped the card with a yellow fingernail.

"We have decided to allow you full worker's citizenship rights with all of the benefits that entails. A man-size monthly credit. Full access to all recreational facilities. Your own home—the one, in fact, in which you grew up."

The Counselor leaned forward for the final touch. "Beginning tomorrow, Karl Sten, you take your father's place on the proud assembly lines of Vulcan."

Sten sat silent. Possibly the Counselor thought he was grateful. "Of course, that means you will have to serve out the few years left on your father's contract—nineteen, I believe it was. But the Company has waived the time remaining on your mother's obligation."

"That's very generous of the Company," Sten managed.

"Certainly. Certainly. But as Baron Thoresen has so often pointed out to me in our frequent chats—in *his* garden, I might add—the welfare of our workers must come before all other things. 'A happy worker is a productive worker,' he often says."

"I'm sure he does."

The Counselor smiled again. He patted Sten's hand and rose. Then he hesitated, inserted his card in the slot again and punched buttons. Another drink appeared from the slot. "Have another, Citizen Sten. On me. And let me be the first to offer my congratulations."

He patted Sten again, then turned and walked down the street. Sten stared after him. He picked up the drinks, and slowly poured them on the deck.

CHAPTER FIVE

THE ON-SHIFT WARNING shrilled and Sten sourly sat up. He'd already been awake for nearly two hours. Waiting.

Even after four cycles the three-room apartment was empty. But Sten had learned that the dead must mourn for themselves. That part had been walled off, though sometimes he'd slip, and some of the grief would show itself.

But mostly he was successful at turning himself into the quiet, obedient Mig the Company wanted. Or at least at faking it.

The wallslot clicked, and a tray slid out with the usual quick-shot energy drink, various hangover remedies, and antidepressants.

Sten took a handful at random and dumped them down the waste tube. He didn't want or need any, but he knew better than to ignore the tray.

After a few hours, it would retract and self-inventory. Then some computer would report up the line on Sten's lack of consumption. Which would rate a reprimand from the Counselor.

Sten sighed. There was a quota on everything.

Far up at the head of the line a worker touched his card to the medclock. The machine blinked and the man

31

shoved his arm into its maw. It bleeped his vital signs, noted he was free of alcohol or drugs that might be left over from last off-shift's routine brawl, and clocked him in.

The man disappeared into the factory and the line moved two steps forward.

Sten moved forward with the rest, gossip buzzing around him.

"Considerin' Fran was the loosest man with a quota on the bench, I think it was clottin' fine of the Company—so he lost an arm; only thing he ever did with it is pinch joy-girls. They gave him a month's credits, didn't they? . . ."

"You know me, not a man on Vulcan can match me drink for drink—and next shift I'm rarin' for the line—I'm a quota fool! Bring 'em on, I says, and look out down the line . . ."

It was Sten's turn. He slotted his card, stared at the machine dully as it inspected and approved him, and then walked reluctantly into the factory.

The assembly building was enormous, honeycombed from floor to ceiling with belts, tracks, giant gears, and machines. The Migs had to inch along narrow catwalks to keep from falling or being jerked into the innards of some machine and pounded, pressed, and rolled into some nameless device that would eventually be rejected at the end of the line because it contained odd impurities.

After nearly two months in the factory, Sten had learned to hate his partner almost as much as the job. The robot was a squat gray ovoid with a huge array of sensors bunched into a large insect eye that moved on a combination of wheels and leg stalks that it let down for stairs. Only the eye cluster and the waggling tentacles seemed alive.

Most of all, he hated its high-pitched and nagging voice. Like an old microlibrarian that Sten remembered from his Basic Creche.

"Hurry," it fussed, "we're running behind quota. A good worker never runs behind quota. Last cycle, in the third sector, one Myal Thorkenson actually doubled his quota. Now, isn't *that* an ideal worth emulating?"

Sten looked at the machine and thought about kicking it. Last time he'd tried that, he'd limped for two days.

Sten's robot prodded him with its voice.

"Hurry now. Another chair."

He picked up another seat from the pile in front of the long silver tube. Then he carried it back to where the robot squatted, waiting.

Sten and his robot were at the tail end of a long assembly line of movers, the capsules used in the pneumatic transit systems common to most industrial worlds.

The robot was the technician. Sten was the dot-and-carry man. His job was to pick up a seat from the pile, lug it inside the tube to the properly marked slot, and then position it while the robot heat-sealed the seat to the frame. It was a mind-numbing job that he never seemed to do quite right for his mechanical straw boss.

"Not there," the robot said. "You always do it wrong. The position is clearly marked. Slide it up now. Slide it up."

The robot's heatgun flashed.

"Quickly, now. Another."

Sten lumbered back down the aisle, where he was met by a worker whose name he couldn't remember. "Hey. You hear? I just got promoted!"

"Congratulations."

The man was beaming. "Thanks. I'm throwing a big bash after shift. Everyone's invited. All on me."

Sten looked up at the fellow. "Uh, won't that set you back—I mean, put you even with the promotion?"

The man shrugged.

"So I card it. It'll only add another six months or so to my contract."

Sten considered asking him why it was so important to rush right out and spend every credit—and then some— of his raise. How he could throw away another six months of his life on . . . He already knew the answer. So he didn't bother.

"That's right," he sighed. "You can card it."

The Mig rushed on.

Leta was about the only bright spot in Sten's life those days.

In many ways, she was the typical joygirl. Hired on the same kind of backwater planet Sten's parents had come from, Leta just knew that when her contract ran out and she immigrated to one of the Empire's leisure worlds, she'd meet and sign a life-contract with a member of the royal family. Or at least a merchant prince.

Even though Sten knew better than to believe in the whore with the heart of gold, he felt that she got real pleasure from their talk and sex.

Sten lay silently on the far side of the bed.

The girl slid over to him and stroked his body slowly with her fingertips.

Sten rolled over and looked up at her.

Leta's face was gentle, her pupils wide with pleasure drugs.

"Ssswrong," she muttered.

"Contracts. Contracts and quotas and Migs."

She giggled.

"Nothin' wrong with you. An' you're a Mig."

Sten sat up.

"I won't be forever. When my contract's up, I'll get off this clottin' world and learn what it is to be a free man."

Leta laughed.

"I mean it. No carding it. No contract extensions. No more nights on the dome drinking. I'm just gonna put in my time. Period."

Leta shook her head and got up.

She took several deep breaths, trying to clear her mind. "You can't do it."

"Why not?" Sten asked. "Hell. Even nineteen years isn't forever."

"You can't do it because it's rigged. The whole thing. Controlled. Like your job. Like the games. Like . . . like even this. They set it up so you never get off . . . so you're always tied down to them. And they do it any way they can."

Sten was puzzled.

"But if it's rigged, and nobody ever gets off Vulcan, what about you?"

"What about me?"

"You're always talking about what you'll do when you leave, and the planets you want to see and the men you want to meet who don't smell like machine oil and sweat and . . . and all that."

Leta put a hand over Sten's mouth.

"That's me, Sten. Not you. I'm leaving. I've got a contract, and that gives me money and the drugs and whatever I eat or drink. I can't even gamble at the tables. They won't take my card. It doesn't matter what else I do. Just so long as I stay alive, I've got a guarantee that I'll get off of Vulcan. Just like all the other joygirls. Or the shills and the carders. They're all leaving. So are the Techs and the patrolmen. But not the Migs. Migs never leave."

Sten shook his head, not believing a word she said.

"You're a sweet boy, Sten, but you're gonna die on Vulcan."

He stayed away from Leta's place for a while, telling himself that he didn't need her. He didn't want somebody around that was going to tell him those kinds of . . . well, they had to be lies, didn't they?

But the longer he stayed away, the more he thought and the more he wondered. Finally he decided that he had to talk to her. To show her that maybe she was right about all the other Migs. But not about him.

At first, the people at the joyhouse pretended they'd never heard of her. Then they remembered. Oh, *Leta*. She was transferred or something. Yeah. Kind of sudden. But she seemed real happy about it when they came for her. Must've been a shift over at that new rec area in The Eye, for the Execs. Or something like that.

Sten wondered.

But he didn't wonder anymore when, late that off-shift, he stole into what had been Leta's cubicle and found the tiny mike planted in the ceiling.

He always wondered what they'd done to her for talking.

FIRST MONTH EXPENSES:

Quarters	1,000	credits
Rations	500	"
Foreman fee	225	"
Walkway toll	250	"

TOTAL: 1,975 credits

FIRST MONTH PAY:
2,000 credits less
1,975 credits expenses

25 credits savings

Sten checked the balance column on the screen for the tenth time. He'd budgeted to the bone. Cut out all recreation, and worked on the near-starvation basic diet. But it always came out the same. At twenty-five credits a month, he wouldn't be able to shorten his contract time at all, not by so much as six months. And if he kept on living the way he'd been, he'd go crazy in five years.

Sten decided to go over it one more time. Perhaps there was something he'd missed. Sten tapped the console keys and called up the Company's *Work Guidelines Manual*. He scrolled paragraph after paragraph, looking for an out.

"Clot!" He almost passed it. Sten rolled back up to the paragraph, and read and reread it:

SAFETY LEVY: All migratory workers shall be levied not less than 35 credits nor more than 67 credits each pay cycle, except when performing what the Company deems to be extraordinary labor which increases the chances of accidental injury and/or death, in which case the levy shall be no less than 75 credits and no more than 125 credits each cycle, for which the Company agrees to provide appropriate medical care and/or death benefits not to exceed 750 credits for funeral arrangements and/or . . .

He slammed his fist on the keys and the vid screen did several fast flip-flops, then went blank.

They had you. No matter how you shaved it, every Mig would always be in the hole.

Sten paced back and forth.

The robot finished the mover and dropped out the exit, waiting for the next cigar tube to be on-lined. The completed car whooshed away, into the pneumatic freight tube and away toward the shipping terminal. But there'd been some error. Something or someone didn't have the next pile of seats ready.

Sten yawned as his robot whined at another machine about quotas. The second machine wasn't about to take the blame. They bickered back and forth electronically until, eventually, the ceiling crane slammed a seat consignment down between them. The robot slid into the mover. Sten hoisted a seat to his shoulder and lugged it aboard.

He set the chair in position and listened to the robot natter while he moved the seat back and forth.

The robot bent forward, heatgun ready. Sten felt a sudden bout of nausea wash over him. This would be it for the rest of his life, listening to the gray blob preach.

Sten lurched forward. The seat slid into the robot, and the machine yowled as it welded itself to seat and mover frame.

"Help! Help! I'm trapped," it whined. "Notify master control."

Sten blinked. Then hid a grin.

"Sure. Right away."

He ambled slowly off the mover to the line control panel, took a deep breath, and punched the TASK COMPLETE button. The doors of the tube slid closed, and the mover slid toward the freight tube.

"Notify . . . control . . . help . . . help . . ."

And for the first time since he'd been promoted to full worker, Sten felt the satisfaction of a job well done.

CHAPTER SIX

STEN HAD BEEN "sick" for over a week before the Counselor showed up.

Actually, he really had been sick the first day. Scared sick that somebody might have discovered his little game with the robot. It'd be considered outright sabotage, he was sure. If he was lucky, they'd put him under a mindprobe and just burn away any areas that didn't seem to fit the Ideal Worker Profile.

But there probably was something worse. There usually was on Vulcan. Sten wasn't sure what something worse could be. He had heard stories about hellshops, where incorrigibles were sent. But nobody knew anybody who'd actually been sent to such a shop. Maybe the stories were just that—or maybe nobody ever came back from those places. Sten wondered sometimes if he wouldn't rather just be brainburned and turned into a vegetable.

The second day, Sten woke up smiling. He realized that nobody'd ever figure out what had happened to the robot. So he celebrated by staying home again, lounging in bed until two hours past shift-start. Then he dug out a few of the luxury food items his parents had saved and just stared at the nonsnowing wall mural. He knew better than to stick his card in the vid and watch a reel, or to go out to a rec

38

area. That'd make it even easier for the Company to figure out that he was malingering.

The flakes hanging in the air on the mural fascinated Sten. Frozen water, falling from the sky. It didn't seem very sanitary. Sten wondered if there was any way at all that he could get offworld. Even though those snowflakes didn't look very practical, they might be something to see. Anything might be something to see—as long as it was away from the Company and Vulcan.

By the third day, he'd decided he wasn't going to work anymore. Sten didn't know how long he was going to get away with malingering. Or what would happen to him when they caught him. He just sat. Thinking about the snowflakes and what it would be like to walk in them, with no card in his pocket that said where he was supposed to be and what he was supposed to do when he got there.

He'd just learned that if he squinched his eyes a bit, the snowflakes would almost move again, when the door buzzer went off.

He didn't move. The door buzzed again.

"Sten," the Counselor shouted through the panel, "I know you're there. Let me in. Everything is fine. We'll work it out. Together. Just open the door. Everything is fine."

Sten knew it wasn't. But finally he pulled himself up and walked toward the door. The buzzer sounded again. Then something started fumbling in the Identilock. Sten waited at the door.

Then he hesitated, and moved to one side. The Identilock clicked, and the door slid open. The Counselor stepped inside. His mouth was already open, saying something. Sten leaped, both hands clubbed high above him. The blow caught the Counselor on the side of his head, slamming him into the wall. The Counselor slid down the panel and thumped to the floor. He didn't move. His mouth was still open.

Sten began to shake.

But suddenly, he felt calm; he'd eliminated all the possibilities now. He could do only one thing. He stooped over the unconscious Counselor and riffled quickly through his pockets. Sten found and pocketed the man's card. If he used that instead of his own, it might take Control a little longer to track him down. It'd also give him entry into areas forbidden by Sten's Mig card.

Sten turned and looked around the three bare rooms. Whatever happened next, it would be the last time he'd ever see them. Then he ran out the door, heading for the slideway, the spaceport, and some way off Vulcan.

He felt out of place the moment he stepped off the slideway. The people had begun to change. Only a few Migs were visible, conspicuous in their drab coveralls. The rest were richer and flashier: Techs, clerks, administrators, and here and there the sparkle of strange offworld costumes.

Sten hurried over to a clothes-dispensing machine, slid the Counselor's card into the slot and held his breath. Would the alarms go off now? Were Sociopatrolmen already hurrying to the platform?

The machine burped at him and began displaying its choices. Sten punched the first thing in his size that looked male, and a package plopped into a tray. He grabbed it and pushed his way through the crowd into a rest area.

Sten carded his way into the spaceport administration center, trying to look as if he belonged there. He had to do something about the Counselor's card soon. Everywhere he went, he was leaving a trail as wide as a computer printout sheet.

Nearby, an old, fat clerk was banging at a narcobeer dispenser. "Clotting machine. Telling me I don't have the clotting credits to . . ."

Sten ambled up to him, bored but slightly curious. The man was drunk and probably so broke that the central computer was cutting him off.

"It's sunspots," Sten said.

The clerk bleared up at him. "Think so?"

"Sure. Same thing happened to me last off-shift. Here. Try my card. Maybe a different one will unjam it."

The clerk nodded and Sten pushed a button and the man's card slid out. He took it and inserted the Counselor's card. A minute later the clerk was happily on his way, chugging a narcobeer.

Three hours later they grabbed him. The clerk was sitting in his favorite hangout, getting pleasantly potted when what seemed like six regiments of Sociopatrolmen burst in. Before he had time to lower his glass, he was beaten, trussed, and on his way to an interrogation center.

In front, the chief Sociopatrolman peered victoriously at the clerk's ID card. Except, of course, it wasn't his. It was the Counselor's.

Sten could feel it as soon as he entered the spaceport Visitors' Center. Even on the run, there was a sense of—well, what it was exactly, he couldn't tell. But he thought it might be freedom.

He moved through the exotic crowd—everything from aliens and diplomats to stocky merchantmen and deep-space sailors. Even the talk was strange: star systems and warp drive, antimatter engines and Imperial intrigue.

Sten edged past a joygirl into a seedy tavern. He elbowed his way through the sailors and found an empty space at the bar. A sailor next to him was griping to a buddy.

"The nerf lieutenant just ignores me. Can you believe that? Me! A projector with fifteen damned years at the clotting sig-board."

His friend shook his head. "They're all the same. Two years in the baby brass academy and they think they know it all."

"So get this," said the first man. "I report blips and he says no reason there should be blips. I tell him there's blips anyway. Few minutes later we hit the meteor swarm. We had junk in our teeth and junk comin' out our drive tubes.

"Pilot pulled us out just in time. Slammed us into an evasion spiral almost took the captain's drawers off."

Sten got his drink—paying with one of his few credit tokens—and moved down the bar. A group of sailors caught his eye. They were huddled around a table, talking quietly and sipping at their drinks instead of knocking them back like the others. They were in fresh clothes, clean-shaven, and had the look of men trying to shake off hangovers in a hurry.

They had the look of men going home.

"Time to hoist 'em," one of them said.

In unison, they finished their drinks and rose. Sten pushed in behind them as they moved through the crowd and out the door.

Sten huddled in the nose section of the shuttle. A panel hid him from the sailors. They lifted off from Vulcan, and moments later Sten could see the freighter through the clear bubble nose as the shuttle floated up toward it.

The deep-space freighter—an enormous multisegmented insect—stretched out for kilometers. A swarm of beetlelike tugs towed still more sections into line and nudged them into place. The drive section of the freighter was squat and ugly with horn projections bristling around the face. As the shuttle neared the face, it grinned open.

Just before it swallowed him, Sten thought it was the most beautiful thing he had ever seen.

He barely heard the judge as the man droned on, listing Sten's crimes against the Company. Sten was surrounded by Sociopatrolmen. In front of the judge, the Counselor loomed, his head nearly invisible in plastibandages, nodding painfully as the judge made each legal point.

They had found Sten in the shuttle, huddled under some blankets, stolen ship's stores stacked around him. Even as he messaged Vulcan for someone to pick Sten up, the captain kept apologizing. He had heard stories.

"We can't help you," he said. "Vulcan security sends snoopers on every freighter before it clears, looking for people like you."

Sten was silent.

"Listen," the captain went on, "I can't take the chance. If I tried to help and got caught, the Company'd pull my

trading papers. And I'd be done. It's not just me. I gotta
think of my crew . . ."

Sten came awake as a Sociopatrolman pushed him forward. The judge had finished. It was time for sentencing.
What was it going to be? Brainburn? If that was it, Sten
hoped he had enough mind left to kill himself.

Then the judge was talking. "You are aware, I hope,
of the enormity of your crimes?"

Sten thought about doing the Mig humility. Be damned,
he thought. He didn't have anything to lose. He stared
back at the judge.

"I see. Counselor, do you have anything of an ameliora-
tive nature to add to these proceedings?"

The Counselor started to say something, and then
abruptly shook his head.

"Very well. Karl Sten, since you, at your young age,
are capable of providing many years of service to the
Company and we do not wish to appear unmerciful, recog-
nizing the possibility of redemption, I will merely reassign
you."

For a moment, Sten felt hopeful.

"Your new work assignment will be in the Exotics Section. For an indeterminate period. If—ahem—circumstances warrant, after a suitable length of time I will
review your sentence."

The judge nodded, and touched the INPUT button on his
justice panel. The Sociopatrolmen led Sten away. He wasn't
sure what the judge meant. Or what his sentence was.
Except his mind was intact, and he was alive.

He turned at the door, and realized, from the grin on
the Counselor's face, he might not be for very long.

BOOK TWO

HELLWORLD

CHAPTER SEVEN

"SIMPLY A MATTER a' entropy. Proves it," the older man said. And lifted his mug.

The younger man beside him, who wore the flash coveralls of a driveship officer, snickered and crashed his boots onto the table. His coveralls bore the nametag of RASCHID, H. E., ENGINEERING OFFICER.

"Wha's so funny?" his senior said belligerently. He looked at the other four deep-space men around the tavern's table. "These is me officers, and they didn't hear me say nothin' funny. Did ya?"

Raschid looked around and grinned widely at the drunkenly chorused "yessirs." Picked up his own mug in both hands and drained it.

"Another round—I'll tell you. I been listening to frizzly old bastards like you talk about how things is runnin' down, and how they're gettin' worse and all that since I first was a steward's pup."

The barmaid—the spaceport dive's biggest and only attraction—slid mugs down the long polished aluminum bar. Raschid blew foam off the top of his mug and swallowed.

"Talkin' to fools," he said, "is thirsty work. Even when they're high-credit driveship captains."

The captain's mate flexed his shoulders—a move that

had kept him out of fights in a thousand worlds—and glowered. Raschid laughed again.

"Man gets too old to stump his own pins, he generally finds some punko to do it for him. Tell you what, cap'n. You gimme one good example of how things is goin' to sheol in a handbasket, and maybe, jus' maybe, I'll believe you."

The captain sloshed beer down and wiped the overflow from his already sodden uniform front.

"The way we's treated. Look'a us. We're officers. Contract traders. Billions a' credits rest on our every decision. But look around. We're on Prime World. Heart'a the Empire an' all that clot. But do we get treated wi' the respect due us? Hell no!"

"We's the gears what makes the Empire turn!" one of his officers yelled.

"So, what d'ya expect?"

"Like I said. Respect. Two, three hunnerd years back, we woulda been fawned over when we made planetfall. Ever'body wantin' to know what it was like out there. Women fallin' over us. I tell you . . ."

The captain stood up and pointed one finger, an effect that was ruined by a belch that rattled the walls slightly.

"When an empire forgets how to treat its heroes, it's fallin' apart!" He nodded triumphantly, turned to his officers. "That prove it or not?"

Raschid ignored the shouted agreement. "You think it oughta be like the old days? Say, like when there were torchships?"

"You ain't gotta go back that far, but tha's good example. More beer! Back when they was ion ships and men to match 'em."

"Torchships my ass," Raschid sneered. He spat on the floor. "Those torchships. You know how they worked? Computer-run. From lift-off to set down."

The other spacemen at the table looked puzzled.

"Wha' 'bout the crews?"

"Yeah. The crews! Lemme tell you what those livees don't get around to showin'. Seems most'a those torchships were a little hot. From nozzle right up to Barrier Thirty-three, which is where the cargo and passengers were.

"After a few years, they started havin' trouble gettin' young heroes as crew after these young heroes found their bones turned green an' ran out their sleeves after two-three trips.

"So you know who these crews were? Dockside rummies that had just 'bout enough brains to dump the drive if it got hot beyond Thirty-three. They'd shove enough cheap synthalk in 'em to keep 'em from opening up the lock to see what was on the other side, punch the TAKEOFF button, and run like hell. Those were your clottin' hero torchships an' their hero ossifers.

"An' you think people didn't know about it? You think those drunks got torch parades if they lived through a trip? You think that, you even dumber than you look."

The captain looked around at his crew. They waited for a cue.

"How come you know so much—Barrier Thirty-three—on'y way a man could know that he'd have to crew one." The old man's mug slammed down. "That's it! We come over here for a quiet mug or so—sit around, maybe tell some lies . . . but we ain't standing for nobody who's thinkin' we're dumb enough to believe . . ."

"I did," Raschid said flatly.

The man broke off. His mate stood up.

"You sayin' you're a thousand years old, chief?"

Raschid shook his head and drained his beer.

"Nope. Older."

The captain twitched his head at the mate . . . the mate balled up a fist that should've been subcontracted as a wrecking ball and swung.

Raschid's head wasn't there.

He was diving forward, across the table. The top of his head thudded into the captain's third officer, who, with another man, crashed to the floor in a welter of breaking chairs.

Raschid rolled to his feet as the mate turned. He stepped

inside the mate's second swing and drove three knife-edged fingers into the inside of the mate's upper arm. The mate doubled up.

Raschid spun as the other two men came off the floor . . . ducking. Not far enough. The captain's mug caromed off the back of his head, and Raschid staggered forward, into the bar.

He snap-bounded up . . . his feet coiled and kicking straight back. The third officer's arm snapped and he went down, moaning. Raschid rolled twice down the bar as the mate launched another drive at him. Grabbed the arm and pulled.

The mate slid forward, collected the end of the beer tap in the forehead, and began a good imitation of petrification.

Raschid swung away from the bar, straight-armed a thrown chair away, and snap-kicked the captain in the side.

He lost interest for a few minutes.

Raschid, laughing happily, picked up the fourth man by the lapels . . . and the broken-armed third officer kicked his legs out from under him.

Raschid crashed down, the fourth man flailing punches at him. The old captain, wheezing like a grampus, danced —very deftly for a man his age—around the edge of the roiling mass, occasionally putting the boot into Raschid's ribs.

Two hands came from nowhere and slammed against the captain's ears. He slumped. Pole-axed.

Raschid scrambled to his feet, nodded at the new man in the fight, then picked up the third officer and slung him through the air at his sudden ally, a gray-haired behemoth with a nose that'd been broken too many times for anyone to be interested in setting it. He thoughtfully dangled the third officer with one hand, making up his mind. Then slammed the heel of his hand down just above the bridge of the man's nose, dropped him, and looked around for someone else.

The man who wore the Raschid nametag was sitting atop the fourth spaceman. He had a double handful of the

man's hair, and was systematically dribbling his head on
the bar floor.

The gray-haired man walked over, picked up the mate's
unfinished beer and drained it. Then he grunted.

"I think you've made your point."

Raschid peeled back the man's eyelids, and reluctantly
let the man's head slam finally to the floor and stood.

The two looked each other up and down.

"Well, colonel?"

The gray-haired man snorted. "H. E. Raschid. They get
dumber every year. Or anyway somebody does."

"That smacks of insubordination, colonel."

"Sorry. Would the all-highest Eternal Emperor of a
Billion Suns, Ruler of a Zillion Planets, and Kind Overseer
of Too Many Goddamned People care to accompany his
good and faithful servant back to the palace, where important business awaits, or—or you wanna stay the hell
with it and go look for some more action?"

"Later, colonel. Later. Don't wanna corrupt the young."

The Eternal Emperor threw an arm around his aide—
Col. Ian Mahoney, O. C. Mercury Corps, the shadowy
Imperial force responsible for intelligence, espionage, and
covert operations—and the two men walked, laughing, into
the thin sunlight of Prime World.

CHAPTER EIGHT

THE BARON WAITED in the anteroom, pacing nervously, glancing now and then at the two huge Imperial Guardsmen playing statue at the entrance to the Eternal Emperor's chambers. If he thought about it—and Thoresen was trying hard not to right now—he was scared. Not a familiar emotion for the Baron.

He had been summoned by the Emperor across half the galaxy with none of the usual Imperial Palace formal politeness. The Baron had simply been told to come. Now. With no explanations. Thoresen hoped it had nothing to do with Bravo Project, although he was sure that even the Emperor's elaborate spy system wouldn't have uncovered it. Otherwise Thoresen was as good as dead.

Finally, the doors hissed open and a tiny robed clerk stepped out to bow him in. Thoresen was only slightly relieved when the guards remained at their stations. The clerk withdrew and the Baron was left in an immense chamber filled with exotic items collected by the Emperor over his thousand years of life. Odd mounted beasts from hunting expeditions on alien worlds, strange art objects, ancient books opened to wonderful illustrations far beyond any computer art conceivable.

The Baron gawked about him, feeling very much like some rube from a border world. Eventually he noticed a man waiting far across the chamber. His back was to Thoresen and he was apparently looking out over the Prime World capital through the large curved glass wall. He was dressed in simple white robes.

The Eternal Emperor turned as Thoresen approached and made his bows.

"We were told by our aides," the Emperor said, "that you had a reputation for promptness. Apparently they misinformed us."

The Baron gobbled. "I left as soon as—"

The Emperor waved him into silence. He turned and looked outside again. A long silence. The Baron fidgeted, wondering.

"If it's about the Company's latest prospectus, your highness, I can assure you there was no exaggeration. I'd stake my reputation on—"

"Look at that," the Emperor said.

Confused, Thoresen peered outside. Below, members of the Royal Court flitted about in an elaborate lawn dance on the Palace grounds.

"Simpering fools. They think that because they are titled the Empire revolves around them. Billions of citizens work so they can play."

He turned to Thoresen. A warm smile on his face. "But the two of us know better, don't we, Baron? We know what it is to get our hands dirty. We know what it is to work."

Now Thoresen was *really* confused. The man was blowing hot and cold. What did he want? Were the rumors about his senility true? No, he cautioned himself. How could they be? After all, the Baron had started them.

"Well?" the Emperor asked.

"Well, what, sir?"

"Why did you request this audience? Get to the point, man. We have delegations waiting from twenty or thirty planets."

"Uh, your highness, perhaps there was some mistake—not yours, of course. But—uh . . . I thought you wanted to—"

"We're glad you came, anyway, Baron," the Emperor interrupted. "We've been wanting to talk to you about some rather disturbing reports." He began to stroll through the room and Thoresen fell in beside him, trying hopelessly to get his mind on top of the situation. Whatever that was.

"About what, your highness?"

"We're sure it's nothing, but some of your agents have been making certain comments to select customers that a few of our—ahem—representatives construe as possibly being, shall we say, treasonous?"

"Like what, your highness?" Feigned shock from Thoresen.

"Oh, nothing concrete comes to our mind. Just little suggestions, apparently, that certain services performed by the Empire could possibly be done best by the Company."

"Who? Who said that? I'll have them immediately—"

"We're sure you will, Baron. But don't be too harsh on them. We imagine it's just a case of overzealous loyalty."

"Still. The Company cannot be a party to such talk. Our policy—in fact it's in our bylaws—is absolute."

"Yes. Yes. We know. Your grandfather drew up those bylaws. Approved them myself as a rider to your charter. Quite a man, your grandfather. How is he, by the way?"

"Uh, dead, your highness. A few hundred years—"

"Oh, yes. My sympathies."

They were back at the door and it was opening and the little clerk was stepping forward to lead an absolutely bewildered Thoresen out the door. The Emperor started to turn away and then paused.

"Ah, Baron?"

"Yes, your highness?"

"You forgot to tell us why you were here. Is there some problem, or special favor we can grant?"

Long pause from Thoresen. "No, thank you. I just happened to be on Prime World and I stopped by to inquire —I mean, I just wanted to say . . . hello."

"Very thoughtful of you, Baron. But everything is proceeding exactly as we planned. Now, if you'll excuse us."

The door hissed closed. Behind the Emperor there was a rustling sound, and then the sound of someone choking—perhaps fatally—and a curtain parted. Mahoney stepped out from behind it. Doubled up with laughter.

The Emperor grinned, walked over to an ancient wooden rolltop desk and slid open a drawer. Out came a bottle and two glasses. He poured drinks. "Ever try this?"

Mahoney was suspicious. His boss was known for a perverse sense of humor in certain sodden circles. "What it it?"

"After twenty years of research it's as close as I can come to what I remember as a hell of a drink. Used to call it bourbon."

"You made it, huh?"

"I had help. Lab delivered it this morning."

Mahoney took a deep breath. Then gulped the liquid down. The Emperor watched with great interest. A long pause. Then Mahoney nodded.

"Not bad."

He poured himself another while the Emperor took a sip. Rolled it around on his tongue and then swallowed. "Not even close. In fact, it tastes like crap."

The Emperor drank it down and refilled his glass. "So? What do you think of him?"

"The Baron? He's so crooked he screws his socks on in the morning. He ain't no toady, though, no matter how it looked when you were playing him like a fish."

"You caught that, huh? Tell you what, if I weren't the biggest kid on the block I think he woulda cut my throat. Or tried, anyway."

The Emperor topped off their drinks and then eased back in his chair, feet on his desk. "Okay. We had our face to face—good suggestion, by the way. And I agree the man is just dumb enough and power hungry enough to be dangerous to the Empire. Now. Spit it out. What should I be worrying my royal head about?"

Mahoney scraped up another chair, settled into it and put his feet up beside the Emperor's.

"A whole lot of things. But nothing we can prove. Best bit I got is that a real good source tells me that Thoresen is spending credits by the bundle on a thing he calls Bravo Project."

"What's that?"

"Hell if I know. Couple years ago I had my boy risk his old butt and come right out and ask. Thoresen ain't sayin'. Except that it's, quote, vital to the interests of the Company, endquote."

"Who's your man?"

Mahoney grimaced. "I can't say."

"Colonel! I asked you a question!"

Mahoney sat up straight. He knew where the chain of command started. "Yessir. It's a guy on the board of directors. Named Lester."

"Lester . . . I know him. I was at his birth ceremony. Absolutely trustworthy in matters concerning the Empire. 'Course, in a hand of poker—well, nobody's perfect. So Lester is suspicious of this Bravo Project, huh?"

"Very. Thoresen is practically bleeding the Company dry to pay for it. He's maintaining barely enough profit to keep the stockholders happy. Even then, Lester thinks he's messing with the books."

"That's not much to go on. Even I can't put the Guard on Vulcan on mere suspicion. I'd lose all credibility. Hell, I founded this Empire on the principles of free enterprise and zip government interference."

"Do you have to believe your own propaganda?"

The Emperor thought about it a second. Then answered regretfully, "Yes."

"So what do we do about it?"

The Emperor frowned, then sighed and chugged his drink down. "Hate to do this, but I got no other choice."

"Meaning?"

"Meaning, I'm about to lose a great drinking buddy. For a while, anyway."

Outraged, Mahoney came to his feet. "You're not sending me to that godforsaken hole? Vulcan's so far out of the way even comets duck it!"

"Got any better ideas?"

Mahoney ran it over. Then shook his head. Slugged down his drink. "When do I leave?"

"You mean you're still here?"

CHAPTER NINE

THE AIRLOCK CYCLE clanked to an end. Thick yellow gas billowed into the chamber. Sten could barely see the other workers against the opposite wall.

The interior lock door slid open, and Sten walked toward his job station, across the kilometer-wide hemisphere of Work Area 35.

He figured that two years had passed, plus or minus a cycle or six, since he'd begun his sentence. How the time flies when you're having fun, he thought sourly.

The floor-level vats bubbled and boiled, gray slime crawling up onto the catwalks. Sten threaded his way around the scum, around huge, growing lumps of crystal.

He stopped at his first station, and checked the nutrient gauges feeding into one of the meters-high boulders. It took Sten half a very sweaty hour to torch off the spiraling whorls of a granular cancer from the second boulder in his area. He fed the crumbly residue to the atmosphere plants in the nearest vat, and went on through the roiling yellow atmosphere.

Area 35 was an artificial duplicate of a faraway world, where metals assumed a life of their own. Minerals "grew," "blossomed," and "died."

Samples of the various metals indicated one with rare

properties—incredible lightness, yet with a tensile strength far in excess of any known alloy or element.

The Company's geologists found the mineral interesting and with enormous commercial potential. There were only two problems:

Its homeworld was a man-killer. That was the easiest part. The Company's engineers could duplicate almost any conditions. And with the condemned Migs of the Exotic Section to harvest the minerals, the casualty rate was "unimportant."

The second, and bigger, problem was working the material. After years of experimentation, metal-based "virii" on the mineral's homeworld were mutated, then used as biological tools to machine the crystal.

The shaped metal was used for superstressed applications: driveship emergency overrides and atomic plant core sensor supports as well as the ultimate in snob's jewelry. The cost, of course, was astronomical. Sten's foreman once estimated a fist-size chunk as worth an Exec's contract pay for a year.

The growth rate and size of each boulder were carefully controlled and computer monitored. But Sten had found a way to override the nutrient controls on one boulder. For six cycles, a small, unnoticed lump had been cultured, gram by gram, on one boulder.

Sten checked "his" boulder. The lump was ready for harvesting—and machining into a useful little tool that Sten wasn't planning to tell the Company about.

He unclipped a small canister of a cutting virus from the bulkhead, and triggered its nozzle near the base of his lump. A near-invisible red spray jetted. Sten outlined the base of the growth with it.

He'd once seen what happened when a worker let a bit of the virus spray across his suit. The worker didn't even have time to neutralize the virus before it ate through and he exploded, a greasy fireball barely visible through the roiling yellow haze as the suit's air supply and Area 35's atmosphere combined.

Sten waited a few seconds, then neutralized the virus and tapped the lump free of its mother boulder.

He took the lump to his biomill and clamped it into position, closed and sealed the mill's work area, and hooked his laboriously breadboarded bluebox into circuit so the mill's time wouldn't be logged in Area 35's control section.

Sten set the biomill's controls on manual, and tapped keys. Virus sprayed across the metal lump. Sten waited until the virus was neutralized, then resprayed.

And he waited.

There were only two ways of telling time in Exotic Section. One was by counting deaths. But when the attrition rate was well over 100 percent per year, that just reminded Sten he was riding on the far edge of the statistics.

The other way was with a handful of memories.

The hogjowled foreman had waited until the guards unshackled Sten and hastily exited back into Vulcan's main section. Then he swung a beefy fist into Sten's face.

Sten went down, then climbed back to his feet, tasting blood.

"Ain't you gonna ask what that was for?"

Sten was silent.

"That was for nothing. You do something, and it's a whole lot worse.

"You're in Exotics now. We don't run loose here like they do up North. Here Migs do what they're told.

"Exotic's split up into different areas. Ever' one of them's a different environment. You'll work in sealed suits, mostly. All the areas are what they call High Hazard Envir'ments. Which means only volunteers work in them. That's you. You're a volunteer.

"You mess, sleep, and rec in Barracks. That's the next capsule down from Guard Section, which is where you are now.

"You don't come north of Barracks unless you figure your area ain't killin' you quick enough.

"One more thing. What goes on in Barracks ain't our business. All that matters is the machines are manned every shift and you don't try to get out. Those is the only rules."

He jerked his head, and two of the Exotic Section's guards pulled Sten out.

The lump was almost down to the right dimensions. Sten rechecked his "farm" and corrected the nutrients, then returned to the biomill and set up for the final shaping cut.

Sten's first area was what the foreman called a cinch shift.

It was a prototype high-speed wiremill. Nitrogen atmosphere. Unfortunately, it wasn't quite right yet. Extruder feeds jammed. Drawers put on too much pressure, or, most commonly, the drum-coiler gears stripped.

And every time the plant went down, someone died. Raw wire piling up behind the jammed extruder tore off a man's arm. Broken wire whiplashed through a man like a sword. A coil of wire lifted from its bin curled around a momentarily inattentive inspector's neck and guillotined him.

About a hundred "volunteers" worked in that area. Sten figured there was one death per cycle.

He figured the foreman had been being funny. Until he graduated and found out how fast other areas killed Migs.

The virus had shaped that lump into a dull black rectangle, 10 × 15 × 30 cm. Sten tapped the STORE button, and the neutralizer control, then walked to another console. He quickly built up the three-dimensional model of the tool he would build, which included measurements of the inside of Sten's loosely closed fist.

This tool would fit only one man.

"Ya gon' gimme your synthalk for as long as I want?"

"That's right."

"What'ya want?"

"You know how to fight. Foreman—his bullies—don't mess with you."

"Clottin'-A they don't. Learned how to tight-corner all over the galaxy. Boy, I even had some guards training!" The little man beamed proudly. "You want to be taught?"

"That's it."

"Yeah. Yeah. Why not? Ain't nothin' else to do down here. 'Cept wait to die."

Sten hit the TRANSFER switch and input his model, set up as a machining program, into the biomill. Waited until the PROGRAM ACTIVE light went on, then touched the START button.

Small, medium-power lasers glowed and moved toward the block of metal. Virus sprayed onto the block, and more metal crumbled away. Then the lasers "masked" areas, and the virus shaped that block into the reality of Sten's model.

The shift hours dragged past, and the mill hummed on happily. Once Sten had to shut down when a guard came through. But he didn't stop at Sten's machine.

"Base position. Now. Clot! Stick always goes across your body. Just above the waist. Then you're ready for any kind of defense."

"What about a knife?"

"You know stick—you'll be able to put that knife about eight inches up the lower intestine of the guy what pulled it on you. Now. One—swing your left up. Stick's straight up and down. Step in . . . naw. Naw. Naw! Stick's gonna go into the side of somebody's neck. You ain't askin' to dance with him. Do it again."

An hour before shift-change, the TASK COMPLETE light went on. Sten began flushing the mill's interior with neutralizer. He knew better than to hurry.

"You in a bibshop. Man breaks off a bottle. Comes at you. What'ya do?"

"Kick him."

"Naw. Naw. Naw. Hurt yourself that way. Throw somethin'. Anythin'. His arm's low, throw for his face. He's ice-pickin', slide a chair up his groin. Awright. You hit him. He goes back. What'ya do?"

"Kick. Kneecap. Arch if you can get close. Neck."

"Awright! He goes down. What next?"

"Put his bottle in his face."

"Sten. I'm startin' to get proud of you. Now. Get your tail in the head. Practice for the rest of the off-shift. Next off-shift, I'll show you what to do if *you* got a knife."

Sten unlatched the work-area cover and lifted out his tool.

His. For the first time in his life, he had something that wasn't borrowed or leased from the Company. That the material cost was a merchant prince's ransom and the machining techniques used enough power for an entire dome made it even sweeter.

Sten held a slim double-edged dagger in his clumsy suit gloves. The skeleton handle was custom-fit for Sten's fingers to curl around in the deadly knife-fighter's grip the little man had taught him.

There was no guard, just serrated lateral grooves between the haft and blade that tapered from 5-cm width down 15 cm to a needle tip. The knife was 22 cm long and only 2.5 cm thick.

It was possibly the deadliest fighting blade that had ever been constructed. The crystal tapered to a hairedge barely 15 molecules wide, and the weight of the blade alone was enough pressure to cut a diamond in half.

Sten tucked the knife in an unused suit storage pocket. He already had the sheath built.

Hite had done that for him.

He and Sten had hidden out in a normal-environment disused area. He'd put Sten out with a central anesthetic. And then delicately gone to work.

The sheath was inside Sten's lower arm. With pirated microsurgery tools, Hite laid back a section of Sten's skin down to the dermis. He put an undercoat of living plaskin next to the subcutaneous tissue, then body-cemented into place the alloy U-curve that Sten had already built. That would keep the knife's blade from touching anything—including the U-curve.

A wrist muscle was rerouted across the mouth of the sheath to keep the knife in place. Then Hite replaced the layer of dermis and epidermis over the surgical modifications and body-cemented Sten back together.

It took several cycles to heal. But Hite was satisfied the plaskin was nonirritative, and the skin over the sheath would continue to regenerate.

The shift buzzer in Sten's suit blatted. Sten shut down the mill and headed for the lock.

Nobody knew exactly what Hite had done to get stuck in Exotic Section. It was known that he'd been a pioneer-world doctor. It was known that he'd taken a Tech contract on Vulcan for an unknown reason. And it was obvious that he'd done something incredibly wrong.

Hite never told anyone—including Sten—about what he'd done.

He was not only the only medic the Migs had access to but he'd been in Exotic Section for years.

He was also the only friend Sten ever had.

"Sten, lad. The problem with you is you don't laugh enough."

"Laugh? I'm stuck in the anus of Vulcan . . . everybody's trying to kill me—they're gonna succeed—and you want me to laugh?"

"Of course, boy. Because what could be funnier than all that?"

"I don't get it."

Hite leaned closer. "It's because the gods hate you. Personally."

Sten considered. Then smiled slowly. And started laughing.

"There's your other problem, boy. You laugh too much."

"Huh?"

"What's there to laugh about? You're up the arse of Vulcan and everyone's trying to kill you. I'd get worried if I were you."

Sten stared at him. Then shook his head and started howling.

In the shiftroom, Sten fed high-pressure disinfectant into his suit and resealed it. He waited. There was no leak. Sten dumped the disinfectant into the recycler and pegged the suit. In the Exotic Section, elderly vacuum worksuits, condemned by the Techs, were used. Leaks were very common. And in an area, there wasn't time to patch them. Sten yawned and pushed through the Barracks toward his bunk.

The knife was tucked inside Sten's arm. His open hand held it securely in position. Sten couldn't wait to show it to Hite.

Barracks smelled like The Row. Cubed and recubed. With no Sociopatrolmen. A couple of hulks were going through the meager effects of a young boy who lay sprawled in a pool of blood. One of them grinned up at Sten. "Got fresh meat in today."

Sten shrugged and kept walking. The ethanol stand was crowded as always. He stopped by his bunk. The female Mig who bunked over him had his blanket hung as a curtain, and paired grunts came from behind it.

Sten headed for Hite's square. The old man had been sick, and Sten hoped he was feeling semihuman. He wanted to ask him more about Pioneer Sector.

There was a knot of men around Hite's bunk. The foreman and some of his toadies. And beside them, a robot trundle.

Two of the thugs picked up a gray, frail, still form from the bunk and dumped it unceremoniously onto the trundle.

Sten broke into a run as the trundle automatically swiveled away. He smashed a fist into its control panel and the trundle stopped.

"Ain't no use," one of the toadies said. "Ol' basser's dead."

"What happened?"

"Guess he just died. Natural causes."

Sten started to turn . . . then pulled Hite's body over.

Blood still oozed from the slash in Hite's throat. Sten looked up at the foreman.

"He di'n't want to go on-shift. So, like Malek says, he just died. Naturally."

The foreman made the mistake of laughing.

Sten came off the floor at the foreman. One thug body-checked him and Sten went to the floor, twisted, and came back to his feet.

And the little man echoed in his brain. *You're never angry. You never want anything. You are a response without a mind.*

A toady moved in, and Sten's foot lashed. The man's kneecap shattered audibly and he dropped.

"Take him."

The toadies surged forward. One huge man had Sten from behind, crushing him with both hands. Sten wiggled an arm free and swung a fist back, thumb extended.

The tough dropped Sten and howled back, blood pouring from his eye socket.

Sten spun, his foot coming wide against the base of the bully's neck. It snapped and the man crashed to the deck.

"Get him, you clots!" the foreman thundered.

The two men left looked at the foreman and at Sten, trying to decide which was worse. One of the men ripped a bunk support free, and the second man's hand snaked into his pocket and flicked out with a gleaming knife, honed down from a hand chisel.

Sten dropped his right hand limply. Curled his fingers. The knife dropped into his hand. Cold. Comforting.

The man with the steel bar reached Sten first, swinging. Sten brought the knife up . . . and the blade razored through the steel. The man gaped for a second at the short steel stub he held, then Sten lashed in and cut his throat like soft butter.

The knifeman feinted once as Sten spun, then lunged for Sten's stomach. Sten overhanded a block . . .

The foreman stared, horrified, as his toady's arm, still holding a knife in writhing fingers, thudded to the deck.

Then the foreman turned and ran. The wrong way. Down, away from the guard capsule. Toward the areas.

Sten caught him just before the shiftroom. The foreman turned. Holding out both hands. Panicked eyes wide.

Sten slashed once.

The foreman screamed as his guts bulged out, and slopped wetly to the deck.

"That was for nothing."

Sten ran for his suit as alarms began to shrill.

Inside Area 35, Sten could hear the banging on the lock. He wasn't too worried. He'd dumped the lock air and wedged the inner door open. That'd take them some time to get through.

The guards had to figure Sten was trapped. There was no interconnection to another area. All that was outside Area 35 was hard vacuum.

Sten gingerly lifted the viral spray tank out of his biolathe and muscled it to the dome's curving outer wall. He flipped the bleed valve open and scrambled back toward the overturned gravsled as the red viral spray hissed against the dome's skin.

The gravsled was the biggest thing he could get into position. He'd put all of its anchors down, and hoped it would hold when everything went.

The wall cracked and peeled and bubbled out until . . . the wall dissolved and became exploding blackness. A storm of escaping gasses howled into space. Megacredits' worth of crystal boulders, vehicles, and tools pounded around the hole and then ripped their way out.

The gravsled cracked . . . anchors tore loose, and then, with a grinding crash, the sled came free and thundered toward the hole. It smashed across the hole but was just too large to fit between two main support beams.

And then the howling stopped. And what was left of Area 35 was silent.

Blood ran down into Sten's eyes where he'd slammed into his suit visor rim. He blinked it away and checked his suit carefully for leaks.

Then he slid around the sled and out the hole.

He swayed, momentarily vertiginous as blackness and harsh starlight rose around him.

One way or another, he was out of Exotic Section. And —he managed to grin wryly—achieving one of his dreams. He was out of Vulcan.

And then he was moving. Away from the hole, away from Exotic Section. Headed North, toward the only hole he could maybe hide in—the sprawling main mass of Vulcan.

He had no idea where he was going. First he took steps, then as he became bolder and realized there was enough magnetism left in the suit's boots to keep him from spinning off into space, in great meters-long bounds.

Several times he almost panicked and looked for a nonexistent hiding place, when repair craft and patrol boats speared down toward him.

Then he realized . . . all they were worrying about was the sudden expensive explosion kilometers away in Exotics. If they even spotted him, one man in a worksuit wouldn't be connected with the destruction.

Not yet, anyway.

He held out as long as he could—until his suit's air supply began to rasp in his ears, and he could hear the regulator gurgle at him—then went to the first hatchway he saw. Sten guessed it was for routine maintenance.

He fumbled with its catches, and suddenly the hatch slid smoothly open. He crawled in the tiny lock chamber, closed the outer door, and hit the cycle button.

The inner door creaked open—at least there was air on the other side to carry noise—and Sten stepped out.

A long, deserted corridor stretched away before and behind him. Dust was thick on the walkway, and several of the overheads were burnt out. Sten slumped down against a bulkhead. He was free. He was home.

He considered those two thoughts. And smiled. His smile became laughter.

Free. Until they caught him. Home? On Vulcan?

But he laughed, as Hite had taught him.

It seemed like the right thing to do.

CHAPTER TEN

THORESEN HURRIED OFF the gravsled toward the shuttle. A few more minutes and he would be off Prime World and heading back to Vulcan. He was still nervous about the Emperor and half believed that at any second he would be arrested.

The Baron tensed as several guardsmen walked around a corner. But they were deep in conversation and were obviously not after him. He relaxed.

A certain wild part of him almost wished for a confrontation. Thoresen was not used to bowing to other men. He didn't like the feeling of terror. He walked past the soldiers, thinking that he could take them. Instantly. His mind fingered the possibilities. He would rip the throat out of the first one. The second would die as he broke his nose and drove the cartilage into the brain. The third—he shook off the feeling. He was breathing easier as he started up the loading ramp.

A little later, he was on the shuttle and heading for the liner orbiting around Prime World. Settling back—really relaxing for the first time since he left Vulcan—Thoresen thought over his meeting with the Emperor.

There were several possibilities: (a) The Emperor was senile. Unlikely. (b) The man was really trying to soothe a few aides. Nonsense. It wasn't his style. (c) The Emperor knew about Bravo Project. Wrong. Thoresen was alive, wasn't he? (d) The Emperor suspected something was up but couldn't prove it. Hence the meeting to feel Thoresen out and issue a subtle warning. Now, that was more probable.

All right. What would be the Emperor's next move? That was easy. He'd tighten the investigation. Send more spies to Vulcan.

· The Baron smiled to himself, feeling much better about the situation. He closed his eyes to take a brief nap. Just before he fell asleep he made a note to himself. He'd order Security to clear with him the credentials of all off-worlders. He looked forward to interviewing a few spies personally.

CHAPTER ELEVEN

STEN HAD BEEN on the run for about a month when he met the girl. She was about fifteen and dressed in a shapeless, grimy black coverall. Her face and hands were smeared with grease. And she came within a hair of killing him. Her name was Bet. Sten thought she was the most beautiful woman he had ever seen.

Sten had made it that far by hiding in the ventilation ducts that warrened Vulcan. They varied in size from twenty-meter-wide central ductways to shoulder-wide tubes to individual rooms. The ducts were caked with the grease of years and periodically blocked by huge filter screens. Sten used a small powerdriver he had stolen from a warehouse to get through the screens.

The ventilation ducts went everywhere, giving him quick access to food warehouses and empty apartments when he needed to forage. The only real danger he ever encountered was when he chanced on work parties servicing the filter screens. But they were easy to avoid. He had also heard strange scrabbling and scratching noises which he figured were groups of Delinqs. So far, he had steered clear of them, pretty sure of his reception.

The only thing he feared were the periodic extermination raids mounted by the Company against the Delinqs. From what he had heard back in his Mig days, the few survivors were guaranteed brainburn.

Still, he lived fairly well, and in fact had gained a kilo or two since his escape. He was just getting slightly bored and more than a little picky about his meals when he made a real find.

The hydroponics farm was a glistening green world that stretched out of sight into the mists. Towering purple ferns could be seen and row upon row of every conceivable plant, some in flower, some drooping with ripe vegetables and fruit. Sten had never seen anything like it before except at the vid library.

No humans were about. Only agricultural bots—the lowest form—tending and harvesting the plants. Sten dropped through the duct and landed on the ground. It was soft and green. Sten looked down at his feet. So that's what grass looks like.

He walked through the rows smelling—fresh air? Flowers? Soil? He picked a handful of what he thought might be grapes. Nibbled on them, his face lighting up at the fresh taste. Sten took off his shirt and started stuffing it until the seams nearly split.

A soft footfall. Sten whirled, his knife flashing out. Then he hesitated. It was a girl.

She carried a Sociopatrolman's stun rod, tied to a half-meter-long fiber rod. She hadn't spotted him yet and Sten started to slide back into a row of plants. Then he hesitated. She didn't behave like a Mig or a Tech. She had to be a Delinq.

Sten suddenly remembered one of his father's phrases: "The enemy of my enemy is my friend." He stepped from behind a huge fern into full view.

The girl saw him, froze, then flipped the stun rod on and drew back her arm, ready to hurl the improvised spear at Sten.

"Wait."

The girl stopped. Still ready to throw. No fear at all. Her eyes widened as his knife hand flickered and the blade disappeared from view. He held out his hands, palms up.

"Who are you?"

"I'm Sten."

"You on the run?"

Sten nodded.

"From where?"

"Exotic Section."

The stun rod came up.

"Liar! Nobody's ever—"

"I blew out an area. Came across the outside in a suit. I've been living in the ducts."

The girl frowned.

"We heard there was an accident. But that's impossible."

Sten waited.

"You've got the muscles that come from lifting. And those scars on your legs . . . You're a runaway."

"Then what am I doing here?"

The girl smiled humorlessly. "Who knows? Trying to infiltrate us. Just weird. Maybe a real runner."

Sten shrugged.

"Hold your hands out again," the girl ordered. "Palms up."

Sten did as she asked. The girl inspected Sten's calloused and work-torn hands and looked closely at the grime-encrusted ragged nails.

"You could've faked that. Strip."

"What?" Sten managed.

"Take off your clothes. If you're an infiltrator, you'll have a soft body like a socioslime."

Sten hesitated.

"This stun rod," the girl said evenly, "is power-jumped. It puts out about two hundred percent more force than it should for about two seconds. Then it burns out. But by then whoever it hits is ready for recycling."

Sten fingered the fastener, then stepped out of the suit.

The girl walked completely around him, then stood, considering for a moment, in front of him.

The girl smiled slightly.

"It's a very good body."

Then her smile vanished.

"Come on. Get dressed. I'm Bet."

As he stepped into his clothes, she dumped his "harvest" out of his shirt and handed it to him. She began picking through the vegetables and fruits, tossing some away as too green, stuffing others into a sack.

"You're lucky I came along," she said. "Most runners are caught after the first month."

"You a Delinq?"

She gave him a disgusted look.

"I wouldn't be alive if I weren't. We know how to duck the sweeps. We know the places to hide, where they almost never look. A good Delinq can last . . . maybe five years."

Sten was shocked.

"How long since you ran?" he asked.

"Three years now."

She shouldered the sack and headed for a ventilation duct.

"Come on. I'll take you to Oron."

She slid into the duct, motioned him past her, then replaced the filter screen. Then she pulled what appeared to be a tiny headband from her coveralls, flicked the light on, and wriggled by Sten to take the lead. The soft brush of her body against his turned Sten's mouth dry. He took a deep breath and crawled after her.

The Delinqs paid no attention to Sten and Bet as they dropped from the duct into the long-abandoned warehouse.

About thirty of them, dressed in the stolen finery of Vulcan's warehouses, were celebrating a raid on a particularly rich warehouse, and most of them were drunk or drugged. It was one of the strangest things Sten had ever seen: a party in almost absolute silence. Whispering—even in the safety of home base—was second nature to a Delinq.

Stranger still, they were all children. The youngest, he estimated, was no more than twelve—a girl rubbing oil on the body of a boy about thirteen. The oldest person Sten saw, as Bet led him through them, was in his late teens. Sten felt like an old man.

Oron was sprawled in the office section of the warehouse. At first glance, he appeared to be in his forties. A closer look showed that the white hair and withered arm belonged to a man only a year or so older than Sten.

His face was the worst. Half of it was mobile. The other frozen like a deathmask.

Beside him sat a pudgy girl, busily working her way through a pile of fruit. Behind him, on a fur-piled bed, were two naked girls. Both beautiful and sleeping—or drugged.

"This is Sten," Bet said. "He's a runner."

Oron turned to the fat girl and pointed at Bet. "Who is she?"

"Bet. You sent her out last shift to the hydroponic farm," the girl said, not missing a bite.

Sten froze, arced his wrist, getting ready to spring out his knife. If this was Bet's gang, why didn't Oron know—? Oron caught Sten's expression. Half his face smiled.

"Fadal is my memory," he said, gesturing at the pudgy girl, "I am—am a . . ." His brow furrowed.

"Brainburn," Fadal answered for him.

"Yes. I did something wrong when I was young, for which they . . . brainburned me. But something went wrong. It didn't . . . take. Or rather . . . it only partially worked."

He motioned at his face and withered arm. "My body. And part of my mind . . . So I am an . . . amnesiac."

"Then how do you—?" Sten began.

"All that happens this shift is very clear to me. But the next shift, I do not know what went before. I remember how to talk. That I am a Delinq. That I am Oron. Although sometimes I forget that. And that I am the leader of these people. But . . . I must be reminded of . . . of . . . yes . . . of their names. And what I asked them to do."

"He's the leader," Bet said, "because he can always figure out where to raid. And when to move just before there is another sweep."

"Oron has been a Delinq for twelve years," Fadal said.

She seemed to think it was a compliment. Sten guessed it just might be.

"So you are a runner," Oron said. "And you want to join us?"

Sten hesitated, looked at Bet, and then shrugged.

"Sure. Why not?"

"Do you vouch for him, Bet?"

Bet was surprised. Usually there was a test—and questions. Why was Oron willing to rely solely on her word? She glanced over at Sten, who was waiting for her answer. Then she could see it. The look on his face. He didn't care about the Delinqs or Oron. He was obviously confident in his abilities to survive without them. He was here for . . . her.

Sten felt his heart jump as she nodded.

"Do we team him?"

Bet met Oron's eyes. Suddenly she laughed.

"Yes."

"Bet will be your team partner," he said to Sten. "Do what she . . . shows you . . . and you will live. Now, sit . . . have wine. And tell me . . . your story."

Sten accepted a glass of wine and sprawled on the floor. He began his story, glancing over at Bet now and then as he spoke.

CHAPTER TWELVE

"I WANNA WATCH livee, mommie, I wanna watch livee."

The Creche nurse hustled over to the boy, a warm smile on her face. She hugged him and palmed a button; the wall flickered, became a screen, and cartoon characters scampered in across it. The fourteen-year-old boy giggled in delight.

Bet's parents had sold her to the Company a few cycles before. The price: Their contracts were torn up and the Mig couple was free to leave Vulcan. It was considered a remarkable bargain on both sides.

Normally the Company preferred Mig children to grow up into Mig men and women. But there were exceptions officials constantly sought. The Company psych who tested Bet whistled at her raw intelligence scores. Company reps approached Bet's parents, who told her she was going to a much better place. They kissed her and put her to bed. Bet woke up in a Company Creche, surrounded by mostly younger children. The Company usually started with children of five, but Bet's score had been impressive. It decided to take a chance with the eight-year-old.

For the first time in her life, Bet was smothered by love and attention. The Creche Mothers hugged her, kissed her, and gave her toys. Very few things brought punishment or harsh words. Still, Bet never trusted the Mothers for a minute. No one ever discovered this, because Bet had learned very young to keep quiet, give answers only when asked, and always do what she was told.

It took Bet a long time to figure out what was terrifying her. It was the other children . . . her playmates.

Sten crowded past Bet and looked down into the warehouse. It was exactly like Oron's model. Towering stacks of crates and shipping tubes filled with everything from clothing to luxury food items for the Techs and Execs. It was a place that a human—on legal business—never had to visit as all functions and work were handled by bots, from tiny inventory clerks to giant, idiot-brained skiploaders.

Bet and another Delinq began looking for the alarm system.

Oron had gone over the plan with him and then asked for suggestions.

"No, Sten," he had said after listening. "That way . . . there is no . . . escape. Look."

His fingers traced the model of the warehouse's interior.

"Block the exits with crates. But even if you know they are blocked, you must still . . . think someone will come through. You must be prepared to . . . counter that. To have another . . ."

He fumbled for a word.

"Tactic . . . To be a Delinq, you must know tactics. Even when your plan is . . . perfect . . . you must assume it can go wrong. You must never get in a situation from which there is no . . . escape."

Sten nodded. And Oron began showing him how to protect their backs.

"We will make a backdoor here . . . station lookouts here . . . and here."

Bet had found the first alarm and disarmed it. Another Delinq was already unbelting the duct screen. A rope slithered downward and moments later they were on the floor of the warehouse.

Bet motioned for Sten to follow her to a computer terminal. The other three Delinqs began checking for other alarms.

"We can't leave any sign that we were here," she whispered.

Her fingers flew over the terminal keys. First, she called up the SECURITY INSTRUCTIONS program and ordered the human body detector to ignore their presence. Then she called up the WAREHOUSE INVENTORY. She studied it carefully, made a few notes, and then altered the list.

"We can only take these items. No one will miss them."

She signaled to the other Delinqs and they went to work, gathering their loot.

As a Delinq was lugging the last crate toward the piled loot near an opened vent, the Delinqs heard a slight squeaking noise. They leaped for cover as it grew louder.

The security bot rolled around a corner, feelers extended for signs of human life. The Delinqs held their breath as the feelers waved around in the air. Finally they retracted and the bot rolled toward the exit.

Suddenly, the bot squeaked to a halt. One of the Delinqs smothered a moan. He had left a crate standing in the middle of the warehouse floor when he dove out of sight. The security bot's power-hum rose. A stun rod snicked into view and the bot's sensors peered about, looking for the cause. No alarms. It wasn't sure yet. Although unlikely, a faulty worker bot might have left the crate unstacked.

Bet motioned to Sten. She pointed upward to a high stack of crates. They eased from their hiding place and slithered toward the stack. She clambered up Sten's shoulders, found a foothold and then picked her way up the stack of crates. She reached the top, then flattened as a crate creaked loudly underfoot.

The bot rolled toward the sound.

In a blur, Bet lifted a heavy crate and hurled it downward. The bot's stun rod came up and the crate smashed into it. The entire warehouse clouded with the most horrible odor Sten had ever smelled. Liquid gushed out of the crate, soaking the bot. It immediately began whirling around and around.

Sten caught Bet as she leaped down. Gagging from the smell, they covered their mouths and noses. Sten recognized the stink as Sensimusk. With a mechanical groan, the bot stopped its mad whirling and moved only its stun rod, waving the weapon feebly.

Sten looked over at Bet, who grinned and stepped boldly from behind the stack directly in view of the bot. It didn't even notice her. Sten followed as she walked casually to where the others were hidden. Everyone began shoving booty into the vent. Behind them, the bot waved its weapon indecisively.

Bet hated her doll. It was soft and cuddly and programmed to be the best friend a little girl could have. It made Bet's skin crawl when she held it close to her.

She was ten by then, and had moved to Ward B for the second stage. Love was still dispensed by the Creche Mothers, but it was used as a reward for nongroup participation—the children were encouraged to spend time with themselves. To watch livees instead of playing.

Bet never let on how she felt about the doll. She'd seen other children who maltreated or ignored their dolls punished. It seemed to be the only sin the children could commit. She didn't know why she felt as she did. Her doll was just like all the others—a little girl (boys had male dolls) with tiny, spindly legs and arms and a huge head. The face was a happy grin that Bet had decided was that of an idiot.

But one night she couldn't bear its snuggling up to her in bed and whispering in her ear, begging her to share her little-girl secrets. In a sudden rage, she hurled it to the floor. Instant horror. What had she done?

"Dolly, Dolly, be all right. Don't die—"

The doll opened its eyes again and began to croon.

"Bet, is everything happy?"

Bet nodded.

"Wouldn't you like to go lie down and hold me close and we can tell . . . can tell . . . can tell each other stories."

"Yes, Dolly."

She pulled it into the bunk with her and obediently lay down.

The doll seemed all right after that, even if it did repeat itself a little.

The dolls were actually highly sophisticated remote sensors for the Creche program's main computer. They were complete physical and emotional monitoring facilities. A small proximity director ensured that the computer and its human attendants would know if any child was out of range of her doll, for at night, it was very important that each child cuddle his or her doll close. Only then could the device give its injections. Injections to dull physical perceptivity, to increase emotional dependence, and to reduce physical and, most important, emotional/sexual growth.

When Bet slammed her doll against the wall, she threw its sensors slightly out of kilter. They continued to report her as being at a ten-year-old's level of mental and physical development, so she was eventually classified a rapid-peaking retard and given the bare minimum of injections.

Within two years, Bet could see the change in the other children. The boys stayed round-cheeked and undeveloped. The girls still giggled and played trivial games.

Bet learned always to be alone and last in the refresher as her breasts and pelvic area began to develop. Fortunately she was slow enough maturing that menstruation did not occur.

But Bet knew something was dreadfully wrong. Wrong with the other children and wrong with the Creche Mothers. She felt that things were coming to some kind of awful development—but was powerless to do anything about it.

Sten thought Bet and Fadal had gone a little too far. Dressed as joygirls, they were teasing a brawny, off-duty Tech. Sten peered from his hiding place and shook his head. It wasn't what they were doing—that was part of the plan—it was their idea of what a joygirl looked like. He hadn't seen so much glitter since the crystal vat exploded back in the Exotic Section. He leaned closer, listening.

"You girls is a little young, aincha?" The Tech licked. his lips as he looked them over.

"Don't worry, me and my sister have got lots of experience."

"Your sister, huh? Now, ain't that somethin'. You sure your daddy won't—assumin' I was interested."

"Why should he? It was his idea. He says two more years and his Mig contract will be clear, all the credits we're bringin' in."

"His idea, huh? Well, I heard you Mig kids grew up fast, but I thought that was just stories."

Bet and Fadal looped their arms through his and led him toward the apartment. "Come on. Let's have a party."

The Tech was half out of his clothes by the time Sten kicked in the door.

"The hell! What is this?"

The Tech nearly had a heart attack. He looked like a hairy maiden, trying to cover himself with one hand, struggling with his pants with the other. "Uh— Uh— Whaddya— Who are you?"

Sten brandished a large wrench. "They're my sisters, that's who I am."

He turned to Bet and Fadal, cowering on the bed in mock fear. "Get home."

They hurried out. Sten closed the door and took a step toward the Tech. "Gonna teach you a little lesson. Mess with my sisters, will you?"

"Uh . . . listen . . . they said they was . . ."

"What? Calling them joygirls now? My god, you have a nerve." He lifted the wrench high, getting ready to bring it down on the Tech's balding skull.

"Wait— Couldn't we talk this over?"

Sten lowered the wrench. "Whatcha got in mind?"

The Tech fumbled in his pockets and pulled out his card.

He waved it at Sten. "I got lots of credits . . . lots of 'em. Just name your price."

Sten grinned. Oron was right. This was easy money.

Voices. Bet stirred awake; the sedative the doll gave her was no longer enough for her twelve-year-old body. She leaned out of her bunk and peered across the Creche dorm. Lights. Faint mutterings. She climbed out of the bunk, looked at the doll, and hesitated. The doll "knew" when it was being held. But could it tell by whom?

Bet lifted the blanket on the next bed. She never liked Susi much anyway. She tucked the doll into Susi's arm. Bet slipped into her coveralls and padded through the ward.

The semiforbidden door to the corridor was open. She looked around. All the children were deep in drugged sleep. Bet took a deep breath and then walked through. The central corridor was brightly lit. At one end she saw the open window of what seemed to be a lab. Keeping close to the wall, she crept up to it.

The voices began again. One was high-pitched and sounded like it belonged to a very young child. "I did all right today, didn't I, daddy? I moved that big liner all by myself all the way into the dock. Isn't that good?"

A second voice sounded. This one was deeper. "Of course it is, Tommie. You're the best handler we've got. I told the doctor that, and he promised that he'd see that you got something extra for it."

"Candy? I can have some candy? I like mint. You know I like mint, don't you, daddy? You'll get me some mint, won't you?"

"We'll see, son. We'll see."

Bet looked around the edge of the door. She almost screamed. Sitting in a wheelchair was the emaciated body of a man. It looked just like her doll. A huge head, tottering on a pipe-stem neck. Powered implements lay ready at hand. The head had the hairless face, somehow enlarged, of a young boy. From its lips came the high voice. "I saw some of those Migs you told me about today, daddy. I *am* glad that the Company didn't let *me* grow up like that. They have to walk, and they smell bad. They'll never know what it is to be like me. One day I get to be a crane, and then the next I'm behind the controls of a bot tug. They're so nice to me."

"Of course the Company's nice to you, Tommie," the second voice said. It came from a normal man, wearing the white coat of a lab tech. "That's why we let you in the Creche, and why we help you now. We love you."

"And I love you. You're the best daddy I've ever had."

Bet let the door slip closed noiselessly, turned, and hurtled back down the corridor and out the entrance. She ran. She didn't know where she was running, but she kept going until she was exhausted. She was in a dusty, long-unused corridor. Bet huddled to the wall and tears finally came, then stopped as she noticed the corner had broken off the floor-level ventilating duct grill. She pulled at it and slowly worked the panel loose. Bet crawled into the cavity behind it and curled up. Eventually her sobs died away, and she fell asleep.

When she awoke, the half-dead, kindly face of Oron was staring at her.

The scrawny Delinq peered from the ductway, then motioned behind him. Six other members of the gang dropped quietly down into the empty commercial corridor.

There was a low whistle; the Delinq looked back up. Sten leaned out of the ductway and pointed out the targeted shop. The Delinq moused into the shadows and moved slowly toward it.

Sten settled back to keep watch.

He had been with Oron's gang for nearly nine months. Oron had taught him well and Sten had quickly progressed to trusted raider and now he was planning and leading his own raids. He was proud that none of his raids had taken casualties and very seldom did his Delinqs fail to return fully laden.

Still, he knew such luck couldn't last. Sooner or later,

the Delinqs would be picked up by a sweep and destroyed. It was a fact of life. He'd seen the results of a sweep one time while scouting. The Sociopatrolmen hadn't even bothered to dispose of the bodies. Even though the remains were blackened and half skeletal, he could tell that some of the Delinqs hadn't died easily. Particularly the girls.

He thought about Bet. She was still—despite his friendship with Oron—the only reason he stuck with the gang. Sten loved her. Although he had never had the nerve to tell her. She was— She was . . . He shook himself out of his momentary reverie and went back to watching.

The Delinqs had reached the shop. Small cutting torches flared and the bars fell away. The scrawny Delinq—Rabet—reversed his torch and smashed the window. The Delinqs crowded in, scooping the display contents into their packs.

Sten looked back up the corridor. His eyes widened. Creeping down the corridor was a Sociopatrolman, stun rod ready.

Sten licked his lips, then reversed position. The Sociopatrolman slid into view directly under Sten. Sten levered himself out of the duct, crashing down on the big man, feet slamming into his neck. The Sociopatrolman thudded to the deck, stun rod spinning away.

Big as he was, the Sociopatrolman moved quickly, rolling to his feet, unclipping a riot grenade. Sten landed, spinning over one shoulder, feet coming back under him. Lunging forward, one foot reaching high up, then clear of the ground, the other foot joining, legs curled, snapping his legs out to full lock, as the Sociopatrolman's fingers fumbled with the grenade ring.

Sten's feet slammed into the Sociopatrolman's head. His neck broke with a dull snap. As the man dropped, Sten twisted in midair, bringing his legs back under him, landing, poised and turning, knife-edge hands ready.

There was nothing more to do.

The Delinqs looked at the dead Sociopatrolman, then hastily scooped the rest of the window display into their bags and dashed back toward the vent.

As Rabet clambered into the duct, he gave Sten a thumbs up and a flashing grin.

Sten shifted uncomfortably in his bunk. He couldn't sleep. He kept thinking about the Sociopatrolman he had killed and the scattered long-dead bodies of the Delinq gang. He had to get off Vulcan. He had to take Bet with him. But how? Plans swirled in his head. All carefully considered before. All doomed to failure. There *had* to be a way.

Something rustled. He turned and Bet slid through the curtains and into his room.

"What are you—?"

A soft hand went over his lips, silencing him.

"I've been waiting every night. For you. I couldn't wait any longer." Very slowly, she removed her hand, then took Sten's and guided it to the fastener of her coverall. A moment later, she lifted the coverall off her shoulders and let it fall. Underneath, she was naked.

Bet moved up against Sten and began to unfasten his garment. He took her hand away.

"Wait." He reached behind him, and pulled something from under his pillow. A small bundle. He shook it out. It was a long, flowing glasscloth robe. It danced and gleamed with a kaleidoscope of colors. "For you. A gift."

"How long have you had it?"

"A long time."

"Oh . . . I'll try it on. Later." Then she was in his arms and they sank back into the bunk. Locked together. But still in silence.

Bet followed Sten down the narrow ductway. It narrowed twice and they had to squeeze through. She had no idea where they were going. Sten had said it was a surprise. They turned a corner and the duct ended in a blank metal wall.

"This isn't a surprise," she said. "It's a dead end."

"You'll see." His pocket torch flickered into life and he began cutting. In a few moments he had cut a "door," with only a small piece of metal holding it in place. "Close your eyès."

Bet obeyed and heard the hissing sound of the torch cutting again and then a loud thump as the "door" fell away.

"You can open them now."

And Bet saw "outside" for the first time in her life. A gentle lawn sloping toward a tiny lake. Tall green things that Bet thought were probably trees and at the edge of the lake a small—was it wooden?—house, built in the style of the ancients. Chimney, curl of smoke, and all. Sten tugged at her and she followed him out in a daze.

She looked up and saw a bright blue artificial sky. She shrank back, uneasy. It was so open. Sten put an arm around her and she relaxed.

"For a second I thought I was going to fall . . . off . . . or out."

Sten laughed. "You get used to it."

"Where are we?"

"This is the private rec area of Assistant Personnel Director Gaitson. He left today for a two-cycle recruiting program offworld."

"How do you know?"

"I played with the computer. I'm getting pretty good at it, if I say so myself."

Bet was puzzled. It was nice, but—she looked around—"What are we raiding?"

"We aren't. We're on a vacation."

"A vacation? That's—"

"For the next two cycles we are going to do absolutely nothing except enjoy all the things that Gaitson has laid in. We'll eat the best, drink the best, and play. No raids. No patrolmen. No worrying. No nothing."

Sten led Bet to the lake. He stepped out of his coveralls and slowly waded out. "And right now, I'm taking a bath." He waded out a few meters. Bet watched, waiting for something to happen. Sten turned around and grinned. "Well?"

"How is it?"

"Wet."

Bet smiled. And the smile became a chuckle. And then laughter. Shouting out, loud, full-bellied laughter. The way she used to when she was a child. Before the Creche. It was very un-Delinqlike.

She reached for the fastener of her coveralls.

"Sten?"

"Ummmm?"

"You awake?"

"Ummmmm . . . yeah."

"I was just thinking."

"Yeah?"

"I don't want to ever leave this place."

Long silence.

"We have to. Soon."

"I know that. But it just seems so . . . so . . ."

He hushed her and pulled her close. Brushed away a tear. "I'm getting off," he said.

"Off? What do you mean?"

"Off Vulcan."

"But that's impossible."

"So is living like a Delinq."

"But how?"

"I don't know yet. But I'll find a way."

Bet took his hand. Held it. "Want me with you?"

Sten nodded. "Always." Then he took her in his arms and they held each other all night.

CHAPTER THIRTEEN

MAHONEY ARCED OFF the slideway, over the barrier and into the machine shop's entrance. Balled in midair, hit on his feet, and was running.

He dashed down the assembly row, dodged a transporter, and rolled up onto the waste belt. The belt carried him from the shop, and a few feet over a second, southbound slideway. Mahoney slid to the side, went over the edge, hanging by his hands.

He let go, and rebounded onto the slideway. Took several deep breaths, and dusted off his coveralls. Shucking that tail, he thought, was getting harder and harder. Thoresen and his security section were entirely too interested in the movements of Quartermaster/Sergeant Ian Mahoney, Imperial Guards, Field Ration Quality Control subsection.

So far his tags were nothing more than Vulcan's routine paranoid surveillance on any offworlder. He hoped. But if they nailed him now, he'd be, at the very least, blown. So far Mahoney had managed to borrow a Mig's card long enough to produce an acceptable forgery, scrounge a set of Mig coveralls and head south.

He was miles below The Eye. Far off limits for any non-Company employee.

Down there, if he was uncovered by Security or any

Sociopatrolman, the Company would probably find it simpler just to cycle him through the nearest food plant than go through the formalities of deportation.

Mahoney had put himself into the field quite deliberately. He'd been somewhat less than successful in recruiting local agents. Stuck in The Eye, all he had access to were obvious provocateurs and Migs so terrified they weren't worth the bother. At any rate, going operational was possibly less hazardous than red-lighting his mission and heading back for Prime World.

The Emperor, he felt, would be less than impressed with Mahoney's progress to date:

1. Thoresen was, indeed, in a conspiracy up to the top of his shaved head, and letting no one, including his own board of directors, in on the operation. Big deal. That the Emperor knew a year ago, back on Prime World.

2. Thoresen was working a gray and black propaganda campaign against the Empire, specifically directed at the Migs. But since he was using Counselors as the line-out, and had so many cutouts between himself and the campaign, he was still untouchable. Mahoney figured that operation had been going on, and all he'd been able to get was specifics and intensity.

Mahoney snorted to himself. Any buck private in Mantis Section's rear rank would have come up with that much or gone back to being a slime-pounder.

3. Offworld security systems were being beefed up and there were persistent rumors of some of the Company's production facilities being diverted to arms production. Unprovable, so far. And even if Mahoney could prove the allegations correct, the Company could always blandly claim to be planning expansion in Pioneer Sector.

"Zip-slant nothin' is what I got," Mahoney muttered. And then froze. Far ahead, down the slideway, he could see a cordon of Sociopatrolmen checking cards with a portable computer. Mahoney's forgery wasn't that good. He quickly stepped off the slideway, onto a cross-passage. The slide-passage creaked along, into a large dome. On the other side, there was a second ID-check block.

Mahoney rabbited up a side-passage. Basics. Walk slow. Breathe slow. Look happy. A little zipped. You've just come off shift and are headed for your apartment. He went up a narrower corridor, then slanted off on still a third. Turned at the entrance then giant-stepped around the next curve.

Stopped. Waited. Listening.

Of course. Footsteps behind him.

Mahoney was being steered. But he didn't have a lot of options. Moving as slowly as he could, he let the ferrets push him deeper into the abandoned sectors of Vulcan.

The first man made the mistake of trying to blindside Mahoney from a dead-end passageway. Mahoney went in under the blackjack, and put an elbow through the thug's epiglottis. Mahoney side-kicked the riot gun out of the second tough's hands, one-handed the gun out of the air and hauled in on the powerpack cord. The Sociopatrolman top-spun. Mahoney backpunched knuckles into the base of the man's skull.

Two. He turned, realizing that they were just the blocking element. Three more were coming around the corner. One had a gun up. Aiming.

A stun rod, spear-lashed to a rod, lashed out of the upper vent, burying itself in the gunman's eye. He screamed and went down.

Mahoney drove forward, knowing he wasn't close enough to the others, when a young man dropped out of the vent, right hand blurring back and forth.

Mahoney blinked as the second man's head bounced free, blood fountaining up to paint the overhead. The young man crouched, continuing his spin, and brought the knife completely through a circle, lunging up from the ground.

Mahoney noticed the young man kept his free hand on top of his wrist as a guide. Knows what—

And the third man whimpered at the knife deep in his chest. He toppled. The young man bent, pulled the knife out, and wiped it on the corpse's uniform. Young. Good. A bravo.

Mahoney stood very still and let the young man walk up on him. Another young man—no, a girl—dropped from the vent. She retrieved her spear.

About nineteen, fairly short, say sixty kilos. Second evaluation: nineteen going on forty. He looked like any street kid on any gutter world, except he didn't cringe. Mahoney figured he hadn't done a lot of crawling. A Delinq. Mahoney almost smiled.

Sten eyed Mahoney, then the two corpses behind him. Not bad for an old man. Looked to be in his mid-forties, and big. Sten couldn't place him, in spite of Mahoney's Mig coveralls. Not surprising, since Sten had only known three classes, and only face-to-faced two of them.

"There'll be more of 'em along directly, my friend," Mahoney said. "Let's keep the introductions short."

"There's no hurry. For us. Never seen five patrolmen after one man. What'd you do?"

"It's a bit complicated—"

"Sten. Look."

Sten didn't take his eyes off Mahoney. Bet stood up from the corpses and held three cards out to Sten. "Those weren't patrolmen. They've got Exec cards!"

"Thoresen's security," Mahoney said. "They must've tracked me from The Eye."

"You're not . . . you're offworld!"

"I am that."

Sten made a decision.

"Strip."

Mahoney bristled, then caught himself and swore. The kid had it. He tore off the coveralls, then pulled off his boots. Hefted one experimentally, then slammed it against the wall. The heel shattered, and bits of the tiny transmitter scattered across the deck.

Sten nodded. "That's how they followed you. You can put the coveralls back on."

He stirruped his hands, and launched Bet back into the vent. She reached down, gave him a hand, and he slithered up.

Turned, inside the vent, as Mahoney flat-leaped up,

caught the edges of the vent with both hands and levered himself into the airduct.

"A bit tight for someone my age."

"It isn't your age," Bet said.

"We'll not be making light of our elders and their pot-guts."

"Follow us," Sten said shortly. "And no talking."

Mahoney blinked again as Sten put his knife away . . . seemingly into his arm. Then he ran after Bet and Sten, down the twisting duct.

CHAPTER FOURTEEN

"NO, FADAL. FOR some reason I . . . remember what an empire is," Oron said.

Mahoney started to ask. Sten shook his head.

"Intelligence?"

"Eyes."

"Ah. And you will then want my people . . . and myself to be *your* eyes?"

"No," Mahoney said. "I'm too close to being blown."

Oron looked inquiringly at Fadal. She was blank.

"Thoresen wouldn't have top Security men on me unless he was pretty sure who I was."

"Thoresen . . . head of the Company. Your enemy," Fadal whispered.

"You want?"

"I must have confirmation of Thoresen's plan. I've blue-boxed into the Exec and the central computers, and there was nothing on Bravo Project except inquiry-warning triggers."

"This . . . Thoresen. He must have it personally."

"Probability ninety percent plus."

Sten broke in. "What happens if it's there? And you're right?"

"We'll send in the Guard. The Emperor will set up some

kind of caretaker government. Things will change. For the Migs. For everyone."

"Not good enough," Bet said.

"We'll be dead by the time your clottin' Empire arrives. Or don't you know? Us Delinqs don't live to get old," Sten said.

"Sten is right. A runner from another gang passed the word . . . when?"

"Two shifts ago," Fadal said.

"He saw patrolmen at the warehouses. They were drilling with . . . riot guns," Oron said, and smiled at his successful memory. "They will be conducting an extermination drive soon. And we are now too many to evade them."

"How many in your gang?"

"Fifteen now," Fadal answered.

Mahoney calculated quickly. The tiny Imperial detachment had its own airlock. The inquiry wouldn't be too loud if he got what he wanted . . . "Passage offworld. For *all* of you. To any Imperial world."

Sten discovered he'd stopped breathing. He took a deep breath and looked disbelievingly at Mahoney.

"I can do it. You people raid Thoresen's quarters. Bring me anything that says Bravo Project. Which you can deliver on the ship. The Empire keeps its bargains."

"I do not think there's any need to . . . debate this. Is there?"

Mahoney stood up.

There wasn't.

The patrolman stalked to the end of his beat and stopped. He yawned. Then turned and started back down the corridor.

Sten oozed from the vent in the wall . . . breathe . . . breathe . . . pace . . . pace . . . forward. Moving up on the guard. Keeping in time. Eyes on the patrolman's back. Closing. In step. Inside the three-meter awareness zone. Eyes off target. Mind blank.

Sten's left hand curled around the patrolman's neck.

Cramped the big man's head hard back as he drove his knife deep into kidney. Breath whuffled. The man gargled. Sten sidestepped as the corpse voided, then dragged the patrolman back to the vent and stuffed him in. He ran down the corridor, to the beginning of the Exec section. Found the paneling and pried.

When the Delinqs had pored over the complete plans for The Eye that Mahoney had blind-dropped for them in the Visitors' Center airways, they'd found the key.

Evidently the Execs were more delicate than Techs or Migs. Most of the passageways, particularly those around the higher-echelon areas, were subdivided with an inner, noise-insulating wall.

The paneling came clear, and Sten beckoned.

The other fourteen Delinqs poured out of the vents and streamed toward him. One by one they slithered into the wallspace. Oron was in the middle, blank-faced. Fadal guided him into the inner wall. Sten cursed silently, and hoped Oron's memory would return quickly because if they failed, most of them would die in The Eye. Even if a few managed to get south again, into Mig country, there'd be an endless stream of extermination drives.

Again, Sten realized there was no choice. Bet grudgingly agreed. And then vacillated between eagerness to see new worlds and worry about whether they'd fit in. Sten figured that was a lucky sign.

The wallspace narrowed. Sten sucked his chest in. Must be a collision door. His chest stuck for a minute. Sten nearly panicked, then remembered to empty his lungs. He slid through easily.

They huddled outside the great double doors to Thoresen's quarters. Sten curiously touched the material. Rough. Grainy. Like fatigued steel. But rougher. Sten wondered why Thoresen didn't have the surface—it appeared organic —worked smooth.

Bet set the pickup to another frequency, and touched it to the door. Eyes closed . . . her fingers ran across the pressure switches. Inaudible pressure increased/decreased in Sten's ears. There was a click. The main lock was open.

Bet extracted a plastic rod from her pouch. Touched the heat button, and positioned it carefully in the middle of the door's panel. On the end of the rod, heated to human body temperature, was a duplicate of Thoresen's index fingerprint. Sten wondered how Mahoney had obtained it.

The door chunked—the Delinqs grabbed for weapons—and swung open.

Sten and the others cat-walked inside.

Time stopped. They were in space. They were in an exotic, friendly jungle.

They were in the very top of The Eye. Thoresen's quarters. The cover to the dome top was open, and space glittered down at them. Sten was the only one who'd seen off-Vulcan. He had enough presence to softly close the doors and look around.

There was no one else in the dome.

A garden. With furniture here and there, flowing gently into flowering wildness, as if someone had removed the walls, ceiling, and floor of a very large house, leaving in place all of the implements of living.

The Delinqs moved, recovering.

Sten spotted a motion detector swiveling toward them. He ran forward and leaped, knife plunging through the pickup. Sten spotted other cameras and pointed. The Delinqs nodded. Moved forward, fading into the unfamiliar shrubbery.

Sten, Oron, and Bet kept together, looking for what would be an office. At one side of the dome was an elaborate *salle d'armes*. Blades and guns of many worlds and cultures hung from the dome panels. And, on the other side, an imposing, free-floating slab that had to be a desk. Behind it, the most elaborate computer panel Sten had ever seen. Nearby stood a stylized sculpture of an enormously fat woman. Maybe.

Sten looked at Oron questioningly. His eyes gleamed bright. He waved them at the sculpture.

Sten and Bet slid up to it. It had to be. A narrow UV trip beam crossed in front of it. Sten took a UV projector from his belt, flipped it on, adjusted the intensity, and hung it in front of the pickup across the chamber.

It took several minutes to find the tiny crack in the sculpture. Sten fingered all projections on the sculpture. It wasn't that simple. Probably a sequence release that would take forever to figure out.

Oron turned, and Sten took the small maser projector from the ruck Oron wore. Opened it up, aimed the maser sights at the crack, and flipped it on. A little pressure on the trigger and the sculpture powdered. Underneath was a touch-combinationed door. Sten very carefully took a freeze carrier from his own pack and unclipped a tiny tripod.

He opened the freeze carrier and a white vapor spilled into the room from the near Kelvin-Zero cylinder inside. Sten pulled on an insulated glove and attached the cylinder to the tripod, aiming the release spout at the right side of the safe door. He armed the release and backed away.

Spray jetted from the cylinder and crystallized against the hull-strength steel door to the safe. Then Bet took a hammer from her pouch and tapped. The metal shattered like glass. The three grinned at each other.

They were in.

Papers, more papers, bundles of Imperial credits—Sten started to stuff bills in his pouch but Oron waved at him. No.

Then came a thick red folder. BRAVO PROJECT. They had it!

None of them noticed the young Delinq who'd wandered into the *salle*. Fascinated by an archaic long arm, he took it from the wall. The bracket clicked softly upward.

Sten handed the Bravo folder to Oron. The blank look suddenly returned to Oron's eyes. He looked, puzzled, at the folder and stood up. The folder spilled, papers scattering across the floor. Sten muttered and started gathering papers. No kind of order—scattered all over the floor. Sten worked as fast as he could.

The first blast caught three Delinqs in the chest, and side scatter from the riot gun blistered the foliage. The Sociopatrolman in the door pulled the trigger all the way back and swiveled.

The second blast caught a Delinq as he dived through some brush, burning away half his chest. Coughing screams broke the silence. Sociopatrolmen streamed through the door—guns out.

Bet pulled a grenade from her belt, thumbed the fuse, and pitched it, going flat, as death seared above her head.

Sten rolled toward the *salle,* ducking behind the first shelter he saw.

Three joined tanks, with a long hose and twin handles. Some kind of weapon.

The placard above the museum piece read: EARTH PRE-EMPIRE. RESTORED. FLAME WEAPON. It was Sten's luck that Thoresen, like many collectors, kept his weaponry ready for use. Sten grabbed the hose's two handles, and pulled them both. He saw the puff from the cone head at the nozzle, a small flare of fire, and then greasy, black flame spurted from the nozzle.

It spouted fifty meters across the chamber—a far greater range than its aeons-dead builders planned—and napalm drenched the Sociopatrolmen. They howled, for it was a very unpleasant series of deaths, whether a patrolman was lucky enough to have the oxygen sucked from his lungs by the searing flames, or, worse, as the sticky, petroleum-based napalm burnt through to the bone. But one man stopped screaming long enough to spray a burst from his gun just as a still-bewildered Oron walked forward. His head spattered through the chamber.

Robotlike, Sten stalked forward, hosing the nozzle back and forth. Finger locked on the trigger, eyes wide in panic. And then the flame sputtered and dribbled back to the nozzle.

Sten dropped it and just stood there.

Bet grabbed his arm.

"Come on!"

Sten came back to the world. The patrol team that had been blocking the entrance was gone. All dead.

Sten and Bet ran for the door, and only one other Delinq came out of his hiding place after them.

They went out the door and pelted down the corridor. There wasn't time enough to make it back to their rat paneling. All they could hope to do was put distance between them and Thoresen's quarters.

A running blur—the three of them down corridors, ducking as patrolmen came after them. Panicked Execs back and doors slamming and locking.

A floor grating. Sten and Bet heaving up. The grating coming clear.

Sten looked down. The passage went down, endlessly. No fans or acceleration ducting. He didn't know what it was for, but it didn't matter. A team of patrolmen was jogging down the corridor after them.

Narrow climbing cleats ran down the side, and Sten could make out some kind of tunnel about ten meters below the main passageway. He waved Bet into the hole. She clambered in awkwardly and Sten realized she'd been hit somehow.

Sten followed.

The other Delinq was still shaking his head when the riot gun blast caught him and blew him apart.

Bet slipped, one foot left the cleat and her leg fluttered into the passageway. Gunk. Grease. Something. She clawed at the cleat, lost her handhold. Screamed.

Too late, Sten reached for her as he stared down half a world. Bet, screaming endlessly, fell away from him.

Sten watched her body drop away. Until he couldn't see it. Then, somehow moving quickly, he slid sideways and began working his way down the passageway.

Mahoney paced his office. After he heard the alarms, he had monitored the patrol net and heard the riot squads being sent in.

The door opened suddenly and Sten walked into the

room. Empty-handed. "They caught us. They caught us. Bet's dead."

Mahoney caught himself. "Bet. That girl?"

"Yes. She's dead. Dead. And the file. What you wanted. Oron had it."

"Where's Oron?"

"Oron's dead. Like Bet."

Mahoney squelched his natural reaction to curse. "All right. It's blown. But the bargain still stands. I've got the cruiser standing by."

"No. I don't want to go."

"Then what do you want?"

"A gun. Bet's dead, you see."

"You're going back out there?"

"Bet's dead."

"Yes. I keep two over there. In that desk."

Sten turned around and walked to the desk. He never heard Mahoney's step or saw the meat-ax hand snapping down. Sten crashed forward, across the desk.

Mahoney eased Sten around and gentled him into the chair. Then allowed himself a personal reaction. "Clot!" He brought himself back, and took a copy of the *Articles* from a drawer. He laid Sten's right hand on it.

"I'm not knowing what religion you have. If any. But this'll do. Do you—whatever your name is—*Sten* it is. First name unknown. Swear to defend the Eternal Emperor and the Empire with your life—I know you do, boy. Do you solemnly swear to obey lawful orders given you, and to honor and follow the traditions of the Imperial Guard as the Empire requires? You do that, too. I welcome you, Sten, to the service of the Empire. You've not made a mistake, enlisting in the Guard. And it's a personal honor to me that you've chosen me own mother regiment, the Guard's First Assault."

He put the book down, and stopped. Ruffled Sten's hair.

"You're a poor sorry bastard, and it's a shame things have worked the way they did. The least I can do is get you off this hellworld and let you be alive awhile longer."

He tabbed the communicator switch.

"Lieutenant. In my office. A new recruit for the Guard. Seems to have fainted when he realized the awful majesty of it all."

Mahoney took a bottle of synthalk from his desk and, without bothering with a glass, poured a long drink down his throat.

"With the wind at your back, lad."

CHAPTER FIFTEEN

THORESEN WAS WADING in excuses and assurances from the chief of security. The more he looked at the man's vidscreen image, the more he wanted to smash his earnest face. "No *real* harm done," the man said. How could he know?

Thoresen didn't really give a damn about the damage to his quarters or the charred bodies of the patrolmen. But what about Bravo Project? He had recovered the file. But he'd be a fool not to act on the assumption that someone had seen enough of the file to be dangerous.

Thoresen's head snapped up as he caught something in the drone from his chief of security.

"What did you say?"

"We have recovered the bodies of thirteen Delinqs and full identities have been made."

"Not that. After."

"Uh, one, possibly two of them escaped."

So. He was right to worry.

"Who were they?"

"Well, sir," the chief said, "we recovered a hair particle in your quarters. A chromosome projection estimates the man would have been—"

"Let me see for myself," the Baron snapped.

A computer image began to build on the screen as the

chromoanalysis built the image of a man cell by cell. Finally, there was a complete three-dimensional figure. It was Sten. Thoresen studied the image carefully, then shook his head. He didn't recognize the suspect.

"Who is he?"

"A Mig named Karl Sten, sir. Reported missing in that Exotic Section explosion some cycles—"

"You mean the man responsible for *that* debacle is alive? How could he possibly—oh, never mind. That's all."

"But, sir, there's more infor—"

"I'll go over the report myself. Now. That's all!"

The Baron scrolled the report that was Sten's life. It didn't take him long. There wasn't much to it, really, if you separated out all the legal and psych trash.

Suddenly, the connection was made. The Bravo Project. Sten was an orphan of Recreational Area 26. The Row had come back to haunt him.

He palmed the console board and the startled face of the chief leaped on the screen.

"I want this man found. Immediately. I want every person available on this."

"Uh, I'm afraid that's impossible, sir."

"Why is that?" Thoresen hissed.

"Well, we—uh . . . have located him. He's on an Imperial troop ship, bound for—"

Thoresen blanked the man out. It was impossible. How could—? Then he pulled himself together. He'd find this Sten. And then . . .

A few moments later the Baron was talking quietly to a little gray man on a little gray world. The hunt for Sten had begun.

BOOK THREE

THE GUARD

CHAPTER SIXTEEN

NUCLEAR FIRES BLOOMED up from the planet, silhouetting the warships hanging just out of the atmosphere.

"H minus fifty seconds and counting. Red One, Red Two detached to individual control. Begin entry maneuvers." The command ship's transmission crackled in the assault ship's control chambers.

Controls went live, and the fleet transports swung in from their orbital stations. Braking rockets flared as the ships killed velocity and sank closer toward atmosphere's edge.

"Foxfire Six, I have an observed ground launch. Predicted intersection . . . uh, thirty-five seconds. Interception probability eighty-three percent. Beginning diversion . . ." signaled an observation and interdiction satellite.

Foxfire Six's pilot cursed and slammed full power to the drive on his assault transport. He picked a random evasion pattern chip and fed it into the computer.

Deep in the ship's guts, Sten crashed forward against the safety straps. His platoon sergeant slammed against the capsule wall. The ceiling rotated around Sten, swung up crazily, and then went away as the artificial gravity went dead.

Sten and the other men in his platoon wedged themselves more tightly in the shock cocoons as gravity came and went in a dozen directions while the transport veered.

The control room speaker crackled: "Four seconds until atmosphere. H minus thirty . . . antimissile evasion tactics in progress."

Pinpoint flames leaped from the O and I satellite as it launched a dozen intercepts down toward the six pencil lines of smoke curling up for the transport.

Close to the black of space, pure light flashed.

"Foxfire Six, I have a hit on one of your birds. Hit also tumbled gyros on second bird. Suggest you make diversionary launch."

The transport's weapons officer dumped two batteries of gremlins to home on the upcoming missiles. The gremlins spewed chaff as they dropped.

A missile fell for the ruse, and diverted onto a gremlin. The others, probably ground-guided, homed on the huge troop transport.

"Foxfire Six, intercept now ninety-nine percent. Suggest you launch troop caps."

Inside Sten's capsule, the beeper went off, and a computer voice announced, "Capsule launch on short countdown. Surface impact one minute twelve seconds."

The transport pilot hit the launch key and the craft seemed to explode. The huge cone separated from the ship's main body, then spewed twenty long capsules into space. The capsules went to automatic regime, and targeted on the robot homer already in place on the target zone.

The grizzled corporal cocooned next to Sten said thoughtfully, "Guess they got us targeted. Six to five they'll take us out before we ground. Naw. Make that eight to five. Want a piece?"

Sten shook his head, and the capsule rotated around him again.

Forty-six seconds had passed since the invasion elements, Red One and Red Two, had dropped away from the fleet.

The sky around the planet was blazing from nuke and conventional explosions.

Two missiles proximity-detonated on troop capsules. Sten's capsule juddered. "In atmosphere," the corporal said.

An idiot-level radar in the capsule nose tsked and told the capsule's computer to kill speed. Huge wings snapped out from the capsule's sides, and nose rockets bellowed. The capsule's vertical dive shallowed as the wings' leading edges went red then up into white. The air-howl was deafening inside the capsule.

Nearly simultaneously, the capsule's computer dumped three tear-away parachutes out the tail, and pulsed rockets to turn the capsule's course away from the ocean, back on track with the TZ homer. The computer deployed two sets of divebrakes to burn away before the capsule was subsonic.

Short-range ground/air missiles flashed up from the air defenses around the planet's capital below Sten's capsule. One- and two-man tacships skipped and skidded through the black blossoms, then tucked and went in.

Laser sights targeted launch sites, and glidebombs dropped, locked in.

The second wave of tacships swept across the city, scatterbombs cascading down. In the city's heart, a firestorm raged, solid steel and concrete flowing in rivers as the city melted.

A terrain-following missile picked up Sten's incoming capsule, targeted and went to full boost, but lost the capsule in ground clutter. Unable to pull his bird out, the missile's officer manually detonated, hoping to do damage with a near miss.

The capsule pancaked in, up a wide avenue. Touchdown!—and the shockwave caught the capsule, one wing slamming against the street, and then the capsule pinwheeled.

Sten's eyes came open. Blackness. Then the minicharges blew and the capsule's bulkheads dropped away.

The men cascaded out, onto the street.

Sten stumbled, regained his feet, and automatically knocked down his helmet's flare visor. He hit the breakaway harness on the willygun; magazine in; armed; Sten went down on one knee. Ten meters away from his nearest squadmate.

Landing security perimeter complete.

A bellow from the platoon sergeant: "First. Second squads. Maneuver. Third squad. Security. Weapons squad, set up over by that statue."

"Come on. Diamond. Move it."

Sten and his squaddies moved forward, hugging the side of the street. Sten's ears finally decided to return to life, and now he could hear the clatter of bootheels and the creak of his weapons harness.

The first missile from the weapons squad's launchers shushed into the air, and swung, patrolling for a target.

"Come on, you. You ain't got time for bird-watching. Keep your—"

The squad went flat as rubble crashed. Sten rolled through a doorway and came back up.

He ducked down, out of sight as the huge, gray-painted assault tank rumbled through a building and toward his squad.

Sten fumbled a grenade from his belt, armed it, and overhanded the small ovoid toward the track. The grenade burst, meters short, and Sten dove for the deck as one of the tank's two main turrets swiveled toward him.

His eardrums crawled and spine twisted as the tank's maser came up to firing pressure. The wall above him sharded as the soundwaves battered it into nothingness. Sten stayed down as the tank rumbled past.

One tread chattered a meter away from him. Sten heard the long gurgling scream as someone—his team partner—was pulped under the three-meter-wide tracks.

Sten rolled to his feet as the tank passed, caught the dangling end of the track's towing harness, and pulled himself clear of the ground, almost level with the rear was useless. Sten awkwardly crawled from under the tank, bellowing exhaust, Sten unclipped another grenade and rolled it up between the turrets.

He dropped away and thudded to the pavement. The

tank rolled on a few meters, far enough for Sten to be out of the sensor's dead zone.

An antipersonnel cupola spun toward him and the gun depressed, just as the grenade detonated. The blast ripped one main turret away. It cartwheeled through the air to squash two crouching guardsmen.

Sten lay motionless twenty meters behind the tank. Flame spouted from the crater in its top, then was smothered by the extinguishers. The second main turret ground back. Its AP gun sputtered fire, and bullets chattered toward Sten. He screamed as a white-hot wire burned through his shoulder, but came to his feet and dove forward, sliding across the pavement, under the track.

Pain. It hurts. Sten forced himself into the familiar aid mantra, and the nerve ending died, pain faded. His arm was useless. Sten awkwardly crawled from under the tank, then went flat as bullets spattered on the armor beside him.

A column of enemy infantry was infiltrating forward, through the ruins. They opened fire as Sten went around the tank's side.

The engine growled, and the tank rumbled forward. Sten edged along with it, keeping the tank between himself and the enemy troopers. He heard shouted commands, and bent down, peering through the track's idler wheels. He saw legs running toward the tank. Sten picked a bester grenade from its pouch and lobbed it over the tank. His flash visor blackened, covering the light explosion.

The soldiers went down. Stunned, their time sense destroyed, they'd be out of action for at least half an hour.

Gears crashed, and the tank ground down the avenue, toward Sten's platoon headquarters. Sten grabbed a cleat and awkwardly swung himself up onto the tank's skirts. The tank's remaining main turret was firing half-power charges down the avenue. The AP capsules were reconning by fire—spraying the buildings on either side of the track.

Sten crawled across the tank, toward the turret. An eye flickered in an observation slit, and an AP gun swung toward him. Sten jumped onto the top of the tank's main turret. He blinked—

Sten was sitting in a room, a gleaming steel helmet over his head, blocking his vision. Transmission tendrils curled from the helmet. But Sten was riding the top of a heavy tank, in life-or-death battle on a nameless world somewhere.

Sten's fingernails ripped as the turret swung back and forth, trying to throw him off. A hatchway clicked, and Sten shot forward while pulling a combat knife from its boot sheath. He lunged toward the tankman coming out, pistol ready.

The knife caught the man in the mouth. Blood gouted around Sten's hand. The man dropped back inside the tank. Sten levered the hatch completely open then jerked back as bullets rang up from the interior.

Sten yanked off his equipment belt, thumbed into life a time-delay grenade on it, then dropped the whole belt down the hatch.

He jumped. Landed, feeling tendons rip and tear, went to one knee, pushed away again, over a low ruined wall as behind him the tank blew; a world-destroying, all-consuming ball of flame boiled up from the tank over the wall, catching Sten. He felt his body crackle black around him and sear down and down into death.

The recording switched off.

Sten tore the helmet off his head and threw it across the room.

A speaker keyed on.

"You just participated in the first assault wave when your regiment, the Guard's First Assault, landed on Demeter. The regiment suffered sixty-four percent casualties during the three-week operation yet took all assigned objectives within the operations plan timetable.

"To honor their achievement, the Guard's First Assault was granted, by the Eternal Emperor himself, the right to wear an Imperial fourragère in red, white, and green. The battle honors of Demeter were added to the division's colors.

"In addition, many individual awards for heroism were made, including the Galactic Cross, posthumous, to Guardsman Jaime Shavala, whose experiences you were fortunate enough to participate in as part of this test.

"There will be thirty minutes of free time before the evening meal is served. Testing will recommence tomorrow. That is all. You may leave the test chamber."

Sten clambered out of the chair. Odd. He could still feel where that bullet had hit him. The door opened, and Sten headed for the messhall. So that's being a hero. And also that's becoming dead. Neither one of them held any attraction for Sten. Still, he thought to himself, thirty-six percent is a better survival rate than Exotic Section had.

But he still wanted to know what valuable characteristics he could develop to qualify for Guard's First Assault Way Behind the Lines Slackers Detachment.

He sat on the edge of a memorial to some forgotten battle and waited for the long line of prospective recruits to shorten up.

Sten took a deep breath of nonmanufactured air and was mildly surprised to find himself feeling happy. He considered. Bet? That wasn't something he was over. Any more than he had recovered from the death of his family. He guessed, though, that that kind of thing got easier to deal with with practice. Practice, he suddenly realized, he might get a lot of in the Guard.

Ah well. He stood and strolled toward the end of the line. At least he was off Vulcan. And he'd never have to go back. Although he did have dreams about what Vulcan would look like with a sticky planet buster detonated just above The Eye.

Very deliberately he shut the idea off, and concentrated on being hungry.

CHAPTER SEVENTEEN

RYKOR, TOO, WAS happy. Wild arctic seas boomed in her mind. Waves climbed toward the gray, overcast sky as glaciers calved huge bergs.

She rolled as she surfaced, exultantly spouting, then crashed her flukes against the water, and leapt free from wave to wave in powerful, graceful dives. There was a gentle tap on her shoulder.

Rykor rolled one eye open and sourly looked up at Frazer, one of her assistants. "You want?" she rumbled.

"There's a vid for you. From Prime World."

Rykor whuffled through her whiskers and braced both arms on the sides of the tank. She levered her enormous bulk up and over into the gravchair. Folds of blubber slopped over the sides until the frantic chair tucked them all safely in place. She tapped controls, and the chair slid her across the chamber to the main screen. Frazer fussed beside her.

"It's in reference to that new Guards recruit. The one you put the personal key on."

"Figures," Rykor muttered. "Now I'll get more walrus jokes. Whatever a walrus is."

The screen was blank, except for a single line of blinking letters. Rykor was mildly surprised, but touched the

CIPHER button, and added the code line. She motioned Frazer away from the screen.

It cleared, and Mahoney beamed out at her.

"Thought I'd take a moment of your time, Rykor, and ask you to check on one of my lads."

Rykor touched a button, and a second screen lit. "Sten?"

"Now that'd be a good guess."

"Guess? With your personal code added to the computer key?"

"That's always been my problem. Never known for bein' subtle."

Rykor didn't bother with a retort. Too easy a target. "You want his scores?"

"Now would I be bothering a chief psychologist if all I needed was a clerk to recite to me? You know what I'd like."

Rykor took a deep breath. "Overall, he should be what I've heard you call a 'nest of snakes.'" Mahoney looked puzzled, but decided to let it pass. "Exceptionally high intelligence level, well integrated into temporal planning and personnel assessment.

"Which does not compute. He should be either catatonic or a raving psychopath. Instead, he's far too sane. We can test more intensively, but I believe he's primarily functional because his experiences are unassimilated."

"Explain."

"Analysis—bringing these problems, and his unexpressed emotions into the open—would be suggested."

"Suggested for what," Mahoney said. "We're not building a poet. All I want is a soldier. Will he fall apart in training?"

"Impossible to predict with any certainty. Personal feeling—probably not. He's already been stressed far beyond our limits."

"What kind of soldier will he be?"

"Execrable."

Mahoney looked surprised.

"He has little emotional response to the conventional

stimuli of peer approval, little if any interest in the conventional rewards of the Guard. A high probability of disobeying an order he feels to be nonsensical or needlessly dangerous."

Mahoney shook his head mournfully. "Makes one wonder why I recruited him. And into my own dearly beloved regiment."

"Very possibly," Rykor said dryly, "it's because his profile is very similar to your own."

"Mmm. Perhaps that's why I try to stay away from my own beloved regiment. Except at Colors Day."

Rykor suddenly laughed. It rolled out like a sonic boom, and her body moved in undulating waves, almost driving the chair into a breakdown. She shut the laugh off.

"I get the feeling, Ian, that you are tapping the Old Beings Network."

Mahoney shook his head.

"Wrong. I don't want the boy cuddled through training. If he doesn't make it . . ."

"You'd send him back to his homeworld?"

"If he doesn't make it," Mahoney said quietly, "he's of no interest to me."

Rykor moved her shoulders.

"By the way. You should be aware that the boy has a knife up his arm."

Mahoney picked his words carefully. "Generally the phrase is knife up his sleeve, if you'll permit me."

"I meant what I said. He has a small knife, made of some unknown crystalline material, sheathed in a surgical-modification to his lower right arm."

Mahoney scratched his chin. He hadn't been seeing things back on Vulcan.

"Do you want us to remove it?"

"Negative." Mahoney grinned. "If the instructors can't handle it—and if he's dumb enough to pull it on any of them—that gives a very convenient escape hatch. Doesn't it?"

"You will want his progress monitored, of course?"

"Of course. And I'm aware it's not a chief psychologist's duties, but I'd appreciate it if his file was sealed. And if you, personally, were to handle him."

Rykor stared at the image. "Ah. I understand."

Mahoney half smiled. "Of course. I knew you would."

CHAPTER EIGHTEEN

"MY NAME IS Lanzotta," the voice purred. "Training Master Sergeant Lanzotta. For the next Imperial Year, you may consider me God."

Sten, safely buried in the motley formation of recruits, glanced out of the corner of his eye at the slender middle-aged man standing in front of him. Lanzotta wore the mottled brown uniform of a Guards Combat Division and the pinned-up slouch hat of Training Command. The only decoration he wore, besides small black rank tabs, was the wreathed multiple stars of a Planetary Assault Combat Veteran.

He was flanked by two hulking corporals.

"Bowing and burnt offerings are not necessary," Lanzotta went on. "Simple worship and absolute obedience will make me more than happy."

Lanzotta smiled gently around at the trainees. One man, who wore the gaily colored civilian silks of a tourist world, made the mistake of returning the smile.

"Ah. We have a man with a sense of humor." Lanzotta paced forward until he was standing in front of the man. "You find me amusing, son?"

The smile had disappeared from the boy's face. He said nothing.

"I thought I asked the man a question," Lanzotta said. "Didn't I speak clearly enough, Corporal Carruthers?"

One hulk beside him stirred slightly. "I heard you fine, sergeant," she said.

Lanzotta nodded. His hand shot forward and grabbed the recruit by the throat. Seemingly without effort, he lifted the trainee clear of the ground and held him, feet dangling. "I do like to have my questions answered," he mused. "I asked if you found me amusing."

"N-no," the boy gurgled.

"I much prefer to be addressed by my rank," Lanzotta said. He suddenly hurled the recruit away. The trainee fell heavily to the ground. "You'll find a sense of humor very useful," Lanzotta added.

"There are one hundred of you today. You've been chosen to enter the ranks of the Guard's First Assault Regiment.

"I welcome you.

"You know, our regimental screening section is very proud. They tell me that less than one out of a hundred thousand qualify for the Guard.

"Under those conditions, you men and women might consider yourselves elite. Corporal Halstead, do these— whatever they are—look like they're elite to you?"

"No, Sergeant Lanzotta," the second behemoth rumbled. "They look like what's at the bottom of a suit recycler."

"Umm." Lanzotta considered. "Perhaps not that low."

He walked down the motionless ranks, looking at the trainees closely. He paused by Sten, looked him up and down, and smiled slightly. Then walked down a few more ranks. "My apologies, corporal. You were right."

Lanzotta went back to the head of the formation, shaking his head sorrowfully. "The Imperial Guard is the finest fighting formation in the history of man. And the Guard's First Assault is the best of the Guard. We have never lost a battle and we never will."

He paused.

"Some general or other said a soldier's job is not to fight, but die. If any of you fungus scrapings live to graduate, you'll be ready to help the soldier on the other side die for his country. We aren't interested in cannon fodder in the Guard. We build killers, not losers.

"You'll be in training for one full year here at the regimental depot. Then if I pass you, you'll be shipped to the field assault regiment.

"Now you beings have three choices for that year. You can quit at any time, and we'll quite happily wash you out into a scum general duty battalion.

"Or else you can learn to be soldiers."

He waited.

"Are any of you curious as to the third alternative?"

There was no sound except the wind blowing across the huge parade ground.

"The third option is that you can die." Lanzotta smiled again. "Corporal Halstead, Corporal Carruthers, or myself will quite cheerfully kill you if we think for one moment that you would endanger your teammates in combat, and there's no other way to get rid of you.

"I believe, people. I believe in the Empire and I serve the Eternal Emperor. He took me off the garbage pit of a world that I was born on and made me what I am. I've fought for the Empire on a hundred different worlds and I'll fight on a hundred more before some skeek burns me down." Lanzotta's eyes glittered.

"But I'll be the most expensive piece of meat he ever butchered."

Lanzotta, as if unconsciously, touched the assault badge on his breast.

"Now, I will give you the first four rules for staying alive and happy. First, you should think of yourselves as two stages below latrine waste. I will let you know when I think you are qualified to consider yourselves sentient beings. Right now, I don't think that will ever happen.

"Second, when a cadreperson addresses you, you will come to attention, you will salute, you will address him by his rank, and you will do exactly what he tells you to do."

He nodded sideways to Carruthers. The corporal ran forward to one recruit.

"YOU!" she shouted.

"Yes."

The corporal's fist sank into the trainee's stomach, and he collapsed to his knees, retching.

Carruthers took one step to the side.

"YOU!" she screamed at the trembling woman.

"Yes . . . corporal," the trainee faltered.

"JUMP!"

The girl gaped. Carruthers' fist blurred into her chin, and she went down.

"THEY AREN'T LISTENING, SERGEANT." She sidestepped.

"YOU!"

"Yes, corporal," the third trainee managed.

"JUMP!"

"Yes, corporal!"

The recruit started bounding up and down.

"THAT'S NOT HIGH ENOUGH!"

The trainee jumped higher.

Carruthers watched, then shook her head in satisfaction. She rank back to her position beside Lanzotta.

"Third," Lanzotta went on as if nothing had happened. "You will run everywhere except inside a building or when otherwise ordered.

"And fourth—" Lanzotta stopped. "The fourth rule is that everything you can do is wrong. You walk wrong, you talk wrong, you think wrong, and you *are* wrong. We are here to help you start doing things right."

Lanzotta turned to Halstead.

"Corporal. Take this trash out of my sight and see if there's anything you can do to improve them."

"YES, SERGEANT." The corporal snapped a salute, then ran to one side of the formation.

"Right . . . face!" he shouted.

Sten blinked as he found his body responding to hypno conditioning he'd been programmed with in the sleep lectures.

"Forward . . . *harch!* . . . double-time . . . *harch!*"

The formation of trainees stumbled forward.

"This is your home, children," Halstead's voice boomed down the long squad barracks. Sten and the other recruits each stood next to a bunk.

"We give you a bed, which you'll be lucky to see four hours a night," Halstead went on. "You got one cabinet to put your equipment in. We will show you how to store it.

"I know most of you were brought up in a sewer works. You *will* keep this barracks clean. But it will *never* be clean enough."

Halstead walked to the door. "You have two minutes to gape around. Then fall outside to draw clothing and equipment."

The barracks door slammed shut. There was silence for a moment, then the excited buzz of conversation. Sten looked around the room at his fellow trainees. They looked fit, healthy, and terrified. He wasn't quite the smallest of the group, but close.

"Farmers. All farmers," the trainee beside the next bunk said. Sten looked at him. It was the young man from the tourist world. He held out a vertical palm to Sten. "Gregor."

Sten touched palms, and introduced himself. "Is there something the matter with farmers?" he asked curiously.

"Not a thing. Just what the Empire needs to make into heroes." Gregor might have curled a lip.

"But not you?"

Gregor smiled. "You are on it. Not me."

Sten lifted an eyebrow."

"Officer. That's the ticket. You hide and watch. When they start combing the losers out . . ." Gregor smiled again.

Halstead's whistle shrilled suddenly. Boots clattered as the trainees dashed for the door.

"YOU'RE TOO SLOW, CHILDREN. WAY . . . TOO

". . . SLOW. THE LAST FIVE OUT ARE ON MESS DUTY!" Halstead bellowed.

"NEXT!" the corporal screamed. Sten, standing naked in the long line, wondered if Halstead could talk normally. Probably not, he decided. The trainee in front of Sten dashed to the large coffin, ran inside, put his toes on the mark, and Halstead banged the door shut.

He waited, then jerked it open. "OUT OUT OUT," he bellowed.

The man jumped out, and ran down the corridor to a dispenser trough that was already filling with packaged uniforms.

Sten pulled his head out of the ultrasonic barber. He ran his fingers dubiously over his suddenly bare skull.

Carruthers grinned at him and growled, "Yeah, you look even dumber than you feel."

"Thank you, corporal," Sten shouted, and ran back to the waiting formation.

Sten, the clumsy transport bag dangling from one shoulder, ran back toward the barracks.

"FASTER, FASTER," screamed Halstead. "THAT ONLY WEIGHS FORTY KILOS, SCUM."

Out of the corner of his eye Sten saw Carruthers kneeling on the chest of one recruit who'd gone down under the weight of the bag.

"You've got to understand," Carruthers crooned, "we're just trying to help you, skeek." She suddenly bellowed, without getting off the panting man, "NOW ON YOUR FEET!"

"Oooh," Lanzotta moaned as he walked down the long line of trainees. "You think you look like soldiers?"

He stopped in front of one trainee. Instantly Carruthers and Halstead were beside him. "Son, your tunic lines up with your pants fastening."

"DID YOU HEAR THE SERGEANT?" Halstead

howled as he yanked the trainee's cap down over his eyes. "HE SAID YOU LOOKED LIKE DRAKH," Carruthers screamed in the boy's other ear. Lanzotta went on, as if the two bellowing corporals weren't there. "We want you to look your best." He shook his head sadly and walked on, as Halstead straight-armed the recruit back across his bunk, which collapsed sideways.

Lanzotta stopped in front of Sten.

Sten waited.

Lanzotta looked him up and down, then stared into Sten's eyes. A smile touched the corners of his mouth again, and he walked on.

There was a heavy whisper in his ear. "I think the sergeant likes you," said Carruthers. "He thinks you'll make a fine soldier. I do too. I think you ought to show us all just how good you are."

Pause.

"DROP! DO PUSHUPS! DO MANY, MANY PUSH-UPS!"

Sten went down, caught himself on his hands, and started down. Carruthers sat on his shoulders, and Sten collapsed to the floor. "I SAID DO PUSHUPS," Carruthers shouted.

Sten fought to lift himself clear of the ground. Carruthers got up.

"ON YOUR FEET," she howled. Sten snapped up, back at attention.

"I THINK WE WERE WRONG. I DON'T THINK YOU'LL EVER MAKE A SOLDIER," Carruthers shouted. "YOU WON'T EVEN MAKE A GOOD CORPSE."

Sten stood motionless.

Carruthers glowered at him for a moment, then went on to the next victim.

"Your father didn't love you, did he, trooper?"

"NO, CORPORAL."

"Your mother hated you, didn't she?"

"YES, CORPORAL."

"Why didn't your mother love you?"

"I DON'T KNOW, CORPORAL."

"She hated you because she was losing business until she had you aborted. Isn't that right, recruit?"

"YES, CORPORAL."

"Who is the only person who loves you, trainee?"

"YOU ARE, CORPORAL."

Sten winced as Carruthers hurled the recruit against the wall.

"WHERE ARE YOU FROM, SCUM?"

"Ryersbad Four, corporal."

"WHAT? WHAT DID YOU SAY?"

"Ry—Ryersbad Four, corporal."

"GET THAT TRASHCAN, RECRUIT."

"Yes, corporal."

"PICK IT UP. OVER YOUR HEAD."

The garbage cascaded over the recruit's shoulders.

"GET IN IT."

The trainee knelt, lowering the steel container over his body. Instantly Carruthers and Halstead thudded kicks into the can.

"SCUM—*crash*—YOU DON'T HAVE ANY HOME —*crash*—THE GUARD IS YOUR ONLY HOME— *crash*—WHERE ARE YOU FROM—*crash*."

"Nowhere, corporal," came the muffled voice from inside the can.

Halstead moaned, and tried to tear his cropped hair.

"It's hopeless," he said quietly. "Absolutely hopeless."

Screaming again:

"RECRUIT, YOU WILL GET OUT OF THAT TRASHCAN."

He helpfully kicked the container over. The trainee crawled out, his uniform stained and smeared.

"YOU LOOK LIKE YOU JUST FOUND A HOME, RECRUIT. NOW YOU TAKE THAT CAN OUT OF HERE TO THE MESSHALL. AND I WANT YOU TO STAND IN IT AND TELL EVERYONE WHO COMES BY THAT THAT'S YOUR HOME."

"Yes, corporal."

The recruit shouldered the container and stumbled toward the door.

"In your bunks," Lanzotta snapped.

The naked recruits dove for their beds. Lanzotta walked toward the door.

"I want you to know something, children," he said. "I can truthfully say that I have never spent a worse first training day with a sorrier group of scum. I'm not even going to enjoy killing you. Don't you agree?"

"YES, SERGEANT," came the shout from a hundred bunks.

"I really can't stand it. Good night, children."

Lanzotta flipped off the light switch.

"Are you all exhausted?" came the question in the blackness.

"YES, SERGEANT."

"What?"

"NO, SERGEANT."

The light came back on.

"That's nice," Lanzotta said. "Five minutes. Fall outside dressed for physical training."

He smiled and walked out of the barracks as the recruits stared at each other, stunned.

Sten ran the depil stick over his face again, just to make sure, reslotted it, and picked up his shower gear. He hurried out of the refresher to his bunk. Flipped open the cabinet and, checking the layout chart pinned to the inside wall, put everything away.

He checked the clock. He had a whole minute and a half until he had to dress. He sat down on the floor with a happy moan. His bunk was already S-rolled for the day, blanket folded in the prescribed manner on top of it.

"Sten. Gimme a hand." Sten pulled himself back up, and grabbed the other end of Gregor's mattress.

The two men looked at each other, and both of them

suddenly snickered. "Definitely material for a recruiting livee," Gregor grinned. "By the way. You notice something interesting?"

"There's nothin' interesting on this clottin' world. Except that bed if I could crawl back in it."

"Look around. Somethin' interestin'. There's women in this unit, right?"

"Good thinkin', Gregor. Guess they'll have to make you an officer."

"Shaddup. But you know somethin' more interestin'? Everybody sleeps alone."

"Probably some rule against anything else."

"Rules ever stop anybody who's in the mood?"

Sten shook his head.

"They put something in the food. That's what it is. Chemicals. 'Cause they don't want anybody getting attached to somebody who probably's gonna wash out."

Sten thought about it. Not likely. If everybody was like he was, they were just too tired to raise even a smile. He decided to change the subject. "Gregor. You said something about you're gonna be an officer?"

"Sure."

"How?"

"I have three things on my side. First, my dad. Don't say anything, 'cause I don't want to sound like I'm bragging, but he's a wheel. Our family owns most of Lasker XII. He's got touch. We've even been presented at court."

Sten looked at Gregor thoughtfully. He guessed that was pretty significant.

"Second. I went to military schools. So I know what they're talking about. And I'll tell you, that's a lot better than the conditioning they pour in us while we're trying to sleep."

"Military schools. Doesn't the Guard have some kind of academy? Just for officers?"

Gregor looked a little uncomfortable. "Yeah, but my dad .·. . I decided it'd be better to start at the bottom. You know, so you understand the troops that you're gonna command. Be one of them, and all that."

"Uh-huh."

"Third. Every now and then, they make an outstanding recruit award and commission the lucky choice. Right out of basic."

"Which you think is gonna be you?"

"Pick somebody else. Look around. Go ahead. Pick somebody."

Sten eyed the recruits, milling into their uniforms.

"Like Lanzotta said. They're just cannon fodder. I'm not saying I'm great, but I don't see competition. Unless . . . maybe you."

Sten laughed. "Not me, Gregor. Not me. I learned a long time ago, you keep your head down you don't get caught by the big pieces."

The door crashed open. "AWRIGHT, LISTEN UP. WE GOT A CHANGE IN THE TRAINING SCHEDULE SINCE IT'S GETTIN' COLD OUTSIDE. IT'S ALMOST TWENTY DEGREES CENTIGRADE, AND SO WE'RE GONNA PRACTICE. UNIFORM OF THE DAY WILL BE COLD-WEATHER GEAR."

Gregor's mouth hung open. "Cold-weather gear? It's the middle of summer!"

Sten jerked his cabinet door open and started pawing an arctic uniform out.

"Thought you'd already learned what Lanzotta said about us thinking."

Gregor wearily nodded, and started changing.

"Report!"

"Sten. Recruit in training!"

Lanzotta leaned back in his chair.

"Relax, boy. This is just routine. As you know, the Empire takes a great deal of interest in seeing that its soldiers are well treated."

"Yessir!"

"Therefore, I've got some questions to ask you. These will be filed with the rights commission. First question: Have you, since your arrival on Klisura, seen any instances of physical maltreatment?"

"I don't understand, sir."

"Have you seen any of the cadre abuse any trainee? It's a severely punishable offense."

"Nossir!"

"Have you witnessed any cadre member addressing any trainee in derogatory tones?"

"Nossir!"

"Do you consider yourself happy, trainee?"

"Yessir!"

"Dismissed."

Sten saluted, whirled, and ran out. Lanzotta scratched his chin thoughtfully and looked at Halstead.

"Him?"

"Not sure yet. But probably."

CHAPTER NINETEEN

THE ASSASSIN WAS methodical.

Mental notes: Sten; Thoresen; Time . . . time a question; Thoresen more so. Motive: personal. Possible—no, probable danger to me. Assignment questionable unless . . .

"There's a matter of payment," the assassin said finally.

"We've already settled that. You'll be well paid."

"I'm always well paid. It's a question of delivery. Uh . . . my back door?"

"You don't trust us?"

"No."

The Baron eased back in his chair, closed his eyes. There were no worries. He was just relaxing and taking in a bit more UV.

"It seems, at this point, your problems aren't a back door—a way out—as much as they are your knowledge."

"Knowledge?"

"Yes. If you choose to not accept the assignment . . . well, you're privy to a great deal, you must realize. Need I go further?"

The assassin casually reached over the desk and picked up an antique pen. "If you even look at one of the alarms," the killer whispered, "I'll bury this pen in your brain."

The Baron was still, then pushed a smile across his face. "Do you have your own way out?"

"Always," the assassin said. "Now, when I complete the task, I have a bank in—"

Thoresen waved languidly. "Done. Whatever the arrangements. Done."

"It's not enough money."

"Why not?"

"To begin. I must get inside the Imperial Guard. That may mean other deaths than your target."

"You're thinking of joining the Guard?"

"Possibly. There is also the matter of the man who recruited Sten, this Imperial intelligence operative."

"A minor agent."

"Are you sure?"

The Baron hesitated. "Yes."

"I still need more money."

"That is not a problem."

"The time?"

"Yes. This must be done immediately."

The assassin stood up to leave. "Then I can't do it. No one can. If you'd still like to try, I'll give you a few names, but no one who would take the job is competent. Be warned of that."

The Baron looked at him thoughtfully. "How much time?"

"As much as I need."

Thoresen was running ahead of the assassin. He had the best here. So . . . yes. It was the only way. "Very well."

The assassin started for the door.

"A moment, please," Thoresen said.

The assassin stopped.

"The matter of the pen. How would you have killed me?"

The assassin shook his head. "No."

"I collect martial trivia—I'm quite willing to pay . . ."

The assassin named a price and Thoresen agreed. A few minutes later he was holding his elbow crooked in just the right position.

CHAPTER TWENTY

STEN FOUR-HANDED BEERMUGS and pushed away from the vendor. He clattered the mugs down on the table, drained one, and grabbed another before the other two trainees could get to it.

"Whaddaya think, Big Time Trainee Corporal Sten?" Morghhan asked.

"Just like the clottin' world I came off. Anytime you get promoted, you end up payin'. Only difference is they take the credits now instead of later."

"Y'got a bad attitude, troop," Morghhan said as he sluiced down beer.

Sten poured more down his own throat and considered. Bad attitude? Not hardly. He was still pretty happy, in spite of the best efforts of Lanzotta and company. Maybe he was stuck in the Guard. But it was just for a few years. And nothing he did could extend that contract.

Also Sten had, if not friends, at least people he could sit and talk with. Even though most of their time was spent deciding what sewer pit Lanzotta crawled out of, he wasn't alone anymore. The new jargon everybody used wasn't much different from Mig-talk.

He put Bet back behind the wall quickly and turned to Morghhan, the skinny recruit he'd been sure wasn't

134

going to make it through the last weeks of physical conditioning on that three-gee world.

"Damn right I got a bad attitude. I didn't ask for no stripes. They don't pay me better 'cause I gotta tell you clots when to wipe, do they?"

"If I was you," Bjhalstred said softly, "I'd be honored. Shows how much cadre thinks of you. Shows they think you'll make a real hero guardsman type."

Sten snorted at Bjhalstred. He couldn't figure the agri-world boy out. Nobody could be so dumb. Or could they? Not that it mattered. Sten shrugged and dumped the spare beer in Bjhalstred's lap.

He yelped and grabbed at his crotch. "Noncoms ain't permitted to discipline trainees. Ain't you listened to the regs? You wanna go outside?"

Sten stood up. "You first."

"Naw. You g'wan an' start without me. I'll work on your beer while you're gone."

Morghhan interrupted. "Chop it. Here. Take Gregor's. Looks like he ain't gonna show."

They drained their mugs, and Sten sourly held out another handful of credits. "I'm buyin', somebody else is flyin'." Bjhalstred headed for the machine.

"You got any idea why they gave you the stripes?" Morghhan asked.

Sten shook his head. "I sure ain't been leechin' Lanzotta. Maybe they figure on trainee rank to wash out the weak ones, now they're finally gonna start teachin' us soldiering."

"That don't compute."

"Why not? We been nine weeks just doin' muscle-puffs, and we're down, what?"

"Seventy-three left. Out of a hundred."

"Way too high, Carruthers was tellin' me. They only graduate ten per company. Should've dumped forty percent by now, she said. Said they was gonna put everybody under the fine-line startin' right away."

"So what? Either way they're gonna get you if they want."

"Now there's a high-prob thought," Bjhalstred agreed, coming back with the next round. "Speakin' of high, here's ol' Lord Gregor himself."

Gregor slid into a spare seat.

"Looks like you're nursin' a case of the hips," Morghhan said. "Who put it to you?"

"I was with Lanzotta."

"For almost an hour? An' the bloodstains don't hardly show."

Gregor smiled grimly. "I'm not the one with bloodstains. But Lanzotta's gonna be."

Sten waited.

"You went to him?"

"You have it locked. To tell him I'm sending off a letter to my father."

"I'll bet he was very interested," Bjhalstred said solemnly. "Very important for a young trainee to keep his family posted."

"It was about this clotting trainee stripe thing."

Sten eyed Gregor over his beer. "You still think you got raw 'cause they didn't give you any acting rank?"

"Straight. Hell, I deserve at least as much of a chance as anybody. They say these jack stripes are to pick out potential leaders. Why not me?"

"Maybe they figure you're nothin' but a potential wipe," Morghhan said.

"Try me," Gregor glowered.

"Shaddup, the both of you," Sten put in before Morghhan had time to bristle. "We are sittin' here, quietly drinkin' beer, and celebratin' that we can now get out of barracks for two hours a night an' get swilled."

"Cadre gives us enough grief, we don't have to go out and synthesize our own," Bjhalstred agreed.

Morghhan added a massive belch and went for more beer.

"I ain't just blowin'," Gregor said. "You know my father's got influence. All I want is justice. Tell you what. I see all they gave you is a double stripe. Since you and

I are the only ones in this company with any intelligence—"

"Appreciate the thought," Bjhalstred said. "Glad you two fleet admirals decided to split a beer with an ol' scrunchie like me."

"That's not what I mean," Gregor said irritably. "Sten and I are the only two who're aware how much your whole military career depends on what happens right here in training."

"Military career," Morghhan said as he came back to the table. "Whoo. Things getting serious around here."

"Let 'im finish," Sten said.

"So I told my father to go straight to the Imperial Court. Get an investigation. Why is the Guard wasting its finest potential because the instructors couldn't pour piss out of a spaceboot unless there was a printout on the heel?"

"Come on, Gregor. You mentioned my name. What's this got to do with me?"

"I'll use you as an example. You only got two stripes. You ought to have been trainee platoon leader. Or better. If I hadn't had training already, I got to admit you'd be almost as good a troop as me."

"Yuh."

"So I'm gonna mention you in my letter. Make a stronger case, and when my father takes care of things, it'll do you some good too."

Sten started to say something, then decided to spend a few seconds unhooking Morghhan's fingers from the spare mug and inhaling it. Then he put the mug down.

"I don't think I want that," he said, just as quietly as he could manage. "I'll make my own way, thanks."

"But—"

"Gregor. That's what it is, like you say. End program."

Gregor stared at Sten, then nodded. "Whatever you want. But you're making a mistake."

"My mistake."

Gregor got to his feet. "Anyway. I got a letter to write." And he was gone.

"Trainee Corporal Sten?"

Sten looked back from the doorway at Bjhalstred, who had snapped to rigid attention.

"You have my permission to speak, Trainee Bunghole Bjhalstred."

"Request plus or minus reading on that last, over."

"Stand by. Computing. Prog 1—somebody's either gonna be trainee fleet general or Guard cesspool orderly with thirty years' time in grade. I dunno. Prog 2—I'm gonna get imploded. Halstead said training was really gonna start tomorrow mornin', an' that's more than I can face without a hangover."

Three mugs clanked solemnly.

"Awright," Carruthers said in what were almost human tones. "What you're about to get is the most carefully engineered way of killing someone known to man. Imperial engineers designed it so not even maggotbrains like you could screw it up. Which is almost unbelievable.

"I need one idiot volunteer. You." She waved at Sten. "Post."

Sten slid out of the bleacher bench, double-timed to a position in front of the low stand, and waited at attention.

In the distance, behind Carruthers, ran the thousand-meter tree- and bush-studded emptiness of a firing range, lane-marked at its far end.

Carruthers opened the top of the lecture stand and took out a weapon. A smooth black triangle formed the stock/pistol grip, and a stubby inverted cone ended the seventy-centimeter-long barrel.

Carruthers handled the rifle reverently.

"You probably seen this, and handled it in the livees. This is assault rifle Mark XI. We call it the willygun. Tell you something strange about this. This was invented more'n a thousand years ago, on Terra, by a designer named Robert Willy.

"It was a fine design," Carruthers said. "On'y problem was that lasers weren't that good and nobody knew for sure how to handle hunks of antimatter, which is what makes this piece so deadly."

She touched a stud, and a long tube slid out of the rifle's butt. "This is the ammunition. Antimatter Two—AM_2—the same stuff that powers spaceships. One tube contains fourteen hundred rounds. The bullet's a one-millimeter ball of AM_2, which is inside an Imperium shield, which is the only thing that keeps the whole magazine from exploding when it touches conventional matter.

"We once calculated, as a matter of interest, that one of these tubes has enough energy to power a scoutship all the way around this system at full drive level.

"Ain't that interesting, Bjhalstred?"

Bjhalstred jumped awake.

"You wasn't sleeping on me, was you, Bjhalstred?"

"NO, CORPORAL."

"That's good. That's very good. But why don't you come on out here and get down in pushup position to make sure you don't *get* sleepy.

"Anyway. Fourteen hundred rounds. If the Empire ever sold these guns on the open market, which of course they never will, each little tiny AM_2 ball would cost a guardsman three weeks' salary. You see how good the Empire is to us?"

Carruthers waited.

"YES, CORPORAL," came the shout.

"Aren't you all glad you went and joined up?"

"YES, CORPORAL."

"You sounded a little weak on that one," Carruthers growled. "Assault rifle Mark XI. You got two controls. One is for your safety/single-shot/automatic fire mode selection, the other is the trigger. You got one dial, here on the butt, which shows you the state of battery charge. Each battery will give the laser enough energy for about ten thousand rounds, depending on atmospheric pressure, if any, and conditions.

"The laser is what is used to fire the particles. This means the only sight you got is this crosshair. You don't have to worry about trajectory or bullet drop or any of that other dust that's important with a conventional weapon.

"Which is what is special about the willygun. If you can point it at something, you hit that something.

"Demonstrator!"

Sten mounted the platform. Carruthers handed him the rifle. Sten handled it curiously. Light. Almost too light, like a toy. Carruthers grinned at him. "That ain't nothing you'd give your kid brother on Empire Day," she said, seeming to read Sten's thoughts.

Curruthers opened the stand again and took out an object wrapped in plastic and about fifty centimeters to a side. She jumped down from the stand and walked ten meters to a low table. Carruthers unwrapped the parcel.

"This here is meat," she said. "The stuff that soyacrap in the messhall is supposed to taste like. It's got about the same consistency as a humanoid."

Carruthers set the blood-oozing meat on the table and walked back to the stand. "Shoot me that deadly charging chunk of beef, trainee," she said.

Sten raised the weapon awkwardly to his shoulder, and aimed through the sight. He pulled the trigger. Nothing happened.

"Helps if you take the safety off first," Carruthers snarled.

Sten flipped the switch just above the trigger, reaimed, and fired. There was the low crackle as air ionized.

His eyes jumped open, and the recruits semidozing through the lecture snapped awake. The minute particle hit the meat. It looked as if the beef exploded, blood spattering for several meters to the side.

"Go take a close look, trainee," Carruthers invited.

Sten climbed down from the stand and walked to the table. There were only a few chunks of the meat left. Sten stared at the spattered table and ground, then came back to the stand.

"Makes you think," Carruthers said, "just how healthy anybody on the receiving end of that round would be. The answer is," she said, raising her voice, "they wouldn't be. You hit anything humanoid or even anything close to it with one of those anywhere and they're dead. If the round don't make a hole big enough to stick your fist through, the shock will."

Carruthers stood silently, letting the idea sink in.

"Something to think about, isn't it?" she said soberly.

"AWRIGHT, SLUGS, YOU SAT ON IT LONG ENOUGH. NOW UNASS THOSE BLEACHERS AND GIMME A COMPANY FORMATION. We're gonna let you kill some targets today."

Carruthers waited until the recruits were on line, then added softly, "So far we dumped less'n a third of you skeeks back to your home cesspits. Here's where we cut some more dead tissue out.

"Children, there ain't never been a soldier who couldn't shoot. If there was an army that'd let him, that army wasn't around long—and the Guard has been around for a thousand years. This is where we start cuttin' clean.

"You either qualify on the willygun or you're out. Simple as that. If you more'n just qualify, there's bennies for that. More pay and better training.

"But first you best qualify. 'Cause I hear they're jumpin' those duty battalions into terraforming these days. I'd ruther be making a first-wave drop myself. Figure the chances are better.

"Now. FIRST RANK, 'TEN-HUT. ONE MAN PER POST. AT A RUN. MOVE OUT!"

Ten recruits, in spite of extensive individual attention and minor batterings, failed to qualify. Their bunks were rolled and empty the next day.

Sten couldn't understand why anybody had problems. Carruthers had been right. Point the willygun, and you hit. Every time.

When the rifle course ended, Sten was qualified for the next stage: SNIPER-RATED.

It got him ten more credits a month, his first ribbon, and more training.

Carruthers thunked down beside him.

"You got the target?"

Sten peered through the sights of the rifle. "Yes, corporal."

Carruthers touched the control box beside him. The target shot sideways, out of sight behind the stone wall a thousand meters from Sten.

"Awright. Now. Focus on the wall. The crosshairs go out of focus, right? Use the first knob on your sight. Twist until you get the sight focused."

Sten followed instructions.

"Got it? Now use the knob below your sight, and turn until the crosshairs are about where you think that target is, even though you can't see it. Got it? Fire one."

Sten touched the trigger.

Sten's fortieth-century sniper rifle was, in essence, quite simple. The round was still the AM2 shielded particle. But instead of using a laser as propellant, a modified linear accelerator hung around the barrel. The sight was used to give exact range to the target, then, when the scope was twisted to fix on the out-of-sight target, the accelerator "spun" the round so that it could execute up to a ninety-degree angle if necessary.

A gun that could shoot around corners.

Sten heard the explosion and saw the wall crumble.

"Hit."

Carruthers slammed Sten on the back.

"Y'know, troop, you keep up like this and Guard's First may get themselves a trooper."

And for some reason, Sten felt very proud of himself.

Sten crashed the garbage bin down on the dump, then upended it. Clean enough. He shoved the nozzle of the ultrasonic cleaner to the bottom and touched the trigger. Then banged the can a few more times on the concrete and lugged it back into the messhall. Most of the Guard's menial jobs were handled either by civilians or by the time-servers of the duty battalions. Except for the real scutwork. The Guard reserved those chores for punishment detail. It didn't bother Sten that much. It was still better than any on-shift back on Vulcan.

Besides, he didn't figure he could have gotten around the problem.

He'd been quite happy, sitting there on the sand watching Halstead posture at Lanzotta's commands.

"We are not building technicians," Lanzotta had said. "I've told you that. We're building killers. We want people who want to listen to the sound of their enemies' eyeballs pop, who want to see what happens when you rip somebody's throat out with your teeth."

Sten looked around at the other trainees. Most of them looked mildly aghast. Sten blanked. He remembered quite well, thank you, sergeant.

"We need a demonstrator."

Silence. The company had learned by now what volunteering generally got you. And then somebody said, "Corp' Sten."

Sten had a pretty good idea it was Gregor, but didn't worry about it. He was seriously into being invisible. Lanzotta heard the voice.

"Sten. Post."

Sten grunted, snapped to his feet and ran forward.

"Yes, corporal."

Halstead did another fast one-two move. Fair, Sten analyzed. He's open down low, though.

"Recruit Corporal Sten. That man is your most dangerous enemy. Your mission is to close with and destroy him!"

Sten ambled in. Held up his hands in what he hoped would look like an offensive move and went airborne. Sten rolled in midair, recovered, and held back as his feet touched. Allowed himself to crumple forward, face first in the sand.

That should do it. And he heard Lanzotta's whisper in his ear.

"You are faking it, recruit corporal. You know how to do it better. Now I want you to get back up, without letting your fellow skinks know what you're doing, and attack Corporal Halstead."

Sten didn't move.

"The alternative is three days on garbage detail."

Sten sighed and picked himself up.

Halstead moved in, hands grabbing. Poor, Sten flashed, and rolled toward the ground. Legs in the air, scissored about Halstead's hips.

Halstead crashed, Sten locked, using Halstead's momentum to bring him back up. Halstead rolling up, Sten incoming, shoulder under Halstead's waist.

Halstead went straight up in a curving flight. Sten had time enough to consider if he'd put a cadre into suborbital, then he was moving. Halstead slammed back down, still moving, and Sten slammed two toe kicks into his ribs.

Halstead stayed down.

Sten recovered and turned.

There was awed silence from the trainees. Sten looked at Lanzotta, who heaved a sigh and jerked a thumb.

"Hup, sergeant!"

Sten picked up his cap and double-timed toward the messhall.

There it was. Spaced if you did, spaced if you didn't. Sten grabbed the other garbage can and lugged them back into the messhall.

The mess sergeant grinned at Sten as he came through the tiny office.

"Guess you're glad to be goin' back to trainin' tomorrow, hey?"

Sten shook his head.

"Ya like it here?"

"Negatory, sergeant."

"What's the problem, 'cruit?"

"Tomorrow we start knife training, sergeant."

"So?"

Yeah. So. Sten suddenly started laughing as he dragged

the cans back toward their racks. So? It was still better than Vulcan.

Even Sten felt a little sick as the medic worked swiftly on the gaping wounds. The body was riddled with shrapnel and gouting blood.

"The procedure hasn't changed in thousands of years," the medic instructor said. "First get the casualty breathing again. Second, stop the bleeding. Third, treat for shock."

He finished, covered the humanoid simulacrum with an insul-blanket, and stood up. Looked around the class.

"Then you yell as loud as you can for a medic. Assuming some bork hasn't decided we're the most important target he can hit and there's any of us left."

"What then?" Pech, the fat recruit, asked.

"If there's no professional treatment, use your belt medpak. If the bleeding's stopped and the insides are more or less together, the antis in the kit should keep your buddy from getting the creeping crud."

He laughed.

" 'Course if you're on some world where we don't know anything about the bugs, best you can do is try to leave a good-looking corpse." The medic looked over Pech's steadily diminishing chubbiness. "Which will be hard enough in your case, Pech."

Sten and the others chuckled. The medic was the first instructor they'd had who'd treated them even vaguely like sentient beings.

The medic opened a large cabinet and motioned to Sten, who helped him lift out another simulacrum. This one was dressed in a battle suit.

"In a suit, things are different," the medic said. "The medpak should already be hooked up inside the suit and work automatically. Sometimes it does."

Another snort of laughter from the medic.

"But if the suit's holed, all you can do is seal it and get the casualty to a medshelter. You get more on that in suit drill. Now, I need a sucker—I mean a volunteer."

He glanced around the audience, and his eyes lit on Pech. "Come on up, troop."

Pech double-timed up to the stand and waited at attention. "Relax, relax. You make me nervous. Okay. This dummy here is your best buddy. You went through training together. You chased . . ." He pretended to study Pech closely. ". . . uh—ameboids together. Now his arm has just been blown off. What are you going to do?"

The medic stepped back. Pech shifted nervously.

"Come on, soldier. Your best friend's bleeding to death. Move!"

Pech took a tentative step forward as the medic pressed the switch concealed in his palm and the simulacrum's arm exploded. "Blood" sprayed across Pech and the stand.

Pech froze. "Come on, man. Move."

Pech fumbled for the medpak on his belt and moved closer. More pulsing "blood" dyed his face. Pech unclipped the pak's base and took a pressure bandage off.

"Thirty-four, thirty-five, thirty-six, thirty-seven . . . forget it, soldier."

Pech seemed not to hear him and fought to get the bandage in position. Finally, the gout of "blood" stopped.

"Your friend just died," the medic said harshly. "Now, on your feet."

Pech clambered up, numb. The medic stared around at the trainees to make sure they got his point. Then he turned back to Pech.

"The dye used in that blood won't wear off for two days. Maybe that'll help you think about how you'd feel if that dummy had really been your teammate."

Pech never did recover from the incident. A few weeks later, after a series of foul-ups, he disappeared. Washed out.

Sten blinked as the world came back into focus. He and the five other recruits stared at each other blankly. Halstead flipped up the flash visor on his shock helmet.

"How long were you out?" he asked.

Sten shrugged. "A second or two, corporal?"

Halstead held out his watch finger. Two hours had passed. He unclipped another of the tiny bester grenades from his pocket.

"Instant time loss. You don't know what's happened to you, and you don't think anything's gone wrong. These are some of the most effective infiltration weapons you'll use.

"The company's out on the dexterity course. Report to Corporal Carruthers."

Sten saluted and the recruits ran off.

Sten couldn't get the man out of his mind. There had been nothing unusual about the incident, but for some reason the officer's image kept poking up from his brain at odd moments.

It had been his day as company runner and he had been dozing at the desk. He didn't hear the door open or close.

"You the only one here, guardsman?"

Sten snapped awake and was on his feet.

The man standing in front of him was tall and slender. Sten blinked and found himself staring at the uniform. Almost imperceptibly, it was changing shade to match the paneled wall background. The man wore a soft hat of the same kind of strange material that Sten later learned was a beret. It was tilted rakishly over one eye.

A winged dagger was pinned to the beret. The only other insignia on the uniform were captain's stars on one shoulder and on the other the black outline of some kind of insect.

For some reason, Sten found himself stammering.

"Uh, yessir—they're—they're all out in the field."

The officer handed Sten a sealed envelope.

"This is for Sergeant Lanzotta. It's personal, so see it's delivered directly to him."

"Yessir."

Then he was gone.

A week later, Sten got a chance to ask Carruthers who

the man was. The corporal whistled when Sten described the uniform.

"That's Mantis Section!"

Sten looked at her blankly.

"You mean you ain't heard?"

Sten shook his head, feeling like a pioneer-world idiot.

"They're the nastiest bunch of soldiers in the Imperial Army," Carruthers said. *"Real* elite. They work alone— humanoids, ETs. The Empire takes the best the Guard has and then disappears them into the Mercury Corps—Intelligence."

Sten remembered Mahoney and nodded.

"Anyway. Mantis wears those fancy trop-camouflage uniforms when you see them. Mostly, you don't see 'em at all and you'd better hope it stays that way."

"Why is that?"

"If you see one of those boys in the field you know you're about to be in deep trouble. Any one of 'em's probably got about two thousand and three of the enemy on his butt."

Carruthers smiled a rare smile. There was nothing she liked better than war stories. "I remember one time on Altair V. We were down with a regiment on a peace-keeping mission and somehow we'd got ourselves surrounded.

"We were screaming for help on every wavelength we could reach and tryin' to hang on. We figured the next thing that'd happen is we'd have to die a lot."

Carruthers laughed. Sten figured that she had just made some kind of a joke and laughed back.

"So, one night this woman shows up at the command post. A Mantis Section troopie. She'd come through the enemy lines, through our pickets, through the support lines and first thing we know she's sitting down with our CO eating dinner. When she finished, she borrowed some AM_2 tubes and bester grenades and disappeared again.

"I dunno what she did, or how she did it, but about twelve G hours later six Imperial destroyers showed up and bailed our tails out."

Carruthers glared at Sten, which made him feel a whole lot better. A smiling Carruthers was something he didn't think he wanted to get used to.

"But that's not the way it usually works," she told him. "You ever see one of those guys again, troop, you crawl under something. 'Cause as sure as your tail is where your head ought to be, there's something big and nasty about to come screaming in—you just remember that, hear?"

Sten heard her real well.

"You will *all* learn about the fighting suit," Lanzotta said. "Chances are, some of you will even die in one. And you will discover, as I did, that the suit will kill you faster than the enemy, more often than not."

At that point, Sten and the others turned their minds to "doze." They all thought they had Lanzotta figured now. All of his little lectures were structured the same. First, an introduction. Then—Lanzotta's favorite part— a history lesson. Followed by the information they really needed to know. At which point they snapped awake again.

"I am particularly fond of this subject," Lanzotta continued. "In fact, I have made a personal study of the suit. Because it was with this piece of equipment that the technicians reached the absolute height of absurdity."

Click. Snap. Every recruit mind instantly slipped into a deeper state of unconsciousness. Lanzotta motioned to Halstead, who walked to a terminal and rapped on a few keys. There was a loud clanking and grinding and all the recruits came awake as a long rack of fighting suits ratcheted out into the lecture area.

Sten looked over the suits, and for once, he didn't have to fake interest. Many of them he recognized from the war feelies. They were huge, armored things shaped vaguely like humanoids. Some had what could pass for arms, but were track-based.

The first thing he noticed was they all seemed to be graded by size. At the beginning of the rack, they were small and flimsy-looking. From there they got larger and larger and more complex-appearing, until about two-thirds of the way down the line. Then they got smaller again, but with a more durable look about them.

Lanzotta paced along the line of suits, stopping at the largest one. "Now here, as I can personally attest, is where the Techs really outdid themselves. It was all so logical, you see. To anyone but a guardsman. They made bullets, therefore they made bulletproof vests."

Lanzotta looked his captive group over, as if anticipating a question. No one was that dumb.

"Now, I'm not going to explain what a bullet was," Lanzotta said, "except to say it was a projectile that was capable of creating a hole in you as big as the willygun. In some ways, it was worse."

The way Lanzotta grinned at that, Sten *knew* he meant "worse."

"The larger the antipersonnel weapon," Lanzotta continued, "the more the Techs loaded on the armor. Until, finally, with this suit we could take anything. Lasers, nukes, bugs, null bombs, you name it, we were just about invulnerable."

Sten was starting to get the drift of what was wrong with the suit.

"About fifty years ago, I had the great pleasure of testing this suit in action. Myself and about two thousand comrades in arms."

Lanzotta laughed. And it was instant tension time for the recruits. Should they laugh? He obviously thought he had made a funny. But Carruthers and Halstead were stony-faced. They didn't think it was funny. Lanzotta ended their agony by not noticing anything and going on.

"Our orders were to put down a rebellion on a godforsaken planet called Moros. Besides the troops, we were supplied with everything known to modern military science—including the latest fighting suit."

Sten studied it more closely. It was the largest, non-tracked piece of equipment on the rack. There were tubes and wires, minividscreens, and knobs and bulges everywhere. It looked like it weighed about five hundred kilos and would take a whole battery of Techs to operate.

"I love this suit," Lanzotta said. "It can do anything. "It's AM2-powered and pseudomuscled. Anyone inside it would be equal to thirty beings in strength. A small company dressed in these could advance through any kind of fire the enemy threw at them. It's impervious to almost anything and you can live in it for months without outside support."

Lanzotta shook his head with the wonder of it all.

"Of course, no one thought to brief the natives on Moros. They weren't told what brave and fierce warriors we were. They didn't even know the word technology, so what could they think?

"We landed and they ran into the jungle. We advanced under fire—mostly spears and blowguns—and burned their villages. Then one day they grew tired of running."

Lanzotta laughed again. But this time, Sten and the others were too caught up with his story to notice.

"What they discovered was this: Yes, we were big strong soldiers with the fire power of a small tank. But we couldn't maneuver. And we were cut off from our environment. So, they worked out this simple little trick.

"They dug pits, camouflaged them, and then fled before our advance. Of course, many of us fell in. The pits were lined with nets that tangled us up."

Lanzotta wasn't laughing.

"And while we were struggling out of the nets, they'd run up to the pit and stick a big long spear through the suit's waste vent. The spear made large holes in the trooper inside.

"Naturally, the excrement was carried into the body. The wound festered so badly that the medpaks froze up—and many of us rotted to death."

Lanzotta shook his head.

"We lost two-thirds of the guardsmen that made the assault. And more in another landing. Finally the only solution was to dust the planet, sit back, and watch Moros glow."

Lanzotta patted the suit.

"Destroying planets isn't done in polite diplomatic circles. The Emperor was very unhappy."

Lanzotta grinned as he came to his final point.

"The *new* Techs," he said, "started redesigning the suit."

Sten wished he could find a place to hide. From the look on Lanzotta's face, he knew it would have to be very deep and made of something at least as strong as titanium.

"It is a sin and an abomination in the eyes of the Lord," Smathers frothed. "It was my duty to report their behavior to you."

Lanzotta stared at him, then at the two men standing at attention nearby. Sten, he ignored—for the moment.

"Colrath, Rnarak, is he telling the truth?"

"YES, SERGEANT."

Lanzotta sighed and turned to Smathers.

"Smathers, I have a distinct surprise for you. The Guard doesn't care about what beings do with each other when they're off duty, so long as everyone falls out for formation the next morning."

"But—"

"But you come from a world settled by the Plymouth Brethren. Fine. Some excellent guardsmen have been produced by your beliefs. But all of them learned their ideas are not to be applied to anyone but themselves. And since when have you ever interrupted your sergeant?"

Smathers stared at the floor. "Sorry. Sergeant."

"Your apology is accepted. But have you ever been to bed with a man?"

Smathers looked horrified. "Of course not."

"If you don't know about it, did you ever consider that you're missing something?" Lanzotta said.

Smathers' eyes bulged.

"In any event," Lanzotta said briskly. "You are spending time worrying about something that is none of your business. And since you seem so preoccupied ferreting cesspools, I think we need one volunteer to clean the one in the barracks. You're accepted."

"You're not going to—"

"I'm not going to," Lanzotta agreed. "Now move out."

Smathers walked down the barracks toward the latrine. Lanzotta turned to Colrath and Rnarak.

"While the Guard isn't concerned with what you do or don't do with each other, we still must respect the beliefs of the other trooper. I am deeply distressed by the fact that you two couldn't be bothered to find a private place for your recreation, and instead disturbed the sleep and happiness of other trainees. Go help him clean the cesspool."

The two shame-faced men walked slowly away. Now Lanzotta turned his attention to Sten.

"Recruit Corporal Sten!"

"Yes, sergeant."

"Why didn't you deal with this matter yourself?"

"I tried to, sergeant. Smathers insisted on seeing you."

"As is his right. Especially when confronted with a recruit corporal incapable of handling a simple barracks dispute."

"Yes, sergeant."

"First, you will remove those stripes."

"Yes, sergeant."

"Second, you will join those three on the cesspool detail."

"Yes, sergeant."

"Dismissed."

Sten followed the others out. Next time, he thought, he'd save everyone a whole lot of trouble and just tear Smathers in half.

CHAPTER TWENTY-ONE

BASICALLY, STEN DECIDED, he didn't give a Mig's ass. He touched the anodizer to the last bit of exposed metal on his weapons belt, then tucked it back in his cabinet.

Then looked up .

Tomika stood there, kitbag in hand.

He decided, for about the gigatime, she was the nicest-looking thing about training. And he'd tried. Indeed he'd tried.

"Who's paired with you, Sten?"

"My left hand," he said.

She tossed her ditty on his bunk and started patting the pillow into shape. Sten's mouth dropped.

"Uh, Tomika? I asked before and—"

"I don't bag with NCOs. I got standards."

Sten suddenly decided it not only wasn't important, but it was funny. Broke his laugh off as he looked at Gregor.

"You see what I meant," Gregor said. "And you were wrong."

"I'm always wrong, Gregor. Howcum this time?"

"They are arbitrary. They wouldn't give me the rank I deserve. And they broke you. You see?"

"Nope. Far as I can see, I stepped on it."

"It's right there. In front of you." Sten decided that Gregor was getting a little shrill.

"DNC, troop. Does not compute."

"My father taught me that any business that doesn't respond to new stimuli is doomed. That's the Guard. All they want is cannon fodder. Anybody who doesn't fit their idea of a moron hero, they'll put to scutwork. And if they make a mistake, like they did with you, they'll bust him down as soon as they see it."

"You really believe that, Gregor," Tomika said.

"Dash-A right I do," Gregor said. "I've written another letter to my father, Sten. He'll see things are rectified."

Sten sat up. "You, uh, mention me?"

"No, I did not. Just like you would have wanted. But you will regret it. You'll see."

And Gregor laughed, turned, and walked back toward his bunk.

"Hey, Ex Recruit Trainee Small Time Corporal Sten? Is he two zeds short of a full count?"

Sten didn't answer her, just listened to Gregor's laughter as he clambered into his bunk.

"And what happens when I do this?"

Tomika giggled. Sten suddenly sat up in his bunk and put a hand over her mouth. Movement. A buried snicker. Tomika reached up and grabbed him, pulling Sten down to the pillow.

"No, Sten," she breathed. "Wait."

Sten did—for a long count of heartbeats.

And then the shouting started.

Somebody hit the lights, and Sten bolted out of the bunk. The shouting came from Gregor's area.

Sten rolled out of his bunk, reflexively sliding up into an attack stance. And then he slumped down again, laughing helplessly.

Gregor screamed louder and started flailing.

Sten and the other recruits gathered around Gregor's area. The man did have problems.

"It's the Giant Spider of Odal," somebody said in a mock hushed voice. "You're in trouble, Gregor."

Gregor was indeed in trouble. Somebody must've snuck a spray can of climbing thread out of the training area the day before. And while Gregor slept, he, she, or they had spun the thread from bunk to cabinet to boots to bunk to combat shoes to cabinet to end up connected to Gregor's nose.

The high-test, incredibly sticky goo made a very effective spider web, Sten decided. Whoever had spun the web had unclipped the hardener from the nozzle tip, so the more Gregor flailed, the more he became enmeshed in the strands.

Gregor by now had trussed himself neatly in the strands and was moaning.

Sten looked at Tomika. "Who's got the real case at Gregor?"

She motioned blankly. "Just about everybody." The woman giggled. "Guess he'll make a fine officer."

"Bet three–one it won't straighten him out," Sten said. "Not just that, but prog—"

"Are we enjoying ourselves, children?" The recruits turned to instant statuary.

Sten could never figure how Carruthers managed a 116-dB(A) whisper. "Is there any particular reason we aren't all at attention?"

"Ten-hup!" somebody managed. Carruthers waddled forward through the cluster. Looked at Gregor and clucked thoughtfully.

"The Giant Spider of Odal. Knew we had lice and a few rats, but thought we fumigated those spiders last cycle."

Carruthers turned.

"Morghhan! Why don't you stroll down to supply and draw a tank of solvent. If you wouldn't mind."

The squadbay door slammed on Morghhan before Carruthers finished her sentence.

"Giant spiders, hmm. Serious business." Whisper into shout. "Recruit Sten, what's the uniform of the day for spider hunts?"

"Uh . . . I dunno, corporal."

"DROP, DROP, DROP. YOU ARE AN EXNONCOM
AND YOU ARE SUPPOSED TO KNOW THAT!
TRAINEE TOMIKA, YOU SHOULD HAVE TOLD
HIM—DROP, DROP, DROP!"

Carruthers walked back to the door.

"You will fall out in five minutes in full spider-hunt
dress, and prepare to spend the remainder of the night
looking for what I estimate is five giant spiders."

She slammed out. The recruits looked around. Bewildered. The door creaked open again.

"Anyone who is not in the proper uniform draws two
days' kitchen detail. That is all, children. Time's a-wast-
ing."

When Bjhalstred ran over Corporal Halstead with a
combat car, Sten knew he had been right all along. There
was nothing stupid about the farmboy. Now, no one ever
accused Bjhalstred of crunching Halstead on purpose. It
was an accident. Sure, Sten thought to himself, sure.

"This," Halstead proclaimed, "is another Empire tool
for wormbrains. One gauge shows you battery charge.
Turn this switch, and the car starts. You adjust the lift
level stick to the desired altitude. One to one-grand
meters. Doppler radar keeps you automatically that far
off the ground.

"Shove the control stick forward, you lift up. Farther
forward, the faster. Max speed, two hundred kph. Move
the stick to the side, the combat car turns. Do we have a
volunteer?"

Halstead looked around the trainees until he saw someone trying to be invisible.

"Bjhalstred," he crooned. "Come on up here, my boy."

Bjhalstred locked his heels in front of the corporal.

"Never driven a car, hmm?"

"NO, CORPORAL!"

"Why not, trainee?"

"We don't believe in them on Outremer, corporal. We're
Amish."

"I see." Halstead considered for a minute, then evidently decided not to say anything. "In the car."

Bjhalstred clambered in.

"You don't have any religious objections to driving, do you?" Halstead asked.

"NO, CORPORAL."

"Fine. Start it, set it for two meters height, and drive out across the parade ground. Turn it around and come back."

Bjhalstred fumbled with the controls, and the car silently lifted clear of the ground and hung there.

"Well?"

Bjhalstred looked puzzledly at the controls, then firmly took the control stick in his hand and yanked it to the right.

Halstead had just time to scream *"NOO"* as the combat car pivoted on its own axis, the bumper catching Halstead in the head and sending him spinning off the stand to the ground, and the car smoothly soared forward. Its radar had enough range to pick up the trainee-filled (but rapidly emptying) bleachers, and lifted the vehicle neatly up and over the bleachers, after which it turned neat fifteen-meter circles. Bjhalstred sat petrified at the controls.

Eventually Lanzotta and Carruthers got a second car and maneuvered alongside the aimlessly circling first vehicle. Lanzotta jumped lightly into the troop compartment, reached over Bjhalstred's shoulder, and turned the power off. The car settled down to the ground. Lanzotta levered Bjhalstred out.

"At the moment," Lanzotta said, "I do not love you, trainee. You have knocked one of my cadremen unconscious, and this is a Bad Thing.

"I am sure you will want to make Corporal Halstead happy when he finally comes to, won't you?"

Bjhalstred nodded.

"Otherwise he is liable to kill you, trainee. And then I'll have to write up a report on why he did that. So I'm sure you want to volunteer to do the poor corporal a personal favor, don't you?"

Bjhalstred nodded again.

"You see that mountain," Lanzotta said, pointing at the kilometers-distant ridge. "There is a creek on that mountain, trainee. Corporal Halstead is particularly fond of the water from that creek. So why don't you get a bucket and run up there and get him a bucket of water?"

"Huh?" Bjhalstred managed.

"That is, 'Huh, Sergeant,'" Lanzotta said. "And I think you heard me."

Bjhalstred nodded, got slowly up from the seat, and started for the barracks.

Lanzotta watched him run into the building, dash out carrying a bucket, and disappear in the distance. Sten, watching from the company formation meters away, thought he saw Lanzotta's shoulders shake slightly. No, Bjhalstred wasn't that dumb.

CHAPTER TWENTY-TWO

LANZOTTA LOOKED HAPPY.

Sten shuddered and wished he'd hit formation in the rear ranks. This would be a bad one.

Halstead started to call the company to attention. Lanzotta waved him into silence. "Something very interesting just happened, children," he said smoothly.

Pacing back and forth. This would be very bad.

"I just received the notification from, shall we say, a higher authority. It seems that I may not be performing my duty to best suit the needs of the Empire."

Sten wanted to find a very deep, very heavily shielded shelter. He hoped he didn't know what was going on.

"I may not be giving some of my trainees the proper attention. Particularly in the area of acting rank. It seems this authority wonders if some very capable leadership might be squelched by this suppression.

"Yes. A very interesting letter."

Lanzotta's smile vanished, replaced with a look of sincerity. "I would hate to err on the Emperor's service, would I not? Gregor! Post!"

Sten thought right then would be a very good time to die. Gregor double-timed to the head of the formation, snapped-to and saluted.

"Recruit Gregor? You are now recruit company commander."

Someone in the rear rank said "Clot!" very loudly.

Lanzotta evidently decided to be deaf momentarily.

"Take charge of the company, Recruit Company Commander Gregor. You have one hour to prepare the unit for transshipment and combat training."

It was possible, Sten decided, to think somebody had bad breath just by listening to them wheeze on a radio. He itched between his shoulder blades. It didn't do any good. Some genius had designed vacuum assault suits to itch a soldier everywhere it was impossible to scratch. Sten told himself he didn't itch, and went back to listening to Gregor wheeze on the command circuit.

Come on, he thought. Make up your mind.

"First Pla—I mean one-one."

Sten keyed his mike.

"Go."

"The ship is a Class-C patrolcraft. That means we go in through the drive tubes. I had my first sergeant take a reading. They're cool."

Sten unclipped from the asteroid he and his platoon were "hiding" behind and drifted out a little.

The old hulk hanging in blackness two kilometers away had been more or less tarted up to look like a C-Class, right enough. But . . .

Sten went on command. "Six? This is one-one. Request seal."

Gregor grunted and shut the rest of the company off the circuit.

"Going in the tubes is a manual attack, sir."

"Of course, Sten. That's why . . ."

"You don't figure those bad guys maybe read the book? And have a prog?"

"DNC, troop. What do you want? Some weird frontal shot?"

"Clot, Gregor! We go up the pipe, somebody'll be waiting for us, I figure. If you could put out a screen, I'll take my platoon on the flank."

"Continue . . . one."

Sten shrugged. No harm in trying.

"We'll tin-can it. Peel the skin and bleed internal pressure off. That'll throw 'em off, and maybe we can double-prong them."

More wheezing. Sten wondered why Gregor's father couldn't afford to get his son an operation."

"Cancel, one. I gave orders."

Sten deliberately unsealed the circuit.

"Certainly, captain. Whatever the captain desires. Clear." Carruthers' voice crackled.

"One. Breaking circuit security. Kitchen detail."

Sten heard Gregor bury a laugh in his open mike.

"This is six. By the numbers . . . leapfrog attack . . . maneuver element . . . go."

Sten's platoon jetted into the open. Sten checked the readout and automatically corrected the line.

Diversion fire lasered overhead from the other two platoons. Sten tucked a random zig program into the platoon's computer. They continued for the hulk.

By the time they closed on the hulk's stern, half the platoon hung helplessly in space, shut down as casualties by the problem's computer.

Sten rotated the huge projector from his equipment rack and positioned it. He figured to go in just below the venturi and—

And there was a massive flash in his eyes, Sten's filter went up through the ranges to black, and Sten stared at the flashing CASUALTY light on his suit's control panel.

By now he'd gotten used to being "killed." As a matter of fact, this was the first time he'd enjoyed it. He did not think any of the casualties would collect the usual scut details when they got back to the troop area.

Lanzotta had a much bigger fish to barbecue. Or maybe much smaller, now.

* * *

Lanzotta was stone-faced and standing very still.

Sten relaxed, and flickered an eye toward Gregor.

"You went in by the book, recruit company commander?"

"Yes, sergeant."

"Did you bother to check EM range?"

"No, sergeant."

"If you had, you could have seen that your enemy modified those solar screens into projectors. Aimed straight back at their normally undefended stern. Why didn't you check, recruit company commander?"

"No excuse, sergeant."

"Did you consider an alternate assault?"

"No, sergeant."

"Why not?"

"Because—because that's how the fiche said to assault a C-ship, sergeant."

"And if you didn't do it by the manual, you might have gotten yourself in trouble. Correct, Recruit Company Commander Gregor?"

"Uh . . ."

"ANSWER THE GODDAMNED QUESTION."

Sten and the others jumped about a meter. It was the first time Lanzotta had ever shouted.

"I don't know, sergeant."

"I do. Because you were thinking that as long as you stuck by the book, you were safe. You didn't dare risk your rank tabs. And so you killed half a company of guardsmen. Am I correct?"

Gregor didn't say anything.

"Roll your gear, mister," Lanzotta said. And ripped the Guard Trainee patch off Gregor's coveralls. Then he was gone.

Carruthers double-timed to the head of the formation.

"Fall out for chow. Suit inspection at twenty-one hundred hours."

Nobody looked at Gregor as they filed back into the barracks. He stood outside a very long time by himself.

But by the time Sten and the others got back from

chow, Gregor and his gear had disappeared as if they'd never existed.

"First sergeant! Report!"

"Sir! Trainee Companies A, B, and C all present and accounted for. Fifty-three percent and accounted six in hospital, two detached for testing."

The trainee topkick saluted. Sten returned the salute, about-faced to Lanzotta, and saluted again.

"All present and accounted for, sergeant!"

"It is now eighteen hundred hours, recruit captain. You are to take charge of your company and move them via road to Training Area Sixteen. You will disperse your men in standard perimeter defense. You are to have them in position by dusk, which is at nineteen-seventeen hours. Any questions?"

"No, Sergeant Lanzotta!"

"Take charge of your company."

Sten saluted and spun again.

"COMPANY . . ."

"Platoon . . . 'toon . . . 'toon . . ." chanted Sten's platoon leaders.

"Right *HACE!* Arms at the carry! Forward . . . *harch* . . . double-time . . . *harch.*"

The long column snaked off into the gathering twilight. Sten double-timed easily beside them. By now he could walk, march, or run—eyes open, seventy percent alert—and be completely asleep. Lanzotta had been exaggerating when he said the trainees would only get about four hours' sleep a night.

Maybe that'd been so at the beginning. But as the training went downhill toward graduation, the pace got harder. There were fewer washouts now, but it was far easier to go under.

Lanzotta had explained to Sten after he'd given him the tabs of a recruit company commander. "First few months, we tried to break you physically. We got rid of the losers, the accident prone, and the dummies. Now we're fine-lining. The mistakes you make in combat training are ones that would get you or other guardsmen cycled for fertilizer.

"Besides, there are still too many people in this cycle." Too many people. Assuming—which Sten didn't necessarily—the one-in-a-hundred-thousand selection process, three companies of a hundred men each had been cut down to sixty-one.

Great odds.

Not everybody had been washed out. A combat car collision had accounted for four deaths, falls during the mountain training killed two more trainees, and a holed suit had put still another recruit in the awesomely large regimental ceremony.

Lanzotta thought it was impressive that a trainee was made a full member of the regiment before burial. Sten thought it was a very small clotting deal. Dead, he was pretty sure, was a very long time, and worm food isn't much interested in ceremony.

Ah, well.

By now they'd progressed from squad through platoon to full company-size maneuvers.

Sten wondered what joyful surprises Lanzotta had planned for the evening. Then he put the dampers back in his mind. He needed the rest. He let his mouth start a jody, put his feet on autopilot, and went to sleep.

Eyes closed, Sten sonared his ears around the hilltop. Four minutes, twenty-seven seconds. All night animal sounds back to normal. All troops in stand-to positions. Not bad.

Lanzotta crawled up beside Sten and flickered on a mapboard light. "Fair. You got them out and down nicely enough. Second Platoon still bunches up too much. And I think you should've put your CP closer to the military crest. But . . . not bad."

Sten braced. Lanzotta was being very polite. He knew for sure this exercise would be a cruncher.

Lanzotta: "Briefing. Your company has been on an offensive sweep for two local days. You have taken, let's see, fifty-six—about seventy-five percent casualties. Tsk. Tsk.

"You were ordered to assault a strongly held enemy position—there!"

Lanzotta took a simulator minicontrol from its belt pouch and tapped a button. On the hill across from them, a few lights flickered.

"Unfortunately, the position was too strongly garrisoned, and you were forced to withdraw to this hilltop. You are far in advance of artillery support, and, for operational reasons, normal air or satellite support is nonexistent.

"You medvacked your casualties, so you have no wounded to worry about. The problem is quite simple. Very, very soon, the enemy will counterattack in strength. You probably will not be able to hold this position.

"Your regimental commander has given you local option command. Friendly positions are"—He pointed behind him and touched the panel. At the top of the ridgecrest simulators set up a strong, not particularly well blacked-out position—"there. Between your company and friendly lines are an esimated two-brigade strength of bandits, operating with light armor and in small strike-patrol elements. All the options are yours. Are there any questions?"

Sten whistled silently.

"Recruit captain, take charge of your men. You have two minutes until the problem commences."

Lanzotta slid away into darkness.

Sten motioned to Morghhan, his recruit first sergeant. They slithered away from the CP area. Sten dropped a UV filter over his eyes and flicked on a shielded maplight.

"*Sauve qui peut* and all that crud," Morghhan whispered. "You wanna surrender right now and avoid the morning rush?"

"Us killer guards never surrender."

"You think he's setting you up?"

"Damfino. Prog—no. Retrograde movement's supposed to be a bitch, they told us."

"You figure it, Sten. I'm gonna go practice up speaking fluent Enemy." Morghhan low-crawled back to the CP and waiting runners.

"Four and three and two and one," Lanzotta said, somewhere in the darkness. "Begin."

He must've started the simulator program. High whining . . . "Incoming!" somebody shouted, and the ground rocked under him. Violet light laserd just overhead. Sten hoped the sweep-track automatic weapons which provided the "enemy fire" weren't set too low or with random-center fire or with a movement homer.

Sten tapped the channel selector on his chest to ALL CHANNELS, and briefly outlined the plan to the listening troops.

"Six . . . this is two-one. We have movement on our front." That was Tomika, acting-jack platoon leader of Second Platoon.

Sten overrode onto the command net.

"Estimation, two-one?"

"Probe attack. Possible feint. Approximate strength two platoons. One hundred meters out, on line."

"Two-one . . . this is six. Hold fire. One-one? Any activity on your front?"

"Not—hang on. That's affirm. Got infiltrators working up the hill—will—aw clot!"

Lanzotta's voice broke in. "Unfortunately the First Platoon leader exposed himself and was hit. Fatal."

Sten ignored Lanzotta. "One-two. Assume command. Estimation?"

"Affirm. Infiltrators. Company size. Prog—first prong attack. Shall we open fire?"

Sten thought quickly. "Negative. When they cross fifty-meter line, they'll probably open fire. Prog—artillery support. First and third squads will withdraw twenty-five meters noisily. Second and fourth squads engage when they reach your positions and first and third counterattack. Prog—another feint. Top! Get weapons platoon to blanket their rear and break up the second wave. Take the CP, I'm shifting to Third Platoon."

Clicked the mike off. "Runner! Let's go!"

They went off into darkness, Sten navigating by treetop shadows. Fire intensified, and the ground under them quivered.

Sten jumped as what sounded like a thousand sirens went off. "Psych," he told the runner. "Just noise. Let's move it!"

Sten dropped into the Third Platoon leader's dugout.

"What's out there?"

Sten held his breath and closed his eyes again. Listening. Sweeping his head from side to side. He swore. "Clot hell! Armor!"

"I don't hear anything!"

"You will. Sounds like two units. Scrunchies pigback for support."

Tagged the radio.

"Weapons . . . I want illumination. Stand by . . ."

The air hummed.

"Weapons, this is six. Do you receive?"

A runner materialized out of the night and slid into the hole.

"All units. Stand by. Scramble R-Seven."

The communicator selected a simple code and keyed the company's transmitters to it. The code would be broken in a few seconds if the enemy had analyzers. But by then Sten would've finished the plan.

"Two-one. Sequence your troops past the CP, and reinforce one-two. Move! Two. On command, you will begin a frontal assault straight forward."

Sten took a deep breath. This training was just real enough to make even simulated suicide work creepy.

"Three-one. Your men will hold the armor below your position. Your orders are to hold regardless. If we break out, you and your men are to exfiltrate solo.

"All units. The company will make a frontal assault against the feint in Second Platoon's sector. We will break out, and each man is on his own. You have the correct bearing on friendly lines. You will evade capture and join the regiment by dawn.

"That is all. Keep only water, basic weapon, and two

tubes. Dump everything, including radios. Good luck. Move!"

Sten cut the radio. Lanzotta appeared beside him.

"Administrative note, Recruit Captain Sten. With dead radios, maneuver control can't inflict casualties."

Sten found time for a grin, "Sergeant, that never crossed my mind." He was being honest.

Sten turned to his CP unit.

"You heard it. Drop 'em and let's chogie."

"Lanzotta just wiped out weapons platoon. Sez it was counterbattery off your fire mission."

Sten groaned.

"Lenden."

"Go, Sten."

"Honk down about five meters and gimme a hand-held."

"Then I'm gonna be dead?"

"Then you're gonna be dead."

"Maybe they'll give us corpses a ride back." The runner hunched out of the hole, pulling a launcher from his weapons belt. He touched the fire key, and the flare hissed upward. A scanner caught him, and pulled the plug. Simulator-transponder went red, and Lenden swore and started back for the assembly area.

The flare bloomed, and Sten saw two . . . five . . . seven assault tracks grinding up the base of the hill.

"Flash 'em."

The platoon leader keyed his central weapons board, and high-pressure tanks, emplaced at the hill's base, sprayed into life. The gas mixed with the atmosphere, and the acting lieutenant fired the mixture.

A fireball roared across the hill's base, and three of the tracks caught and exploded.

"Leapfrog back. About sixty meters and set up an interior perimeter."

Sten rolled out of the hole and skittered back toward the CP.

By the time he flattened beside Morghhan, he had a plan.

Shadows went across his front toward Second Platoon's

area. Firing suddenly redoubled in volume from the Third's last-stand perimeter.

Sten gratefully shed his pack and command net, port-armed his weapon and went after them.

There was dead silence in the office.

Sten stared straight ahead.

"Four survivors, recruit company commander. You were wiped out."

"Yes, Sergeant Lanzotta."

"I would be interested in your prognosis of the effects of such an action in real combat. On the rest of the regiment."

"I . . . guess very bad."

"I guess very obvious. But you don't know why. Troops will take massive casualties and maintain full combat efficiency under two circumstances only: First, those casualties must be taken in a short period of time. Slow decimation destroys any unit, no matter how elite."

"Secondly, those casualties must be taken with an accomplishment. Do you understand, Sten?"

"Not exactly, sergeant."

"I will be more explicit. Using last night's debacle. If you had held on that hilltop, and died to the last man, the regiment would have been proud. That would have been a battle honor and probably a drinking song. The men would have felt uplifted that there were such heroes among them. Even though they'd be clotting glad they weren't there to be with them."

"I understand."

"Instead, your unit was lost trying to save itself. It's very well and good to talk about living to fight another day. But that is not the spirit that ultimately wins wars. Failing to understand that is your failure as a company commander. Do you understand?"

Sten was silent.

"I did not say you had to agree. But do you understand?"

"Yes, sergeant."

"Very well. But I did not relieve you and confine you to barracks for that reason. Your test scores indicate a high level of intelligence. I broke you because you showed me you are completely unsuited for the Guard or to be a guardsman. Effective immediately, you are removed from the training rolls."

Sten's mouth hung open.

"I will explain this, too. You have a soldier. He takes a knife, blackens his face, leaves all his weapons behind. He slips through the enemy lines by himself, into the shelter of an enemy general. Kills him and returns. Is that man a hero? Of one kind. But he is not a guardsman."

Lanzotta inhaled.

"The Guard exists as the ultimate arm of the Emperor. A way of putting massive force into a precise spot to accomplish a mission. The Guard will fight and die for the Emperor. As a fighting body, not as individuals."

Sten puzzled.

"As a guardsman, you are expected to show bravery. In return, the Guard will provide you with backing. Moral and spiritual in training and garrison, physical in combat. For most of us, the bargain is more than fair. Are you tracking me?"

Most of Sten was wondering what would happen to him next—washed out to a duty battalion? Or would they dump him straight back to Vulcan? Sten tried to pay attention to Lanzotta.

"I will continue. A guardsman is always training to be more. He should be able to assume the duties of his platoon sergeant and accomplish the mission if his sergeant becomes a casualty. A sergeant must be able to assume the duties of his company commander.

"And that means no matter how tactically brilliant he is, if he does not instinctively understand the nature of the men he commands, he is worse than useless. He is a danger. And I have told you time and again . . . my job is to not just make guardsmen. But to help those men stay alive."

"Is that all, sergeant?" Sten said tonelessly.

"Four survivors. Of fifty-six men. Yes, Sten. That's all."

Sten lifted his hand toward the salute.

"No. I don't take salutes—or return them—from wash-outs. Dismissed."

Sten ate, turned in his training gear and went to bed in a thick blanket of isolation. Emotionally, he wanted one of his friends to say something. Just good-bye. But it was better like this. Sten had seen too many people wash, and knew it was easier on everyone if the failure simply became invisible.

He wondered why they were waiting so long to get him. Usually a washout was gone in an hour or two after being dumped. He guessed it was the seriousness of what he'd done. The cadre wanted him around for a while as an object lesson.

It gave Sten time to make some plans of his own.

If they were sending him to a duty battalion . . . he shrugged. That was one thing. He didn't owe anything more to the Empire, so as soon as he could, he'd desert. Maybe. Or maybe it'd be easier to finish his hitch and take discharge into Pioneer Sector. Supposedly they never could get enough men on the frontiers, and anyone who'd been even partially through Guard training could be an asset.

But Vulcan . . . Sten's fingers automatically touched the knife haft in his arm. If he went back, the Company would kill him. He'd as soon go out quick before they got there. Besides, there was always a chance . . .

Not much of one, he decided, and stared blankly up at the dark ceiling.

Sten half felt a movement—his fingers curled for the sheath—and Carruthers' arm clamped on him.

"Follow me."

Sten, still dressed, stepped out of the bunk. Automatically, he S-rolled the mattress and picked up his small ditty.

Carruthers motioned him toward the door. Sten followed. Dazed. He had just realized Carruthers had

stopped him as if she knew about the knife. He wondered why they'd never confiscated it.

Carruthers stopped beside an automated weapons carrier. Indicated the single seat, and Sten climbed in.

Carruthers tapped a destination code, and the car
hummed. Carruthers stepped back. And saluted.

Sten stared. Washouts didn't rate, but Carruthers was
holding the salute. Sten was lost. He automatically returned it.

Carruthers turned and was double-timing away as the
car lifted.

Sten looked ahead. The car angled out of the training
area a few feet clear of the ground, then lifted to about
twenty meters. Its screen flashed: DESTINATION RESTRICTED
AREA. REQUEST CODE CLEARANCE. The car's computer
chuckled, and printed numbers across the screen. The
screen blanked, then: M-SECTION CLEARANCE GRANTED.
NOTIFICATION. ON LANDING AWAIT ESCORT.

Sten was completely lost.

CHAPTER TWENTY-THREE

MAHONEY CEREMONIOUSLY POURED the pure-quill medal-cohol into the shooter, and dumped the pewter container into the two-liter beermug. He handed the mug to Car-ruthers, and turned to the other three in the room. "Any-one else need refueling?"

Rykor lifted a fluke and propelled a minicascade from her tank at Mahoney. "I have a mind that needs no further altering, thank you," she rumbled.

Lanzotta shook his head.

Mahoney picked up his own mug. "Here's to failure." They drank.

"How did he take it, corporal?"

"Dunno, colonel. Kid's a little shocky. Prob'ly thought we was gonna ship his butt back for recycling on that armpit he came from."

"He's that dumb?"

"I crucified him, colonel," Lanzotta said. "I would as-sume he isn't guilty of any thinking at this moment."

"Quite likely. You're pretty good at slow torture, Lan." Mahoney paused. "Rykor, sorry to bore you for a minute. But I got to tell these two. Obviously all this is sealed—saying that's a formality. But since it's closed, we can knock off the colonel drekh for a while."

174

Carruthers shifted uncomfortably and buried her nose in her mug.

"I need a very fast final assessment. Rykor?"

"I have no reason to change my initial evaluation. His training performance, as predicted, was near record. His profile did not alter significantly. In no way could Sten have become a successful Guard soldier. His independence, instinctual animosity to authority, and attraction toward independent action are especially jagged on the curve. For your purposes, he seems ideal.

"The peculiar individual traumas we discussed when he entered training are maintained at close to the same level in some ways. But in others, since he has proven himself successful in training and in dealing with other people, he is far more stable an entity."

"Carruthers?"

"I dunno how to put it, sir. But he ain't anybody I'd pick to team with. He ain't a coward. But he ain't for-sure either. At least not in, mebbe, a red-zone assault."

"Only one sir! Thank you. Buy yourself another drink. And me one, too."

Mahoney passed his mug across.

"I could probably elaborate on Carruthers' assessment," Lanzotta said carefully, "but there's no need. Gargle words don't explain things any better than she did."

"Come on, Lanzotta. Like pulling teeth. You know what I want."

"I'd rate Sten first rate for Mantis Section. He reminds me of some of the young thugs I tried to keep under control for you."

Carruthers spun, spilling beer.

"You was in Mantis Section, sergeant?"

"He was my team sergeant," Mahoney said.

"And I got out. Carruthers, you don't know any of this. But there's a clotting difference between going in hot, facing entrenched troops, and cutting the throat of some small-time dictator while he's in bed with a girl. Remember that, colonel?"

"Which one?"

Mahoney gestured, and Carruthers passed Lanzotta his shot/beer. Lanzotta stared into the amber distance, then upended the mug. "I didn't like it. I wasn't any good at it."

"Hell you weren't. You stayed alive. That's the only grade."

Lanzotta didn't say anything.

Mahoney grinned and affectionately scrubbed Lanzotta's close crop. "I'd still trade half a team if you'd come back, friend." Then Mahoney turned business. "Evaluations?"

"Transfer recommended, Psychiatric Section," Rykor put in briefly.

"Recommend transfer," Carruthers aped awkwardly.

"Take him, Mahoney," Lanzotta said, sounding very tired. "He'll be a great killer for you."

Frazer slipped off the slideway and hurried toward the zoo. He was nervous about the meeting and the handivid burned in his pocket. He carded into the zoo and walked past the gate guard, waiting for the hand on his shoulder.

His clerk's mind told him there was nothing to be worried about—Frazer had covered all of his tracks—He was a master at the computer and the Imperial bureaucracy. No way could anyone know why he was there.

Frazer stopped at the saber-tooth tiger cages. He grew more edgy as the beasts paced back and forth. Like all the creatures in the zoo, the tiger was part of the gene history of humankind. If Frazer had gone farther, he would have encountered sloths and giant-winged insects and enormous warm-blooded reptiles. He could smell the reptiles from where he was, rotten meat and bubbling swamps . . .

The assassin moved in beside him. "Got it?"

Frazer nodded and handed the assassin the vidpack. A long wait.

And the assassin said: "Excellent."

"I chose someone whose record could be easily manipulated," Frazer said. "All you have to do is step in."

The assassin smiled. "I knew I could count on you. The best. You have the computer touch."

Someone recognized Frazer's talents. Only he could dip into the informational pile and cut it out, one onion slice of information at a time.

"Ah—the money?"

The assassin handed him a slip of paper. Frazer studied it. "It is untraceable?"

"Of course, pride in my work, and all that. You can see . . ."

Frazer was satisfied. His only regret was that Rykor could never know exactly how clever he was.

The assassin draped an arm over Frazer's shoulder as they walked away from the cages.

"You wonder about loyalty," Frazer began.

"Yes. You do," the assassin said.

The arm draped lower, curling around. Right hand curling around Frazer's chin, left hand snapped against the back of his head. There was a dull *snap!* Frazer went limp. Dead.

No one was around as the assassin dragged the body back to the edge of the cage. Lifted, braced, and Frazer's body lofted down.

The roars and the sound of feeding finished the matter.

CHAPTER TWENTY-FOUR

THE EMPEROR, MAHONEY decided, had finally gone mad. He was hovering over a huge bubbling pot half filled with an evil-looking mixture, muttering to himself.

"A little of this. A little of that. A little garlic and a little fat. Now, the cumin. Just a touch. Maybe a bit more. No, lots more." The Emperor finally noticed Mahoney and smiled. "You're just in time," he said. "Gimme that box."

Mahoney handed him an elaborately carved wooden box. The Emperor opened it and poured out a handful of long reddish objects. They looked like desiccated alien excrement to Mahoney.

"Look at these," he boasted to Mahoney. "Ten years in the biolabs to produce."

"What are they?"

"Peppers, you clot. *Peppers.*"

"Oh, uh, great. Great."

"Don't you know what that means?"

Mahoney had to admit he didn't.

"Chili, man. Chili. You ain't got peppers, you got no chili."

"That's important, huh?"

The Emperor didn't say another word. Just dumped in the peppers, punched a few buttons on his cooking console, stirred, then dipped up a huge spoonful of the mess and offered it to Mahoney. He watched intently as Mahoney tasted. Not ba—then it hit him. His face went on fire, his ears steamed and he choked for breath. The Emperor pounded him on the back, big grin on his face, and then offered him a glass of beer. Mahoney slugged it down. Wheezed.

"Guess I got it just right," the Emperor said.

"You mean you did that on purpose?"

"Sure. It's supposed to scorch the hair off your butt. Otherwise it wouldn't be chili." The Emperor poured them both two beers, motioned to Mahoney to join him, and settled down in a huge, overstuffed couch. "Okay. You earned your check this month. Now, how about the next?"

"You mean Thoresen?"

"Yeah, Thoresen."

"Zero, zero, zero."

"Maybe we should escalate."

"I was gonna recommend that in my report. But it's dangerous. We could blow the whole thing."

"How so?"

"It's Lester. He says there's a lot more motion on Bravo Project. And he's got a way in. Trouble is, if he's caught, we're out an inside man."

The Emperor thought a moment. Then sighed. "Tell him to go ahead." He drained his glass, filled it with more beer. "Now, what about the other matter?"

"The gun smuggling? Well, I still can't prove it."

"But it's happening? That's a fact, right?"

"Yeah," Mahoney said. "We know for sure that four planets—all supposedly our confederates—are shipping weapons to Vulcan."

"Thoresen again. To hell with it. Let's quit playing games with the man. Send in the Guard. Stomp him out."

"Uh, that's not such a hot idea, boss. I mean—"

"I know. I know. Lousy diplomatic move. But what about my 'buddies' on those other four planets? No reason I can't take them out."

"It's done."

The emperor grinned. Finally, a little action. "Mantis Section?"

"I sent in four teams," Mahoney said. "I guarantee those guns will stop."

"Without any diplomatic repercussions?"

"Not a whisper."

The Emperor liked that even better. He got up from his couch and walked over to the bubbling pot. Sniffed it. Nice. He started dishing up two platefuls.

"Join me for dinner, Mahoney?"

Mahoney was out of the couch in a hurry and headed for the door. "Thanks, boss, any night but tonight. I gotta—"

"Hot date?"

"Yeah," Mahoney said. "Whatever that is. Not as hot as that stuff."

And he was gone. The Emperor went back to his chili. Wondering which members of the Royal Court *deserved* to share his company tonight.

CHAPTER TWENTY-FIVE

THE BARON WATCHED the screen anxiously as a swarm of Techs moved quickly about the freighter's hold, making final connections and adjustments. This was it. A few more minutes and he would learn if all the credits and danger were worth it.

The Bravo Project test was taking place light years away from Vulcan, and far away from normal shipping lanes. The picture on Thoresen's screen changed as the Techs finished, then hustled out of the hold, crammed into a shuttle and started moving away from the ancient freighter.

Thoresen turned to the Tech beside him, who was studying swiftly changing figures on his own screen. Then:

"Ready, sir."

Thoresen took a deep breath, then told the Tech to begin.

"Countdown initiated . . ."

The shuttle came to a stop many kilometers away from the freighter. The on-board Techs went to work, changing programs in their computers, getting ready for the final signal.

The inside of the freighter had been gutted, and at opposite ends the Techs had constructed two huge devices

—they would have been called rail guns in ancient times—
each aimed exactly at the electric "bore" of the other.

Thoresen barely heard the countdown. He was concen-
trating on the two images on the screen: One was of a
huge glowing emptiness inside the hold of the freighter.
The other was of the outside of the freighter, the shuttle
in the foreground. The Tech tapped him on a shoulder.
They were ready to go. All of a sudden, the Baron felt
very relaxed. Flashed a rare smile at the Tech, punched
in the code that was the trigger.

The "rail guns" fired, and two subatomic particles of
identical mass were hurled at each other, reaching the
speed of light instantly. Then beyond. Thoresen's screen
flared and then it was over—literally almost before it
began. Then his screen came to life again. Nothing. Just
yawning space. No freighter, no—

"The shuttle," the Tech screamed. "It's gone. They're
all—"

"Clot the shuttle," Thoresen snapped. "What happened?"

His fingers flew over computer keys as he ordered up a
replay of the incident—this time at speeds he could see.

The particles floated toward each other, leaving comet
trails. Pierced the magnetic bubble that was the glowing
spot inside the hold, and then met . . . And met . . . And
met . . . Then they vanished . . . reappeared . . . moved in
and out of time/space . . . until they were replaced by a
single, much different particle. Thoresen laughed—he had
done it. Suddenly, the magnetic envelope began to col-
lapse. There was a blinding flash of light and the freighter
and shuttle disappeared in an enormous explosion.

The Baron turned to the Tech, who was still in shock.
"I want the timetable moved up."

The Tech gaped at him.

"But those men on the shuttle? . . ."

Thoresen frowned, looked at his empty screen, and
then understood.

"Oh, yes. The unfortunate accident. It shouldn't be too
hard to replace them."

He started out of the lab, paused a moment. "Oh, and tell the next crew to back off a little more from the freighter. Techs are expensive."

Lester smiled and patted the Tech on the shoulder. The man babbled something and tears began to roll down his cheeks. Lester leaned forward to listen. Just baby talk. And nothing more to learn.

It had been easy, Lester thought. Easier than he had expected. He had been working on the Tech for half a dozen cycles. Subtle hints of money, a new identity, a lifetime residence paid up on some playworld. The man had been interested, but too afraid of Thoresen to do much more than listen and drink Lester's booze. Then one day he had cracked. He had been almost hysterical when he called Lester and asked to come to his quarters.

There had been some awful accident, he had told Lester, but when pressed he shook his head. No, the Baron . . . And Lester knew he had to take a chance.

He slipped up beside the man, pressed a hypo against his neck, and a moment later the Tech was a babbling idiot. But an idiot who would tell Lester everything he needed to know. Lester eased the man down on the bed. He'd sleep for a while, and then wake up with a huge narcobeer hangover. The Tech wouldn't remember a thing.

Now, all Lester had to do was contact Mahoney. What he would tell him about Bravo Project would guarantee an early end to Thoresen's career.

There was a loud smash and splintering of plastic. Lester whirled, then froze as the Baron stepped through his ruined door. He was flanked by two Sociopatrolmen. Thoresen looked at the sleeping Tech, grinned.

"A little party, Lester?"

Lester didn't say anything. What could he say? Thoresen motioned to his guards; they picked the Tech up and carried him out.

"So, now you know?"

"Yes," Lester said.

"Too bad. I rather liked you." He took a step forward,

looming over the old man, and took him by the throat. Squeezed. Lester fought for air, felt his throat crush. Minutes passed before the Baron dropped Lester's corpse. He turned as one of the guards stepped back into the room. "Make it look good," Thoresen said. "A sudden illness, *et cetera, et cetera.* And don't worry about his family. I'll take care of them."

CHAPTER TWENTY-SIX

STEN WHISTLED SOUNDLESSLY and booted the door behind him shut. Flies were already starting to buzz around H'mid's severed head atop the counter.

Sten bent, touched his fingers to the blood pool around the body. Still a little sticky . . . no more than an hour. Sten reached over his shoulder and palmed out the tiny w-piece that hung between his shoulder blades.

Sten dodged around the counter and silently ran up the steps to the shopkeeper's living quarters. Deserted as well. No sign of search or looting. Very, very bad. He cautiously peered out one window, then ducked back in.

Two rooftops away, three Q'riya flattened, peering down on the street. And below . . . another one, down Sten's escape route. Very badly disguised, polished boot tips protruding from under the striped robes he was wearing.

Were they trying to drive him or was he trapped? Sten tried again. They were going to take him. The foodshop across the narrow dirty street was shuttered. Not at this time of day. Inside there'd be a squad of M'lan—the Q'riya tribe's private thugs.

Sten leaned back against the wall . . . inhale for count of four, exhale for count of four, hold for count of six. Ten times. Adrenaline slowed down. Sten started trying to figure a way out. He scooped up a handful of bracelets,

185

the gems still unset, from H'mid's workbench, then the small carboy of acid from its shelf. Went back to the window and waited. He would probably have ten minutes or so before they decided they'd have to winkle the rat out.

A cart rumbled past below. Ideal. He carefully lobbed the carboy out, into the middle of its dry grain load. Aimed . . . hand bobbing, synched with the unsprung cart.

Fired. The carboy shattered. Smoke curled, and the car seared into flames.

Shouts. Screams . . . smoke coiling back up the street. The best he could do.

Sten tucked his robe ends up into his waistband, kicked off his sandals, and swung over the edge of the window. Hung by his hands, then dropped.

He thudded down, letting himself flatten. The shutter crashed open and a slug whanged out into the mud wall just above him. Sten came up . . . three hurtling paces across the street and a long dive through the open shutters.

Hit on the inside, rolling, and trigger held back to continuous fire as he sprayed the inside of the window.

Three M'lan gurgled down, the second howled air through a ripped open throat. Sten threw a second slug through the center of the man's forehead and was moving, out toward the back door. He burst out then swore. Typical rabbit warren, creaky stairs leading down, past the tiny Fal'ici hovels. Sten went over the railing, and dodged into their midst. Shouts, screams, and shots from the street.

Sten wasn't worried. The Fal'ici wouldn't give any information to help the M'lan, even at gunpoint.

He came out of the slum maze onto another street. Excellent. First luck. Marketing. Thronged . . . including a heavy patrol of M'lan. They must have been tipped. When they saw the running figure, they went after him.

Sten yanked over a pushcart, leaped over a cart's tongue, then turned and tossed H'mid's bracelets high into the air. The gold caught the glittering sun and there was instant chaos. People came out of openings in the walls that Sten couldn't even see.

Somewhere in the boiling mob were the M'lan. Sten thought it very possible that one or another of the Fal'ici might just turn away from the gold for a chance to slip a couple of centimeters of polished glass into a trooper's throat.

He slowed to a walk, pulled his robe down, and casually strolled on. Tossed a flower vendor a coin, and pulled the biggest flower on her cart off. Shoved his nose into it, and minced onward.

How . . . epi? Epi . . . clot it! He'd ask Doc when he got back to the cover house.

Sten took an hour to make sure he wasn't tailed. He didn't think much of the Q'riya's intelligence squads, but there were more than enough of them to run a successful multitail operation.

He was clean, so he walked quickly up to the gate of the unobtrusive house the Mantis Section team was working out of and went in.

To more chaos. Gear was going into packs neatly, but very, very quickly. Alex stood near the door, holding a breakdown willygun ready. Sten took it all in.

"We're blown?" Sten guessed.

"Aye, laddie," Alex said. " Th' clark Vinnettsa's been tryin' t' convince she's got buttons down her back wae taken."

"And talked?"

"Wouldna you? Word is they could make a tombstone confess."

"Somebody took H'mid's head off and left it for me to find," Sten said. He crossed to a table and picked up a glass winer. Thumb over the cover, he eased the spout into his mouth and swallowed. After he'd set it down, he looked at the half-meter teddy bear sitting at ease in the room's only comfortable chair. The creature bore a near-benevolent scowl on his face.

"Doc?"

"Typical humans," the teddy bear purred happily. "You

people could clot up a rock fight. Proof of the existence of divinity, I take it. You would still be in your jungles peeling fruit with your toes if there weren't a God of some sort or another. One with a rather nasty sense of humor, I might add."

Vinnettsa hurried down the stairs coiling wire to the broadcast antenna on the roof.

"Come on, Doc. We don't have time for making love."

Doc held his hands out in what he had learned was a human gesture, jumped off the chair, and began stuffing the hookup into a lift pack.

Ida came unhurriedly out from the closet that concealed the entrance to the comroom. Hefted her compack experimentally. "Doc's right. You can't expect subtlety from anything other than us. Now, why they don't field an all-Rom team—"

Alex chuckled. "For our Emp'rer whidny like havin' a worl' stole from under him, is why."

Ida thought. "If we did steal it—and that's a thought worthy of a Rom—then he wouldn't have to worry, would he?"

Sten looked around. Frick and Frack hung from the room's eaves, waiting.

"Do they have us spotted?"

"Negative," Frick squeaked. "We overflew ten minutes ago. We saw nothing."

Maybe. The two batlike beings weren't high on anyone's intelligence list. Or maybe Sten hadn't worded the question correctly. But the information was probably correct.

The team was ready to roll. They huddled.

"We ken we're blown," Alex said softly. "D'ye think we redline an' evac?"

Jorgensen yawned. He was sprawled beside his pack, stocked pistol ready.

"Y'all sure we want to just pull pitch? Mahoney'll torch our tail for an incomp."

Sten looked at Doc, who wiggled tendrils.

"Myitkina," Sten said. It was Jorgensen's trance word. The rangy blonde sat immobile.

"Possibilities," Vinnettsa snapped.

"A. Mission abort and withdrawal. B. Continue mission and assume nondiscovery. C. Begin alternate program."

"Analyze it," Sten said.

"Possibility A. Mission priority high. Currently incomplete. Consider as last resort. Survival probability ninety percent if accomplished within five hours."

"Continue," Vinnettsa said.

"Possibility B. Insufficient data to give absolute prediction. Assumption that local agent broke under interrogation. Not recommended. Survival probability less than twenty percent."

The team members looked at each other. Voting silently. As usual, no one bothered to consult Frick and Frack.

"Two Myitkina." Jorgensen came out of the trance.

"What's the plan?" he asked.

"Mobs 'n heroes," Alex said.

"That ain't too bad," Jorgensen said. "All I gotta do is run a lot."

Sten snorted. Alex clapped him on the back, a friendly gesture that almost drove Sten through the wall. Sometimes the tubby little man from the three-gee world forgot.

Sten wheezed air back into his lungs.

"Sten, you're a braw lad. A' they say, the bleatin' o' the kid frees the tiger. Or some'at like that."

Sten glumly nodded and started shedding weaponry.

The assassin watched him from across the room. It would have to wait for a while. For better or worse, the assassin's future rode on the team's successes. For a while.

M-PRIORITY
OPERATION BANZI

Do not log in Guard General Orders; do not log in Imperial Archives; do not multex any than source and OC Mercury; do not release in any form. IMPERIAL PROSCRIPT.

OPERATIONS ORDER

1. *Situation:*

Saxon. Plus-or-minus well within Earth-condition parameters. Largely desert. Extensive nomadic culture (SEE FICHE A), predominant. Only port, major city and manufacturing complex Atlan (SEE FICHE B), situated in one of Saxon's few fertile valleys. Existence of large river and introduction of hydropower responsible for growth of Atlan. Atlan, and therefore Saxon's offworld policies, controlled by an extended tribe-family, the Q'riya (SEE FICHE C), believed to be an offshoot of main bedou culture Fal'ici. Manufacturing and all offworld trading controlled by Q'riya. In Atlan, their authority is enforced by the probably created semihereditary group known as the M'lan (SEE FICHE D). Q'riya authority does not extend beyond Atlan's limits, and semianarchy exists among the nomad tribes. Atlan's main export is weaponry, largely created by the introduction of major machinery by DELETED . . . DELETED . . . DELETED. Some primitive art, generally lowly regarded, also transshipped.

2. *Mission:*

To prevent offworld shipment of currently produced arms and, if possible, to significantly reduce or destroy that production capability.

3. *Execution:*

The team-in-place shall exercise the option of how the mission is to be carried out, hopefully by political means but, if necessary, militarily. Factors—this must not be attributed to an Imperial Mission. All extremes shall be taken to prevent evidence of Imperial involvement. Reiterate: All extremes (SEE ATTACHED, MISSION EQUIPMENT). Mission limitations: preference casualty rate among Fal'ici to be kept as low as possible. Continued existence of Q'riya in present position not significant. Alteration of existing social order not significant.

4. *Coordination:*

Little support can be given, due to the obvious conditions of OPERATION BANZI (see above), beyond standard evacuation deployment, which shall consist of . . .

5. *Command & Signal:*

OPERATION BANZI will be under the direct control of IXAL Code, Mantis Team operating under code schedule . . .

CHAPTER TWENTY-SEVEN

THE GUARDS NEATLY lofted Sten into the cell's blackness. He thunked down on an uncomplaining body. Sten rolled off and started to apologize, then sniffed the air. About three days beyond listening, he estimated.

He got to his feet. The cavernous cell was very dark. Sten kept his eyes moving, hyperventilating. His irises widened. The view wasn't worth even one candle, he decided.

The prison was well within the anthro profile that fit Saxon. Build an unbreakable cell, and throw everybody into it you don't like. Feed them enough so they don't starve noisily, and then forget them. What happens in the cell is no one's concern.

He just hoped that Sa'fail was still alive.

Sten found a wall and put his back to it. Waiting. Lousy, he decided. It took about ten minutes for the bully-boy and his thugs to loom up in the blackness.

Sten didn't bother asking. The heel of his hand snapped the head villain's neck back, a sideslash dropped him while he gargled the ruins of his larynx. The second received a fist behind the ear as Sten bounced off the man's dead leader.

He threw the second corpse into the third man's incoming fists, then half turned, foot poised. The third man decided to stay down.

"Sa'fail. Of the Black Tents. Where is he?"

The toady grimaced. Thought was obviously not one of his major operational abilities. Sten was patient.

The toady looked at Sten's ready strike, grunted. "In that corner. The dreadful ones keep their own."

Sten grinned his thanks and snapped his foot out. Cartilage smashed, the man howled and went down. Sten bent over the man. He decided he wouldn't have to kill him. The toady would be too busy bleeding for an hour or so to backjump Sten—and that, he hoped sincerely, was all it would take.

He worked his way through the bodies, softly calling the nomad's name. And found him. Sa'fail had an entourage. Sten looked them up and down. Surprisingly healthy for prisoners. He wondered if they'd gotten to recycling their fellow prisoners to stay healthy yet.

The nomad sat up and stroked his beard.

"You are not of the People," the one who must have been Sa'fail's lieutenant said.

"I am not that, O Hero of the Desert and Man Who Makes the Slime Q'riya Tremble," Sten said fluently in the desert dialect. "But I have long admired you from afar."

The nomad chuckled. "I am honored that you found your admiration so overwhelming you must join me here in my palace."

"Much as I would like to exchange compliments, O He Who Makes the Wadihs Tremble," Sten said, "I would suggest that you and your men get very close to that wall over there. You have"—Sten thought a moment—"not very long."

"What will happen?" the lieutenant asked.

"Very shortly most of this prison will cease to exist."

The nomads buzzed then snapped silent as Sa'fail motioned.

"This is not a jest, I assume?"

"If it were, I would find it less funny than even you."

"Even so, although your consideration might be for a brief time."

Sa'fail considered. Then lithely came to his feet.

"We shall do what the outlander wishes. No matter what happens, boredom shall be relieved."

The drom spat at Alex. He ducked and thumped four fingers against the beast's sides. It whuffed air and wobbled on its feet. The other members of the Mantis team hated droms, the stinking, recalcitrant transport beast of Saxon. They didn't bother Alex. He'd once been unlucky enough to serve with a Guard ceremonial attachment on Earth and had encountered camels.

But he didn't regret what was about to happen to this particular drom. The animal belched.

"Ye'll naught be forgettin' yer last meal," he thought, and strolled away from the tethered beast. In trader's robes, carrying a forged day-pass plate, he'd been shaken down by the security guards surrounding the prison.

Search aboot as ye will, he thought. It's nae easy to find a bomb when it's digestin' in a beastie's guts. An' ye no saw the guns in that garbage in the wee cart.

He squatted by the wall and let the last few seconds tick away.

Frick banked closer to Frack. Half-verbal, half-instinct communication, nonwords: Nothing unusual. The other team members were in place. Frick's prehensile wing finger triggered the transceiver.

"Nothing. Nothing." Flipped the com off and he and his mate banked for the city walls.

If there were any team members to link up with, they'd meet outside. In a few seconds.

Possibly when the charge goes, the assassin thought. Thought discarded. We will need every gun we have.

Jorgensen nervously fondled the S-charge looped around his neck. If life signs weren't continuously picked up by the internal monitors the ensuing blast would leave nothing to ID a Mantis trooper or his equipment.

One day closer to the farm, Jorgensen thought morosely. That's the only way to look at it. He unrolled the rug and lifted out the willygun.

"I realize you did this deliberately," Doc purred. "You know the antipathy we of Altair have toward death."

"Nope," Vinnettsa said. "I didn't. But if I had, it's a clottin' good idea."

Doc sat just in the entrance to a mausoleum, pistol clutched in his fat little paws. Vinnettsa made her final checks on the launcher and willygun, then let the elastic sling snap the willygun back under her arm.

"Revenge. A typical, unpleasant human trait," Doc said.

"Your people never get even?"

"Of course not. Anthropomorphism. Occasionally we are forced personally to readjust the measure the—your word is fates—have made."

Vinnettsa started to answer, and then the first blast whiplashed across the cemetery.

And the two of them were running from the tomb toward the guard quarters that ran inside a tunnel ahead of them.

A week before, bribed guardsmen had cemented the charge into the guardshack on the main gates.

The first explosion was minor. Alex had built it up of explosive, a clay shaping and, bedded into the clay, as many glass marbles as he could buy in the bazaar. Now the marbles cannoned out, quite thoroughly incapacitating the ten guards lounging around the gates.

Alex had set the charge below waist level. "The more howlin' an' fa'in' an' carrin' on wi' wounded, the greater they'll be distracted."

Vinnettsa set the range-and-charge fuse on the launcher's handle, brought it up. Aimed. As she counted ten, she heard the shouting of the officers who were mustering their riot squads to run them down the tunnel into the prison . . .

She touched the stud. The rocket chuffed out, cleared its throat experimentally, then the solid charge caught.

Vinnettsa flattened as the shaped charge blasted through the solid brick and exploded in the tunnel.

She picked herself up and watched the roof drop in. An added dividend, she thought. She headed for Alex's position.

"If Ah hadna been stupid, Ah wouldna been here. Second and third charges." Alex hit the det panel under his robes. Two more diversionary charges blew on different sides of the prison.

"The Guard is mah home, Ah nae want for more. Fourth and fifth charges." He blew those.

"An' noo 'tis time for us a' to be gone." He fingered the main charge switch. And turned. Interested.

The drom ceased to exist. As did the wall.

The shock wave blew the main wall out, huge bricks hurtling across the brief space to shatter the inner wall of the prison. *It* crashed down. Prisoners howled in fear and agony.

Alex grabbed the willygun from the ground. Held it ready.

Dazed, blinking prisoners stumbled out.

"Go! Go!" he bellowed. They didn't need much encouragement. "C'mon, Sten, m'lad. Time's a-draggin'. Ma mither's nae raised awkward bairns."

Sten, an older, bearded man, and several men wearing the tatters of nomad gear ran into the street.

Alex saw a platoon of guards double around the corner toward him. "Ye'll nae credit I thought a' that," he grumbled, and hit the last switch. A snake charge positioned on the pavement moments before blew straight up, into the oncoming guards.

He flipped Sten a gun as he ran up. "C'n we be goin'?" he said. " 'M gettin' bored lurkin' aroun' wi' nothin' much to do."

Sten laughed, dropped on one knee and sprayed bullets down the street. Then the nomads, still bewildered, followed the two soldiers at a dead run.

Doc waved his paw idly. Two willyguns crackled. The four guards at the gate dropped as the bullets exploded in their chests.

Jorgensen and Vinnettsa went down, guns ready, as Sten, Alex, and the nomads ran up. Alex continued on, up to the gates, unslinging a satchel charge. He bent over with it, and touched the timer. Turned and walked back. "Ah suggest we be layin' doon, or we'll be starin' at all our own knackers."

The nomads looked uncomprehending. Sten motioned furiously, and they chewed brick pavement along with the team.

Another blast, and the gates pinwheeled away. Bits of iron and timber crashed around the crouched soldiers.

"Miscalculated a wee on that one," Alex muttered. "Y'kn keek m f'rit."

They were on their feet, running out into the desert.

"We wait here," Sa'fail ordered. "My men watch the city. They will be coming down to see who is stupid enough to come out of Atlan without soldiers to keep them safe."

The team automatically set up a perimeter, then slumped behind rocks. Vinnettsa pulled a canteen from her belt and passed it around.

"The Fal'ici owe you a debt," Sa'fail said to Sten after drinking.

Sten looked at Doc. This was his area. The bear walked into the middle and turned through 180 degrees. Tendrils waving gently.

Sten could feel the tension ebb. Automatically, everyone —soldiers and nomads—felt the small creature to be his best friend. That was Doc's survival mechanism. His species were actually spirited hunters who had nearly destroyed the wildlife of their homeworld. They hated every-

one, including each other except during estrus and for a
short space after a pup was born. But they exuded love.
Trust. Pity the creature that stopped to bathe in the good
feelings from the small creature.

"Why," Sten had once asked, halfway through Mantis
training, "don't you hate us?"

"Because," Doc said gloomily, "they conditioned me.
They condition all of us. I love you because I have to
love you. But that doesn't mean I have to like you."

Doc bowed to Sa'fail. "We honor you, Sa'fail, as a man
of honor, just as your race is honorable."

"We Fal'ici of the desert are such. But those town
scum . . ." Sa'fail's lieutenant spat dustily.

"I assume," Sa'fail went on, "that you liberated me for
a reason."

"Indeed," Doc purred, "there is a favor we wish."

"Yours is anything the People of the Black Tents may
offer. But first we have a debt to settle with the Q'riya."

"You may find," Doc said, "that more than one debt
may be paid at a time."

The tent was smoky, hot, and it smelled. Why is it,
Sten wondered, that a nomad is only romantic downwind?
None of the princelings seemed to have any more water
to spare for bathing than their tribesmen did.

He grinned as he saw Sa'fail, at the head of the table,
ceremoniously bundle a handful of food into Doc's mouth.
Lucky if he pulls back all his fingers, he thought.

But it is going well.

He unobtrusively patted Vinnettsa beside him. The
tribesmen had only grudgingly allowed Ida and Vinnettsa
full status with the other Mantis members. It had helped
that Vinnettsa had been jumped one night by three romantic tribesmen and, in front of witnesses, used four
blows to kill them.

Alex tapped him. "Ah gie ye this as an honor, m'lad."

Sten opened his mouth to ask what it was and Alex
slipped the morsel inside. Sten bit once, and his throat
told him this texture was not exactly right. He braced

and swallowed. His stomach was not pleasant as it rumbled the bit of food down.

"What was it?"

"A wee eyeball. Frae a herdin' animal."

Sten decided to swallow a couple more times, just to make sure.

The tents spread out for miles. The Mantis team and their charges had arrived at Sa'fail's home, and immediately riders had thundered off into the desert. And the tribes had filtered in. It had taken all of Sa'fail's considerable eloquence to convince the anarchic tribesmen to follow him, and only continuous, loud judgings held the tenuous alliances together.

One more day, Sten prayed. That is all we need.

He and Vinnettsa sat companionably on a boulder, high above the black tents and the twinkling campfires. Some meters away, a sentry paced.

"Tomorrow," he said, thinking his way, "if it works—prog not clottin' likely—what happens?"

"We get offworld," Vinnettsa said, "and we spend a week in a bathtub. Washing each other's . . . oh, backs might be a good place to start."

He grinned, eyeballed the sentry, who was looking away, and kissed her.

"And Atlan is a desert and the Q'riya get fed into slow fires."

"Will it be better, you mean?"

Sten nodded.

"Would it be worse is better. And, Sten, my love, do you really care, either way?"

Sten considered carefully. Then got up and pulled Vinnettsa to her feet.

"Nope. I really don't."

And they started down the hill toward their tent.

The assassin watched Sten descend the hill and swore quietly. It would've been possible—and blamable on a tribesman. But that sentry. The chance was still too long.

But tomorrow, there must be an opportunity. The assassin was tired of waiting.

The team split for the assault. Doc, Jorgensen, Frick and Frack went in with the nomad assault. It wasn't exactly Cannae.

The nomads slipped down from the hills in the predawn blackness, carrying scaling ladders. Positioned themselves in attack squads below the walls. The guards were not quite alert. The only advantage the attack had was that it had not been tried in the memory of man. Which meant, Doc told Sten, for at least ten years.

Nomad archers poised secret weapons—simple leatherstrip compound bows that the Mantis troopers had introduced to the tribesmen and helped them build over the month before the assault. Strings twanged and were muted. Guards dropped. And the ladders went into position.

The archers kept firing as long as they could—which meant until somebody successfully reached the walltop without being cut down, then whooped and swarmed up the ladders with the rest.

The four Mantis soldiers kept to Sa'fail. It would be helpful—to the nomads—if he survived the attack. And like most barbarian leaders, he felt his place was three meters ahead of the leading wave.

There were screams, and buildings crackled into flame to the butchershop anvil chorus of clashing swords. Civilians ran noisily for safety. And found none.

The M'lan fought to the last man. Too stupid to know better or, perhaps, smart enough to realize they weren't going to be allowed much bargaining.

Jorgensen shuddered, watching as waves of nomads swept into the Q'riya harem buildings.

Doc pulled at the bottom of the robe.

"Just children," he purred. "Having good, healthy fun." His tendrils flickered, and Jorgensen forgot a transitory desire to put his foot on the pandalike being.

It went on, and on.

志   志   志

Vinnettsa stared down the valley at the burning city three kilometers away. "Probably this is enough. Those nomads will take five years to put anything together."

"Maybe," Sten said. "But these machines are mostly automatic. Cut the power, and we'll make sure."

"Besides," Alex put in, "ye'll nae be denyin' me a great, soul-satisfyin' explosion, widya?"

Sten laughed, and they went to work in the power-house of the dam that bulked at the mouth of the valley, the source of power for all of the elaborate weapons factories scattered below.

At Alex's direction, they positioned charges carefully interconnected with time-fused det cord. They went by a very cautious book and set a complete backup system.

"Gie us two advan'ges," Alex said. "First, we mak siccar, an' second we'll nae hae t'be luggin' a' this home." He effortlessly picked up a concrete block that must've weighed three hundred kilos, and "tamped" his charge.

"Ye gae to yon end, an' final check. Ah'll dae this side."

Sten and Vinnettsa doubled off down the long, echoing concrete corridor.

Sten bent over the first charges, checked the primer tie, tugged gently at the bedded primer, ran his fingers down the fusing for breaks.

Ten meters away, Vinnettsa lifted her pistol. Careful. Two-hand grip. And a job's a job.

Alex swore. Ah'm gettin' careless. Sten had his crimping pliers. He spun and ran lightly down the corridor. He came upon an unexpected tableau. He froze.

Vinnettsa was aiming, savoring the last second of accomplishment.

Alex, without thinking, spun. Ripped a wide disc insulator from the top of a machine, arced it.

The insulator spun . . . arcing . . . wobbling . . . almost too much force . . . as Vinnettsa increased pressure on the stud.

The edge of the insulator caught her just above the elbow. Bone smashed and blood rained as the insulator clipped her arm, gun and all, off.

Sten rose, his gun up, then he saw Vinnettsa. Her face
was clenched in agony as she scrabbled one-handed for
a second gun from her waistband, and swept up—

The first round exploded against the concrete, and Sten
went sideways.

All on automatic, just like he was taught: right hand
up, left hand around the trigger; trigger squeeze; squeeze;
and held all the way back.

Vinnettsa's head exploded in a violet burst of blood
and brains. Her body slumped to the pavement.

Sten's shoulder slammed into the pavement. He just lay
there. Alex pounded up, bending over him.

"Are ye a'right, lad?"

Sten nodded. Not time yet to feel anything.

Alex's eyes were puzzled. "Lass must've been crazy."

Sten pushed himself up on his knees.

"Y'hit, Sten?"

Sten shook his head. Alex lifted him to his feet, then
looked over at Vinnettsa's body.

"We nae got time to greet noo," he said. "But Ah feel
Ah'll be doin' some tears later. She wae a good'un."
Paused. "We hae work, boy. We still hae work."

Alex's shot was a masterwork. The powerhouse shattered, walls crumbling. Huge chunks of the roof sailed
into the lake, and a few thousand liters of water slopped
over the edge.

But the dam held.

The team had time to see their handiwork, and to see
the city of Atlan roaring in flames, before the Imperial
cruiser touched down softly beside them.

CHAPTER TWENTY-EIGHT

THE MANTIS SECTION museum was a small, squat building of polished black marble. There were no inscriptions or signs.

Sten walked slowly up the steps to the door. He inserted his finger in a slot and waited while somewhere a Mantis computer chuckled through its files then buzzed him through. He stepped inside and looked around. Behind him the door snicked closed. Twin beams of light flicked on, probed him swiftly and decided he belonged.

The museum was a single large room, lit only by spotlights on each exhibit. Sten saw Mahoney at the far end and started walking toward him, noting the exhibits as he went by. A twisted battlesuit. Charred documents, carefully framed. Blasted machines. The leg of what appeared to be an enormous reptile. There was nothing to point out what any of them were, or what incidents they commemorated. In fact, the only writing was on the wall where Mahoney stood. It bore names from floor to ceiling, Mantis Section casualties—heroes or failures, depending on your point of view.

Mahoney sighed, turned to Sten.

"I keep looking for my own name up there," he said. "So far, no luck."

"Is that why you called me here, colonel? So I could carve in mine? Save Mantis the trouble and expense?"

Mahoney frowned at him.

"And why would we be doing that?"

Sten shrugged. "I blew it. I killed Vinnettsa."

"And you're thinking there was a choice?

"Battle fatigue? She cracked? And you should have been able to handle it?"

"Something like that."

Mahoney laughed. A grim little laugh. "Well I hate to spoil your romantic delusions, Sten. But Vinnettsa didn't crack. She really tried to kill you."

"But why?"

Mahoney patted him on the shoulder. Then reached into a pocket, pulled out a flask. Handed it to Sten. "Take a nip of that. It'll put you straight."

Sten chugged down several large swallows. He started to hand the flask back to Mahoney, who waved it away.

"Keep it. You'll need it."

"Begging the colonel's pardon, but—"

"She was an assassin, Sten. A very highly paid professional."

"But she was cleared by Mantis security."

Mahoney shook his head. "No, *Vinnettsa* was cleared by security. The woman you killed was not Vinnettsa. It took us a while, but we worked it out. The real Vinnettsa died while on leave. It was a pioneer world, so we didn't get word right away. A clerk, named Frazer, noted the report, then disappeared it. Paving the way for the assassin to step into her place."

"What happened to this Frazer?"

"Killed. Probably your assassin to cover her tracks."

Sten thought it over. It made sense. But it didn't make sense. "But why would anyone go to all that trouble for me? It must have cost a pile of credits."

"We don't know."

Sten thought over his list of enemies, and yeah, he had a few. Maybe even the killing kind. But they would have settled it in a bar or back alley. He shook his head. "I can't think who it would be."

"I can. Vulcan."

"Impossible. Sure, they were after me. But I was a Delinq. A nobody. No, even those clot brains on Vulcan wouldn't plant an assassin just to get somebody like me."

"But they did just the same."

"Who? And why?"

Mahoney gestured at the flask. Sten passed it to him, and he took a big slug.

"There's one way to find out," Mahoney said.

"How?"

"Mindprobe."

Sten's skin crawled as his mind called up images of brainburns and Oron. "No."

"I don't like it any better than you, son," Mahoney said. "But it's the only way."

Sten shook his head.

"Listen. It's got to have something to do with that little mission I sent you and your friends on."

"But we didn't get anything."

"The way I look at it, somebody thinks you did."

"Thoresen?"

"Himself."

"I still don't—"

"I promise I won't look at anything more than I have to. I'll concentrate on the last few hours you were on Vulcan."

Sten took the flask from Mahoney. Drank deep. Thinking. Finally:

"Okay. I'll do it."

Mahoney put an arm on his shoulder, started leading him back toward the door.

"This way," he said. "There's a gravsled waiting."

. . . Sten oozed from the vent in the wall, his eyes on the patrolman's back . . .

"No," Mahoney said, "it's not that."

Sten was lying on an operating table. Electrodes attached to his head, arms, and legs leading to a small steel box. The box drove a computer screen.

Mahoney, Rykor, and a white-coated Tech watched the screen and saw Sten drag the patrolman back to the vent and stuff him in. Rykor checked Sten's vital signs on another display, then motioned to the Tech. He tapped keys and more images appeared on the screen.

. . . Sten and the other Delinqs were at Thoresen's door. Beside him was Bet. She took a plastic rod from a pocket. Positioned it in the middle of the door's panel . . . Bet . . . Bet . . . Bet . . . Be . . .

"Wait," Rykor snapped.

And her Tech put the probe on hold. Bet's image froze on the screen. Rykor leaned over Sten and injected a tranquil. Sten's body relaxed. Rykor checked the medcomputer, then nodded at the Tech to continue.

. . . And Sten stepped into Thoresen's quarters . . . They were in another world . . . an exotic, friendly jungle . . . except . . . Sten spotted a motion detector . . . leaped . . . knife plunging into it.

"Almost there," Mahoney said. "Flip forward a few minutes."

. . . Papers and more papers spilled from Thoresen's safe . . . And then Oron had it, a thick, red folder labeled BRAVO PROJECT.

"Hold it," Mahoney said. "Stop right now."

"Is that what you're looking for?" Rykor asked.

"Yes."

"And you want me—us—out."

"Yes."

Rykor signaled her Tech to wheel her out.

"Watch his vital signs," she said. "If they even flicker, shut the probe off."

"I can run it," Mahoney said.

Reluctantly, Rykor and her Tech left. Mahoney returned to the probe, started flipping through.

Oron's expression went blank and the folder spilled. Sten hastily tried to pick the pages up as they spilled over the floor. He wasn't even reading what was on them, but his mind registered images.

Mahoney cursed at himself as he froze the image of each sheet of paper. His fingers were clumsy at the computer keys as he hardcopied the display. Clot—it was there all the time in Sten's brain!

CHAPTER TWENTY-NINE

MAHONEY STOOD AT full attention before the Emperor.

"AM$_2$," the Emperor whispered to himself. "Yes. Yes, it makes sense. He just might be able . . ."

He looked up at Mahoney, puzzled for a minute, then spoke. "At ease, colonel."

Mahoney slid to a smooth, formal at rest.

"You've told me the facts," the Emperor said. "Thoresen seems to be on the verge of artificially creating Antimatter Two. That's Bravo Project. Fine. Now, what are your feelings? Guesses. Half-thoughts, even."

"The Empire runs on Antimatter Two," Mahoney said. "You control the source. No one, except you, knows where that source is. Therefore—"

"I am the Emperor," the Emperor said. "AM$_2$ makes me that. And since I am sane, and since I am . . . always, I provide absolute stability to the galaxy."

"And Thoresen is thinking he can replace you," Mahoney said.

The Emperor shook his head. "No. You underestimate Thoresen. The Baron is a subtle man. If he could successfully manufacture AM$_2$—which, by the way, no one, not even I, knows how to do—it would still be much more expensive than what I provide."

"So what's his game?" Mahoney asked.

207

"Probably blackmail," the Emperor said. "It would be cheaper and far more rewarding to threaten. If everyone knows how to make AM$_2$, then I am not needed. Of course, he's not bright enough to realize that proliferation of this knowledge would mean the fall of the Empire. Which no one, including Thoresen, wants. But in the meantime, we must be prepared for Thoresen to suddenly quote us a very high price for something."

"Which would be?"

"It doesn't matter," the Emperor said. "What matters is that we stop him. Now."

Mahoney moved to attention again.

"I want this kept quiet," the Emperor said. "So. Use a Mantis Section team. First, foment revolt. Second, capture Thoresen—alive, you understand?"

"Yes, sir."

"Then, with Vulcan in revolt, I shall officially be forced to land the Imperial Guard to restore order. Naturally, someone other than Thoresen will be chosen to head the Company."

The Emperor picked up a drink, toyed with it, took a sip, frowned at the taste and put it down. Looked up at Mahoney again. Raised an eyebrow.

Mahoney snapped a salute. Wheeled. Marched to the door and exited. The Emperor studied his drink. Yes, he had seen to everything. Now it was up to Mahoney.

CHAPTER THIRTY

STEN AND THE other members of his team were gathered around the briefing table. Mahoney was at the head.

"And so," Mahoney said, "with Sten's background on Vulcan, this team would be the logical choice for the mission.

"Now, for the mission itself, I visualize a four-step program . . ."

Sten didn't even hesitate when Mahoney had asked if they would volunteer for the mission. He had a special reason for wanting to go, and even if the others on his team had refused, he would have figured a way out to squirm his way in.

Yes. A very special reason. When Mahoney had been flipping through his mind, he overlooked something. In the Bravo Project folder. Not that there was any reason why he should have noticed. It had been labeled: RECREATIONAL AREA 26: A SUMMARY OF ACTIONS. The Row. Thoresen had ordered it destroyed. And had killed his family.

Mahoney finished. He looked around at the members of the team, his eyes stopping on Sten.

"Any questions?"

"No, sir," Sten said. "No questions at all."

BOOK FOUR

RETURN TO VULCAN

CHAPTER THIRTY-ONE

THORESEN WAS PLEASED with himself. He strolled through his garden, pausing now and then to enjoy a flower. There had been a few glitches, but so far, everything was going according to plan. He was no longer concerned about threats from the Emperor. All possible leaks had been plugged. Even including that little matter of the Mig, Sten.

Sten was dead. Of that he was absolutely sure. Thoresen had just gotten the final information from his main contact on Prime World.

"I've breached Guard security," Crocker had boasted. "So this is straight from their computer."

"What does that mean," the Baron asked, "except that you are going to charge me more?"

"It means your Sten is out of it for good. He was killed in a nasty training accident. A woman trooper was also killed."

Thoresen smiled. How convenient. No final payment due to the assassin.

"Good work. Now, what did you find out about my relations with the Emperor?"

"You're fine, there," Crocker said. "The last time there was a complaint—and it was a minor one—about Vulcan, the Emperor sent a personal reprimand to the complaining party. He said he did not want a patriot such as yourself maligned."

Thoresen plucked a flower. Sniffed at it. That, he didn't believe at all. He was sure the Emperor was playing some sort of game. But he wasn't worried. The only kind he could play was the waiting variety. And Bravo Project was almost complete.

Yes, the Baron had a great deal to be thankful for.

CHAPTER THIRTY-TWO

THE DRONE TUG shifted the huge boulder in its tractor grip and then nosed it against another. Ida cursed as she fought for control, slipped, and the boulders collided. Sten and the others slammed against the rock side, then tumbled toward the other as there was another loud thud.

"Would you get this clotting thing going?" Sten yelled at Ida. "You're turning us into soyamush."

"I'm trying. I'm trying," Ida shouted back. She slid back into her seat and once again began to tap delicately at the computer keys.

Sten and the other members of the Mantis team were inside the boulder. It was actually a huge, hollowed hunk of ore fitted out as a minispaceship. Except, of course, there was no drive unit. Their tug provided that. Which was why everyone was cursing Ida, as she tried to maneuver the drone tug from inside the boulder.

"It's not my fault," she complained. "The damn drone doesn't have the brains of a microbe."

"Dinna be malignin' the wee beastie," Alex said. "Ye're the one giein' the brains—Ouch! Clot you, lass."

Ida grinned back at them. This time the big jolt had been on purpose.

"Maybe we better shut up," Sten said, "and let her drive."

215

Ida caressed the keys. Finally, the tug began to respond more smoothly. The boulder next to them moved away to a safer distance. The drone's drive units flared, and they began to drift slowly after it, toward Vulcan.

Sten had figured the perfect insertion method. Vulcan sent only unmanned tugs to the mining world, where all work was done by bots. A hollow boulder nearby carried their gear.

On the final approach to Vulcan, Ida punched at her computer, setting up an ECM blanket to fool Vulcan's sniffers, then put a finger to her lips, warning them unnecessarily to be quiet. A security capsule sniffed them over, then gave the drone tug clearance.

A jolt, whispered curses, and the tug started to move them toward a huge, yawning port. Then, *slam,* they were down.

"Clot, Ida," Jorgensen groaned. "Gimme a little humanity."

"That's her problem," Doc said. "She has too much of it."

And then they were moving along a slideway toward the thundering sound of grinding, giant teeth.

"This is where we get off," Sten said. "And quick."

They blew the port and scrambled out. About a hundred meters ahead of them waited the enormous jaws of a crusher. Sten and Ida popped the other boulder open and began hauling out gear. Jorgensen patted a knapsack he was carrying. Inside, Frick and Frack were whining to get out.

They carried the gear to the edge of the moving belt, then slid down after it.

"Next time," Ida said as they stacked their things on a gravsled, "you drive."

"Can't," Sten said. "I think you broke my arm."

He ducked under her swinging fist, then jumped up on the sled. As the others climbed on, Sten switched the sled controls to manual and headed for their hiding place.

He had spotted it when he was a Delinq. It was better

than a hideout. It was a home, complete with access to food, drink and not-so-public transportation.

"The Emperor's got nothin' on us," Jorgensen whistled.

Even Doc was gawking at Sten's find. They were standing in the main ballroom of what had once been a luxury passenger liner. It was from the earlier days of interstellar travel, when journeys took months, and competing liners boasted of the diversions they provided their well-heeled customers. There were staterooms, party rooms, and several other ballrooms like the one they were standing in, with glittering chandeliers and polished floors. In the perfect nonenvironment of Vulcan, everything was exactly as the Company had left it centuries earlier when the ship was used to provide quarters to Execs overseeing the construction of Vulcan. It had been bought from a belly-up corporation, bolted into place, and then abandoned as Vulcan grew.

Hundreds of meters up, near the ballroom ceiling, Frick and Frack wheeled about, squealing in delight at their regained freedom.

"Well," Ida said, "the bats like it, so I guess it's okay."

She wasn't quite so happy when Sten showed her the ship's computer and put her to work. "It's so clotting primitive," she said, "it belongs in a museum."

Sten had had enough diplomacy drilled into him by now to know when to keep his mouth shut. And by the time he left, she was huddled over the board, stroking it back to life, and beginning the task of patching them into Vulcan's central computer.

"As I see it," Doc said, "our first objective is recruitment."

He snuggled his tubby body back onto the chair, feet dangling. They were in the captain's quarters, wolfing down the Exec meal Ida had conjured out of the computer.

"Y'mean," Alex said, "Ah canna blow things oop yet?"

"Patience, Alex," Sten said. "We'll get to that soon."
He turned to Doc. "You can't just walk up to a Mig and

wiggle your finger at him. He'll think you're a Company spy and run like hell."

Jorgensen burped, then tossed a couple of Peskagrapes over to Frick and Frack. "Feed me some input, I'll see what I can plow up."

Sten shook his head.

"No. We'll start with the Delinqs."

"From what you told us about them," Ida said, "they'll try to cut our throats."

"A suggestion?" Doc ventured.

Sten was surprised. Doc always stated facts. Never asked. Then he realized that despite their briefings, Doc was still feeling his way through the intricacies of Vulcan.

"Shoot."

"No, no. You don't want to shoot them."

"I mean—Clot! Never mind. Go ahead."

"What we may need to do is establish a suprapeer figure. A hero for them to emulate."

"I don't get it."

"Of course you don't. Listen, and I'll explain . . ."

They didn't have to wait long to put Doc's plan into effect. Ida had patched into the Sociopatrol Headquarters' system, blue-boxed a monitor on it, then left orders for the ship computer to wake her at the appropriate time.

They had been nailed cold. All exits were sealed and the Sociopatrol was moving in reinforcements. It was a large Delinq gang armed with riot guns and obeying orders with almost military precision as the leader snapped out commands.

"You three, behind those crates. You and you, over there."

There was a loud crump as the Sociopatrol peeled the outer lock door. The leader looked around. It was the best she could do. In a few minutes, they would all be dead. She took up position behind a stack of crates and waited.

Another, louder crump and the main door exploded

inward in a shower of metal splinters. Screams from the wounded. The leader recovered, fired a burst at uniformed figures in the doorway. Ragged fire began behind her as the others started to fight back. Hopeless. The patrolmen advanced behind a huge metal shield.

A shout above them.

"Down!"

The leader looked as a slim figure dropped from a duct onto a mountain of crates. He was behind the advancing spearhead of Sociopatrolmen. She lifted her weapon. Almost fired. Again, there was a shout.

"Flatten."

She dropped as Sten sprayed the patrolmen with his willygun. Mass confusion and hysteria began among the attackers. A few tried to fight back. Sten worked his willygun like a hose, spraying from left to right and then left again. And in a moment it was over and there were twenty dead Sociopatrolmen.

Sten jumped down and walked toward the Delinqs. They came out of hiding, dazed. Staring at Sten as he advanced. One boy took a cautious step forward.

"Who's your leader?" Sten asked.

"I am." A voice behind him.

He turned as the woman came from behind the stack of crates. And froze.

Bet.

She fell. And fell. And fell. Screaming for Sten. Every muscle tensed for the hurt. A child again in nightmare fall.

And then there was a softness. Like crashing into a soft pillow, but still falling. And the pillow stiffened, and she hit . . . bottom? And was flung upward, tumbling over and over. Then falling again. Slower.

Until Bet found herself suspended in midair over a huge machine. A McLean gravlift that workmen used to hoist heavy equipment through the ducts.

Cautiously, she slid off the pillow and dropped to the

floor. She peered up into the darkness. Nothing. She shouted for Sten. There were sounds above her, then a beam of light speared down. She threw herself to one side as patrolmen fired at her. Came to her feet and sprinted away.

Bet stretched luxuriously on the bed. Nuzzled up to Sten.

"I never thought—"

He silenced her with a kiss. Drew her closer.

"What's to think? We're alive."

Ida paced back and forth, glaring now and then at the door to Sten's quarters. She was *very* angry. "That's just great," she snarled at Alex. "She bats her eyes and no more. Mantis trooper. Just another loverboy."

"Ye nae hae a sliver a' romance in yer bones, lass?"

Ida snorted but didn't even bother to answer.

"We all ken aboot Bet," Alex said.

"Sure," she snapped. "We all know each other's psych profile. Just like I know you mourn for your mother's home-cooked haggis. But that don't mean I have to let your dear old momma join our team."

"Now, dinna be malignin' me mither. Had an arm a' her could stop a tank wi' one blow."

"You know what I mean."

"Ah do. An' y'be wrong. Wrong a' wee lil body cou' be."

"How so?"

"T'ye nae see it, whidny bother a' explain. Ah'll be havin' Sten do it f'me."

Ida snorted again, then grinned. "To hell with it. Let's have a beer."

"We don't have a chance," Bet pleaded. "Let's just get out. Off Vulcan. Like we always dreamed."

Sten shook his head.

"I can't. And even if the others let me, I wouldn't. Thoresen—"

"Clot Thoresen!"

"Exactly what I plan to do."

Bet started to tell him that killing Thoresen—even if he could—wouldn't bring his family back. But that was obvious. She sighed. "How can I help?"

"You've been running that gang since I . . . left?"

Bet nodded.

"From what I saw, they're pretty good."

"Not as good as Oron's," she said. "But the best, now. We're armed and not running like Oron did."

"And you have the respect of the other Delinq gangs?"

"Yes."

"Good. I want you to set up a meeting."

"A meeting? What for?"

"Listen, and I'll tell you."

The Delinq chieftains eyed each other warily. Even with Bet's assurances, they were suspicious. The meeting could be a setup for the Sociopatrol—or a takeover.

About fifteen of them were spread around the huge table, muttering to each other and trying not to be impressed by the huge banquet or the luxurious dining room.

The meeting place was a new restaurant scheduled for opening in a day or two. The latest servant bots purred around the room offering the Delinqs delicacies reserved for Execs. Ida had found it after Sten had told her he wanted an impressive meeting place for the gang leaders, someplace that would show them just how powerful the Mantis team was. Ida had first patched into the personnel computer, and ordered all of the prospective restaurant employees to remain on their current jobs. The tap of a few more keys showed restaurant construction seriously delayed because of needed materials. And just to make sure, Sten had a few worker bots put a sign on the main entrance: DANGER. DO NOT ENTER. VACUUM CONDITIONS BEYOND.

Bet was at the head of the table. Beside her sat Sten.

She put a hand up for attention and got it. "Look at us all," she said. "Look at the faces around this table."

Puzzled, they did.

"This is the first time the leaders of every gang have been in one room. Better yet, nobody's cut any throats."

True, some of them thought. But maybe not for long.

"Think about what that means. All of us together. Representing a combined strength of maybe three hundred or four hundred Delinqs."

A stir.

"What's that get us?" a gang chief named Patris snarled.

"Normally," Bet said, "nothing. All of us against the Sociopatrol would mean just a little bit more splatter than usual. Normally."

"So who's talkin' about goin' against the patrol?" asked a gang boss named Flynn.

Bet pointed at Sten. "He is."

The muttering became a loud grumbling.

"This is Sten. You've heard about him. He was with Oron."

Even louder grumblings.

"Sten's been offworld. Off Vulcan. And now he's come back to help us."

Stunned silence. But mostly because of the enormity of the lie.

"You all heard about what happened to my gang?" Bet said.

Nods all around.

"And you heard about what happened to the patrol clots that almost got us?"

Slow nods. Glimmers of what she was getting at.

"Sten killed them," Bet said. "All of them. If he wasn't who he says he is, then how could that even be? How could I be here talking to you?"

"She's right," Patris noted. "My best runner saw them cleanin' up the clottin' bodies."

Flynn sneered. "So he's a hero. Big deal. Now, what's he want with us?"

Sten rose. Instant hush.

"It's very simple," he said. "We're gonna take over Vulcan."

The effort to overthrow Vulcan began with a series of what Doc called "gray actions."

"We want to increase the discontent among the Migs," he said. "Then impress on them the vulnerability of the Company."

Doc thought the proposed gray-action incidents his best work yet. Jorgensen thought they were just plain dirty tricks, and what Alex called them was not repeatable, even in his brogue. Only Ida was charmed. She saw infinite possibilities in enriching herself.

"That'll have to wait," Sten warned her.

"For what? I got this computer singin' any song I want."

"Then you found Bravo Project?"

Ida sighed. "Well, almost any song."

Doc glared at her.

"I'll start on the radio broadcasts," she grumped.

Even Doc was impressed with the device she worked out. It took up an entire stateroom aboard the old liner. Basically, it was just a simple radio broadcaster beefed up with enough power circuits to boost Vulcan out of orbit. She rigged it to a Mantis minicomputer and set it to monitoring the Company band that broadcast Mig news and entertainment.

"Flip this switch," she said, "and we're on their band. Anything we say sounds like it's coming from their station."

"You mean like 'Thoresen does it with Xypacas'?" Sten asked.

"A little more subtle than that," Doc broke in. "The idea is to make it *sound* like it's a Company-approved script."

Incomprehension registered on Sten's face. He waved them away in disgust. "Never mind," Doc said. "I'll work out what we're going to say. You just worry about your end."

* * *

Sten and Bet ambled past the factory. They strolled unhurriedly along like two Migs just off-shift and heading for a narcobeer. Several workers came out of the factory and stepped on the slideway beside them.

Sten nudged Bet with an elbow.

"Will you looka that," he said loudly. "That's Bearings Works Twenty-three, ain't it?"

"Yeah," Bet answered. "Sure is. I heard about that place."

Sten shook his head.

"Poor clots. I sure wouldn't wanta work there. Oh, well. Guess the Company's workin' on a cure."

A beefy Mig glared at them. "Cure? Cure for what?"

Sten and Bet casually turned toward him. "Oh, you work there?"

The Mig nodded.

"Sorry," Bet said. "Never mind."

The beefy Mig and his buddies pushed over to them. "Never mind what?"

Sten and Bet appeared a little nervous. "Say," Sten said. "Not so close, if you don't mind. No offense."

"What'sa matter with you? Waddya mean not so close? We got the crawlin' crud or somethin'?"

Bet tugged at Sten. "Let's get out of here. We don't want any trouble."

Sten started away, then stopped. "Somebody's gotta tell them," he said to Bet. He turned back to the puzzled Migs. "We work at the Mig Health Center."

"So?"

"So we been gettin' some real strange cases from that place." He pointed at the factory the men just left.

"What kinda cases?"

"Not sure," Bet said. "Has somethin' to do with the lubricants you use."

The Migs stiffened. "What's wrong with 'em?" the beefy man asked.

"Can't tell. Seems to be some kind of virus. Hits only males."

"What's it do to them?"

Sten shrugged. "Let's just say, they ain't been havin' much of a sex life lately."

"And probably never will," Bet chimed in.

The Migs looked at each other.

Sten grabbed Bet by the arm and pulled her away. "Good luck, boys," he yelled back over his shoulder.

The Migs didn't even notice them leap over the barrier and hurry off down another slideway. They were too busy looking impotent.

Ida positively purred into the microphone. Doc sat beside her, checking his notes, making sure she made the right points in the right untrustworthy tone of voice.

"Before we begin our next request, fellow workers, we have an announcement. This is from the Health Center, and the people over there are very concerned about a rumor that's been going around.

"A silly rumor, really. It has to do with viral contamination of lubricants at Bearing Works Twenty-three.

"Ah, excuse me—I mean with the *non*contamination of lubricants at . . . Never mind. It is totally without foundation, the Health Center informs us. And there is no cause for alarm.

"It is absolutely not true that it causes impotency among males— Correction. There is no contamination—but if there were, it would not affect the potency of males.

"Uh . . . I guess that's it. Now, for our next selection—"

Ida flipped the switch and the regular broadcast boomed in. Just as a song was starting. She turned to Doc, beaming.

"How'd I do?"

"I am happily considering all those poor, suffering Mig libidos."

The following shift, only eight Migs showed up for work at the bearing factory. Within fifteen minutes those eight had also heard about the broadcast denial and were on their way out.

Patris, disguised as a Sociopatrolman, leaned casually against a wall. Watching the Migs at play in the rec area. Another Delinq—a woman dressed like a joygirl—chatted with him. Pretending to be on the make.

A tall, skinny Mig caught their attention. He was working a gambling 'puter. Inserting his card, waiting as lights and wheels flashed. Cursing as he kept coming up empty-handed. In the card went again for another try.

"He's been at it an hour," Patris whispered to the girl.

She glanced over at the Mig.

"Probably just added six months to his contract," she said.

She turned, slipped over to a duct, stumbled against it.

"There's our mark," she whispered to the Delinq inside. A scuttling sound and he was away.

Hours later, the Mig was still at it. Inside the wall, behind the gambling machine, the Delinq manipulated the controls with a bluebox of Ida's evil devise. He kept the Mig just interested enough by feeding him a few wins. But steadily, the man was losing.

"Clot," he finally shouted.

Turned and stalked away from the machine. Patris flicked an invisible speck from his uniform and strolled over to the gambling 'puter. He waited just until the Mig looked his way. Inserted a card. Instant sirens . . . bells . . . lights going wild.

The loser Mig froze.

"Clot," he said to a Mig beside him. "See what that slime just did?"

"Yeah. Got himself a fortune."

"But I been playin' that thing half the day. Don't gimme a clottin' credit. Then he walks up and . . ."

Other Migs gathered at the sound of the winning machine, overheard the loser Mig, then cast nasty looks at Patris. Patris finally pretended to notice. He stalked over to the crowd, swinging his stun rod.

"On your way," he ordered. "Quit gawkin' and git."

The angry crowd hesitated. "Stinkin' cheat, that's what it is," somebody yelled from the back. The somebody being the "joygirl" Delinq.

"You should'a seen him," the loser Mig shouted. "He stole what I should'a won."

More angry grumbling. Patris hit the panic button and in a flash, a squad of patrolmen were rushing to his rescue. He waited until they closed on the crowd, then faded out of sight.

"Fellow workers," Ida said. "We all must be grateful for the marvelous recreational centers provided by the Company. At no small expense, I might add.

"For instance, the gambling 'puters, which give us all good clean, honest fun. Company statistics prove that the machines pay off more credits than they take.

"But there are always losers, who now are spreading a terrible rumor. So terrible it almost embarrasses me to repeat it— However, there is no truth to the story that the machines are set to pay off only to high Company officials. No truth at all. Why, some liars have even indicated that the machines only pay off to Sociopatrolmen. Can you imagine that! The *very* men hired at no small expense by the Company to . . ."

Jorgensen came up with the masterstroke.

"That's lightweight stuff," he said. "You gotta hit a guy where it really hurts."

"Such as," Doc sniffed, a little hurt.

"Like beer."

The following shift break swarms of Migs streamed into the rec domes. Offered their cards and settled back for a cool one. Nothing. Not one drop. The machine merely swallowed the card, deducted credits, and then chuckled at the Mig to go away.

"Clot I will," shouted one big Mig. He shoved his card

in again. Still nothing. He slammed a meaty fist into the machine. "Gimme!"

"I am Company property," the machine informed him. "Violation of my being carries severe penalties."

The Mig kicked the machine in answer. Alarms went off at five Sociopatrol centers. They steamed to the rescue. Only to find empty domes. Empty except for the twisted hulks of beer machines. All looted of their contents and groaning on the floor.

Doc shook his head.

"No. Too obvious. Not gray enough. Skip talking about the beer, Ida, and go to the food situation instead."

Ida turned to her microphone.

"Fellow workers, the Company is pleased to announce a new health program. They have discovered that we are all getting much too overweight.

"Therefore, beginning next shift, all food rations will be reduced thirty percent.

"That thirty— Sorry, we're in error. That program will not take effect until . . . until— What? Wrong announcement? Oh, kill it! The program is no go!

"Fellow workers, there is no truth to the report that food supplies will be cut thirty percent next . . ."

Sten side-stepped a drunken Mig, sloshing a little beer, then pushed through the crowd to Bet. Set down their beers and settled into a seat beside her.

"I'll tell ya," a Mig said to his companions, "they've gone too far now. Too clottin' far."

Sten winked at Bet, who smiled back.

"They cheat us. Mess with our sex lives, try to screw with our beer. Now they're gonna increase all work contracts one year."

"Where'd ja hear that?"

"Just now. From that woman on the radio."

"But she said it was just a rumor."

"Yeah. Sure it is. If it's a rumor, how come they're tryin' to deny it so hard?"

"He's got a point," Sten broke in.

The Mig turned to Sten. Peered at him, then grinned. Slapped him on the shoulder.

"Sure I do. That's the way the Company always works—feed you a rumor, get the reaction, then spring it on you for real."

"Remember last year," Bet said. "There was that rumor we were all gonna lose three paid holidays? What happened?"

"We lost 'em," the Mig said sullenly.

His friends all sipped beer. Thoughtful. Angry.

"What the clot," someone sighed. "Nothin' we do about it 'cept complain?"

Nods of agreement.

"I tell ya," the first Mig said, "I'd sure do something about it if I could. Hell, I got no family, I'd take the risk."

The other Migs glanced about. The conversation was getting dangerous. One by one they excused themselves. Leaving only Sten, Bet, and their Mig friend.

"You mean what you said?" Sten asked.

" 'Bout what?"

"About gettin' even with the Company."

The Mig stared at him suspiciously. "You a spy?"

He started to stand up.

"Well, so what if you are. I'm fed up. Nothin' make me feel better'n to break you—"

Bet took him by the arm. Gently pulled him down and bought him a beer.

"If you're serious," Sten said, "I got some people I want you to meet."

"To do what? Gripe like all the others?" He waved an arm at all the Migs in the bar.

"We gonna do more than gripe," Sten said.

The Mig eyed them. Then smiled a big grin. His hand reached across the table. "I'm your man."

Sten shook his hand.

"What are you called?"

"Lots of things from the clottin' supervisor. But my name's Webb."

They rose and left the bar.

"I think I finally got the idea how this whole thing works," Bet told Ida and Doc.

"The gray actions?" Ida asked.

Bet nodded.

"Poor humans," Doc said, "torturing what little brain they have over the obvious."

Bet gave him a look to shave his tendrils at neck level. Turned, and started out the door.

"Wait," Ida said.

Bet stopped.

"Doc," Ida said. "You're the all-seeing being, but sometimes you miss what's in front of your pudgy little face."

"Such as?"

"Like maybe we ought to find out what Bet has on her mind."

Doc thought about it, tendrils wiggling. Then exuded his warmest feelings at Bet. "My error," he said. "Blame it on genetic tendencies to rip and tear."

Mollified, Bet returned and settled into a chair. "What I was thinking about," she said, "was the ultimate gray action. For Migs."

"Like?" Ida asked.

"Like the old legend that's been going around Vulcan since the first Mig."

"Legends?" Doc said. "I like legends. There's so much to build on."

Bet took a deep breath.

"Story says someday there's gonna be a Mig revolt. A successful revolt led by an offworlder who was once a Mig himself."

Doc was still feeling a little slow—his apology had put him off.

But Ida got it right away. "You mean Sten?"

"Yes. Sten."

"Ah," Doc said, finally getting it. "The mythical redeemer. Sten leads the way to salvation."

"Something like that," Bet said.

"The perfect rumor," Ida said. "We spread the word that the redeemer is here." She looked at Doc. "Have we reached that point yet?"

"Yes," Doc said. "It's the perfect intermediate stage."

Bet hesitated. "One problem."

"Such as?" Doc was anxious to be about his work.

"What will Sten think about it?"

Ida shrugged. "Who cares? Just wish it were me. There's a lot of money in redemption."

The rumor spread like a virus colony on a petri dish. All over Vulcan, Migs were tense, angry, waiting for something to happen. But knowing, still, that nothing ever would. Without prodding, the dissension would dissipate to everyday acceptance.

"You see?" the old Mig told his grandchildren. "It's like I been tellin' your dad all along. There is a way off Vulcan. And clot the Company."

His son and daughter-in-law ignored the obscenity. Nodded to their kids. Gramps was right.

"And like I been sayin' all the time, it's a Mig that'll shove our contracts right up the Company's—"

"*Dad*," his daughter-in-law warned.

"Tell us about him, gramps," a child said. "Tell us about the Mig."

"Well, to begin with, he's just like us. A workin' clot. And then he got offworld. But he never forgot us, and . . ."

"Ah didna ken Ah was servin' wi' th' Redeemer," Alex said. He bowed ceremoniously and held the mug out to Sten.

"Sharrup," Sten growled. Bet giggled.

"Ay, Bet. 'Tis wonderful ye brought th' weenin' hole in m'theology to light. Here Ah was, servin' in darkness, havin' naught save th' Trinity t' keep me safe."

"Trinity?" Bet asked.

"Aye." Alex bent, and picked a struggling Sten up by the hips. Held him high overhead . . . then to either side, then dumped him back in the chair. *"In nomine* Bobby Burns, John Knox, an' me gran'sire."

For once, Sten couldn't find an Imperial obscenity dirty enough to fit the occasion.

CHAPTER THIRTY-THREE

"BEGGING YOUR PARDON, sir," the Counselor said, "but you don't know what it's like out there. Lies. Rumors. Every Mig ready to cut your throat."

"Nonsense," the Baron said. "It's a normal Mig stage."

The Counselor sat in Thoresen's garden, waiting for the ax to fall. But it wasn't what he expected. Here he was with a drink in his hand, chatting with the Baron. That's not what usually happened when Thoresen summoned an employee. Especially with all those stories going around about the Counselor.

"I asked you here," Thoresen said, "because of your well-known frankness."

The Counselor beamed.

"And that matter," Thoresen continued, "of certain, ah, shall we say alleged indiscretions on your part."

The Counselor's face fell. It was all a setup after all.

"There have been accusations," Thoresen said, "that you have been dipping a bit too deep into Mig credits."

"I never—" the Counselor began.

Thoresen held up a hand, silencing him.

"It's expected," Thoresen said. "It's the way it's always been done. The Counselors make a little extra for their loyal efforts, without cost to the Company, and casual labor contracts are extended without expensive book work."

The Counselor relaxed a bit. The Baron's description was accurate. An informal system that had worked for centuries.

"My difficulty," the Counselor said, "is the rumors. I promise you—on my life—I've never taken the amount I'm being accused of."

Again, Thoresen motioned him to silence. "Of course, you haven't. You are one of my most trustworthy—well, at least, discreet—employees."

"Then why—?"

"Why did I summon you?"

"Yes, sir."

Thoresen rose and began pacing. "Actually, I'm calling in all of my key officers. The Migs are moaning and groaning again. It happened in my grandfather's time. And my father's. I'm not worried about them. What I'm concerned about is the overreaction of my own people."

The Counselor thought about the ugly looks he had seen lately. It was more than Mig grumbling. He started to say something. Then decided not to.

"As I said," Thoresen continued, "it's just a cycle. A normal cycle. But it must be handled delicately."

"Yes, sir," the Counselor said.

"The first thing to remember," Thoresen said, "is not to aggravate them. Let them blow a little hot. Ignore what they say. And identify the leaders. We'll deal with *them* after things calm down." He looked at the Counselor. "Am I understood?"

"Yes, sir."

"Good. Now I plan to take a personal hand in all this."

"Yes, sir."

"I want all incidents—no matter how minor—brought to my attention."

"Yes, sir."

"No action—no matter how minor—is to be taken without my go-ahead."

"Yes, sir."

"Then it's settled. Now, is there anything else I should know about?"

The Counselor hesitated, then said, "Uh, yes. The broadcasts on the Mig radio. They've been a little heavy-handed?"

"An excellent example of what I've been talking about. Overreaction. The people responsible have denied releasing that information, but facts are facts."

"If I may ask—what did you do?"

Thoresen smiled. "Dismissed them. And ordered all broadcasts cleared by me."

There was an uncomfortable pause, until the Counselor realized he had been dismissed. He rose, almost bowing.

"Thank you for your time, sir."

"That's what I'm here for," the Baron soothed. "To listen to my people."

He watched the Counselor exit. Measured him. A clumsy man, he thought, but valuable. If things got worse, he could always throw him to the Migs. No. Not necessary. Not now. Events were just being blown out of proportion.

CHAPTER THIRTY-FOUR

FOR A PERSON who had just pulled off a minor coup, Ida looked glum. She had found Bravo Project. Even with Sten's help, it had been a nasty problem. It was, obviously, near The Row. Or, what had been The Row. But the whole area was a warren of corridors, factories, homes. And specially constructed computer dodges, worked out by a genius whom Ida had grown to admire.

"What I did," she told the group gathered around her terminal, "was make the assumption that Bravo Project was sealed from the rest of Vulcan."

"Naturally," Sten said.

Ida glared at him. "That means all the people who worked there have to be kept under ultratight security. But these are special people. Not prisoners. So I figured they gotta be kept happy. The best food. Drink. Sex. The whole shot."

Doc smiled a nasty little teddy-bear smile. Ida had more brains than he gave her credit for.

"I set up a monitor on gourmet food shipments. Livees for highbrows, things like that."

"What's the problem, then?" Sten asked.

Ida tapped some keys. A three-dimensional model of the Bravo Project lab blossomed out. Silence as they all studied it.

"Projection," Jorgensen said. "Direct assault unacceptable casualties. Mission in doubt with conventional tactics."

Doc looked it over. His tendrils waved in agreement. The others waited for his conclusions.

"Under the present circumstances," he said, "Jorgensen is correct. But what if we move it up a stage?"

Jorgensen ran it through his brain. "*Black* operations . . . Input flux increased . . . Bravo target . . . Yes . . . alternatives . . . but too numerous to compute."

They discussed it.

"I vote we push to the next level," Sten said.

"What the clot 'm I supposed to say?" Sten whispered.

Doc was trying to learn a sneer. He didn't have the expression quite right yet. "The usual inspiring drivel. You humans are easy to impress."

"If it's so easy, why don't you get up on those crates?"

"Very simple," Doc said blandly. "As you keep telling me, who believes a teddy bear?"

Sten looked around at the other team members.

"Tell 'em aught but the truth, lad," Alex said. "They're nae Scots so they'd no ken that."

Bet just smiled at him. Sten took a deep breath and clambered to the top of the piled boxes.

The forty-odd assembled Migs in the warehouse stared up at him. Behind them, their Delinq guides eyeballed Sten curiously.

"I don't know what the Company will think of you," Sten said, "but you scare clottin' hell outa me!"

There was a ripple of mild amusement.

"My da told me, most important tool you had was a four-kilo hammer. Used it to tap his foremen 'tween the eyes every once again, just to get their attention.

"I'm lookin' at forty-seven four-kilo hammers just now. You and your cells are gonna get some attention. Starting next shift."

A buzz rose from the cell leaders below him.

"You all got jobs, and you and your folk've run through

them enough. I'm not gonna stand up here and tell master craftsmen how to set your jigs.

"Just remember one thing. There's only a few of us. We're like the apprentice, with half a tool kit. We go breaking our tools early on, we'll end up not getting the job done."

The men nodded. Sten was talking their language. Doc's tendrils wiggled. Correct procedure, he analyzed, even though he didn't understand the analogies.

Sten waited until the talk died. Raised his arm, half salute.

"Free Vulcan."

He waved the Delinqs forward to guide the Mig cell leaders back through the ducts to their own areas, and jumped down from the crates.

"Well, Alex?"

"Ah nae think it's Burns . . . but it'll do. Aye, it'll do."

The Mig eyed the weapon skeptically. It wasn't confidence-inspiring. A collection of 20-mm copper plumbing pipe, brazed together. He unscrewed the buttcap, and took two of the sodium thiosulfate tablets that fell into his palm, shoved the weapon back into his coveralls and went down the corridor.

Breathe . . . breathe . . . breathe . . . normally . . . you're on your way to report a minor glitch to your foreman. There is no hurry . . .

He touched the buzzer outside the man's door. Footsteps, and the bespectacled foreman peered out at him.

He looked puzzled. Asked something that the Mig couldn't hear through the roaring in his ears as he brought the weapon out and touched the firing stud. Electric current ran into tungsten wires; wires flared and touched off the ammonium-nitrate compound.

The compound blew the sealed prussic-acid container apart, whuffing gas into the man's throat. He gargled and stumbled back.

The drill took over. The Mig dropped the gas gun on the dead Tech's chest and walked away. Took the amylnitrate capsule from his coverall pocket and crushed it—completing the prussic-acid antidote—stripped off his gloves and disappeared into a slideway.

Ida swam a hand idly, and the robot's lid opened. She stared in at the ranked desserts in the server.

"Y'all gettin' fat," Jorgensen said.

"Correction. I am not getting fat. I *am* fat. And intend on getting fatter."

She began stuffing some megacaloric concoction into her face with one hand and tapping computer keys with the other.

"Did you wipe them?" Sten asked.

"Hours and hours ago."

"Then what in the clot are you doing now?"

"I randomed, and got the key to the Company's liquid assets pool. Now, if I can get a linkup, I'll be able to transfer whatever I want into some offworld account."

"Like a Free Trader roll?"

"That could—*oops!*" Her hand flashed across the keyboard and cut her board out of circuit. "Suspicious bassids got a security key hidden in there."

Sten started to say something, then turned away. Bet had been watching, confused.

"What's she doing?"

"Setting up her personal retirement fund," Sten said.

"I figured *that*," Bet said disgustedly. "I meant the wiping."

"We figured Company security and the patrol kept records on troublemakers. Migs who didn't rate getting brainburned or pulverized yet. Ida located the records and wiped them."

"I did better than that," Ida said, wiping her hands on the bot's extended towel. "I also put a FORGET IT code in, so any more input will be automatically blanked."

Bet looked impressed. Ida turned back to the keyboard.

"Now. Let's have another squinch at those assets."

*   *   *

"This is Free Vulcan," the voice whispered through a million speakers.

Frantic security Techs tried to lock tracers onto the signal source. Since the signal was initially transmitted via cable to a hundred different broadcast points, randomly changing several times a second, their task was hopeless.

"It has begun. We, the people of Vulcan, are starting to strike back. Seven Company officials were removed this shift for crimes against the workers they've ground down for so many years.

"This is the beginning.

"There will be more."

Sten slumped into the chair and dialed a narcobeer. Drained it, and punched up another.

"Any casualties?"

"Only one. Cell Eighteen. The contact man got stopped on the way in by a patrol spotcheck. His backup panicked and opened up. Killed all three of them."

"We'll need the name of the man," Doc said. "Martyrs are the lubricant of human revolutions."

Sten put his nose in his beer. He wasn't in the mood just yet.

"There goes the little guttersnipe now," Doc said approvingly.

Lying beside the panda in an air vent high above Visitors' Center, Sten focused the glasses. He finally found a Delinq wearing Mig coveralls darting through the crowds of offworlders.

"You had him take a bath, I trust," Doc said. "He is supposed to be the angelic little child every human desires for his very own."

Sten swung the glasses to the four Migs wearing Sociopatrolman uniforms, as they hue-and-cried after the Delinq.

"Slow down, boy," Sten muttered. "You're losing them."

As if listening, the boy zig-zagged aimlessly for a few

seconds and the "patrolmen" closed in on him. Shock batons rose and fell.

"Ah," Doc sighed contentedly. "I can hear the little brute scream from here. What's going on?"

"Mmm . . . here they come."

Spacemen boiled out of the bar the Delinq had allowed himself to be caught at.

"Are they righteously indignant?"

Sten panned the glasses across the spacemen's faces. "Yep."

The offworlders knotted about the struggling group. One of them shouted something about bullies.

"Come on," Sten muttered. "Get 'em moving."

The Delinq was a better actor than the four adults. He went down, but swung his head then dug his teeth into one man's leg. The phony Sociopatrolman yelped and brought the shock baton down.

That did it. The spacemen became an instant mob, grabbing bottles, smashing windows. The four "patrolmen" grabbed the boy and ran for the exit.

Sten hit the key of the minicomputer beside him, and the riot alarm began shrilling.

"Tell me what's happening," Doc said impatiently.

"Our people have cleared the dome. All right, here comes the riot squad in shock formation."

"What are the spaceclots doing?"

"Charging."

"Excellent. Now, we should see the first couple or three real patrolmen going down. Somebody should be panicking and putting his baton on full power and . . ." Doc smiled beatifically.

"Sure did. Took out a first officer. Drakh!"

"What you are telling me is that the morally outraged foreigners, having witnessed the brutal beating of a charming young child, and having been attacked by thugs, are reacting in the most strenuous manner possible. Tell me, Sten. Are they eating the Sociopatrolmen?"

"They aren't cannibals!"

"Pity. That's a human characteristic I haven't been able to observe at firsthand. You may proceed."

Sten grabbed a hose, shoved it through the grill and triggered the tanks of vomit gas into the Visitors' Center, grabbed Doc, and they quickly slithered away.

"Excellent, Sten. Excellent. Free Traders are insatiable rumor-spreaders. At the least, the Company appears in a bad light. With luck, a few of those space sailors are moralists—which I doubt—and will refuse cargo. Especially after they wonder why the Company not only involved them in a riot, but gassed them in the bargain."

Sten decided the only thing that could make Doc happier would be a massacre of orphans.

COMPANY DIRECTIVE—TO BE IMPLEMENTED IMMEDIATELY
Due to poor productivity, the following recreational domes provided for Migrant-Unskilled workers are to be closed immediately: Nos. 7, 93, 70.

There's some'at aboot explosions in vacuum, Alex decided for the hundredth time as he watched the lighter become a ball of flame. Almo' a puirfec' circle it makes.

He picked up his explosives kit and edged out of the loading dock.

Four other crates, besides the one that had just vanished the offworld loading ship, were booby-trapped. With a difference. Only somebody with Alex's experience would realize they would never go off. One explosion was to draw the attention of the Free Traders—destroying only a robot lighter—and the other bombs to discourage Free Traders' shipping Company cargoes.

COMPANY DIRECTIVE—SECURITY PERSONNEL ONLY
Effective immediately all ID cards issued to personnel whose duties are in the following areas: Visitors' Center, Cargo Transshipping, or Warehouse Divisions are rescinded. New passes will be issued on an individual basis. Thereafter, any member of patrol or security staffs failing to detain

persons using old-style (XP-sequence) IDs will be subject to firm disciplinary proceedings.

The secretary checked Gaitsen's desk carefully. Light pen positioned correctly, Exec-only inputs on STANDBY, the chair set carefully so many centimeters from the desk.

Efficiency is all, Stanskill, Gaitsen had said repeatedly. Clottin' surprise, the secretary thought, he never said that in bed. Too busy worryin' about his heart, maybe.

She went to the door, palmed it, and looked around for the last time. Everything familiar and in its place, just the way the Exec wanted. She passed through the doorway, and, as instructed, left her carryall on her desk in the antechamber. She checked the clock. Gaitsen should just about be out of the tube.

She knelt by the duct, and the Delinq waiting impatiently held the screen open. The woman crawled inside and disappeared.

As she awkwardly bent around a ninety-degree turn in the ducting, the secretary was sorry she wouldn't be able to watch as Gaitsen plumped down in his favorite seat.

"Alvor?"

"Yuh?" The bearded cell leader peered over Sten's shoulder.

"Did you have your team take this Braun out?"

"Never heard a' the clot."

Sten nodded, and scrolled on up the security report. Whoever killed Braun—low-level Exec in Product Planning Division—must've been settling a private grudge. He considered a minute. No. Free Vulcan would not claim that killing with the others. Might get the Company even more upset.

COMPANY DIRECTIVE—SECURITY PERSONNEL ONLY

Prior to beginning routine patrols, consult route with shift team director and chart R79L. Areas marked in blue are to be patrolled *only* by four-man teams equipped with riot gear. DISCUSSION OF THIS POLICY MODIFICATION IS FORBIDDEN TO NONCLEARED STAFF.

"This is the voice of Free Vulcan," the speakers resonated. "We would like to know how you Executives and security people feel.

"As if there is a noose tightening around your necks?

"Things have been happening, haven't they? What happened to that Sociopatrol that was sent out to Warehouse Y008? It never reported back, did it?

"And Exec Gaitsen. That must have been very unpleasant. Not a very fast way to die, either. Perhaps you Executives who use your secretaries as joygirls might reflect on Gaitsen for a few moments.

"Yes. There is a noose. And it is getting steadily tighter, is it not?"

"Do you have a tracer?" Thoresen glowered.

"Nossir. And, Baron, I don't think we'll be able to get one." Thoresen blanked the screen, and keyed up another department.

"Semantics. Yes, Baron?"

"Do you have an analysis of that voice?"

"We do. Very tentative, sir. Non-Mig, non-Tech. Even though the voice of Free Vulcan—"

"You have been directed not to use that term, Tech!"

"Sorry, sir. Our theory is that the voice is synthesized. Sorry."

Thoresen flicked off, noted the time, and headed for the *salle d'armes*. He pulled a saber from its hanging and spun on the instructor.

"Come in," he growled. "As if you mean it!"

Sten eyed the hydroponics farm dubiously. It looked just as it had before Alex bustled off. The agribots still lovingly tended the produce intended for Exec consumption. "You sure it's gonna go?" he asked skeptically.

Alex patted him patronizingly. "Ah ken ye dinnae know what ye're glassin', lad. But dinnae tell your gran'sire how to suck eggs."

Sten followed him to the shipping port and ducked inside. Alex let the door almost close, then blocked it with a small metal bar. "Now ye see it—"

He touched off a small emergency flare, lobbed it into the middle of the farm, and yanked the bar out. As the door snapped closed, Sten saw the compartment fill—deck to ceiling—with a mass of flames.

"Ye ken," Alex said, as the shock slammed against the lock, "i's what's known as a dust explosion. Ye mere put the intake in the fertilizer supply, burn awa' the liquidifier, an' dust sprays aboot the room. Touch i' off"—the little man chuckled happily.

> EXECUTIVE PERSONNEL EYES ONLY
> We have noticed an inordinate number of applications for transfer, early retirement, or resignation. We are most disappointed. During this admittedly unsettling time, the Company needs its most skilled personnel to be most attentive to their duties. For this reason, all such applications shall be disapproved until further notice.
>
> >   Thoresen.

Webb slit the dying Sociopatrolman's throat from ear to ear, stood, and brushed his hands off. He walked over to the only survivor of the ten-man patrol, held against the wall by two grim Migs. "Let 'im go, boys."

The surprised Migs released the patrolman.

"We're makin' ya a bargain," Webb said. "You ain't gonna get splattered like the rest of your scum. We're gonna let you go."

Webb's two men looked surprised.

"You just wander back to your barracks sewer, and let your friends know what happened."

The patrolman, near rigid with terror, nodded.

"An' next time they put you out on patrol, you don't have to crud around like you're a clottin' hero. Make a little noise. Don't be too anxious lookin' down a passage where somethin' might be goin' on you don't want to know about. Let 'im run, boys."

The patrolman glanced at the Mig bush section then he backed away. He sidled to the bend in the corridor, whirled and was gone.

"Y'think he's gonna do like you want, Webb?" one of his men asked.

"Don't matter. Either way, he won't be worth drakh anymore. An' don't you think security's gonna wonder why he got away without gettin' banged around?"

"I still don't understand."

"That's why you ain't a cell leader. Yet. C'mon. Let's clear."

The five-man patrol ducked as Frick and Frack hissed down from the overhead girders of the warehouse. One man had time to raise his riot gun and blast a hole through some crates before the white phosphorus minicaps ignited.

The two creatures swooped back over, curiously eyeing the hell below them as the phosphorus seared through flesh and bone, then banked into the waiting duct above.

"You! What's that? The brown drakh?"

"Soybeef stew," Sten replied. "May I offer you some?"

"Nawp. Don't need any extra diseases. I'll help myself." The med-Tech ladled stew from the tureen onto his tray, then slid on down the line.

Sten, face carefully blank, looked down the line of servers to Bet. They both wore white coveralls and were indistinguishable from the other workers in the Creche staff mess. Part of Sten's mind began the countdown, while another caught bits of conversation from the technicians at the tables.

"Clotting little monster! Daddy this, an' daddy that an' daddy I got to be a spacetug today and—"

"If we didn't need 'em, Company oughta space the little clots—"

"Tell 'em stories, pat 'em on the head, wipe their bungs when they mess. The Company don't pay us near enough."

"How you doin' with Billy?"

"Me an' that clot are reaching an understanding. I put him in a sewer supervisor, and just left him there for two shifts. Clottin' booger's gonna learn."

"Actually, doctor, there's no reason the Company has to maintain these creatures in the style it does. I'm theorizing that the program could be implemented with the use of atrophy amputation."

"Hmm. Interesting concept. We might develop it . . ."

Time.

Sten snapped the stock of the willygun to lock and brought it up, finger closing on the trigger. The two Sociopatrolmen lounging at the entrance dropped, fist-size holes in their chests.

"Down! Get down!" Bet shouted . . . the servers stared, then flattened as Sten lobbed two grenades from his pouch into the middle of the hall.

Bet showered a handful of firepills across the room, then the two fell alongside the servers.

Seconds passed and there was stunned silence from the other side of the serving line, then screams. And an all-enveloping blast.

Sten lifted his head and eyed Bet. She was laughing. He scrambled to his feet and pulled her up. Shook her. She came back to reality as he pushed her toward the garbage vent that was their escape hole.

He did, in fact, understand her a little better.

"This is the voice of Free Vulcan. We know what it is to be a Mig. To live under the bootheels of the Company. To know there is no law and no justice, except for those who have the stranglehold of power.

"Now, justice will come to Vulcan. Justice for those who have lived for generations in terror.

"Migs. You know what a terrible joke your Counselors are, and how your grievance committees are echoes of the Company's brutality.

"There is an end to this. From this shift forward, Free Vulcan will enforce the rights that free men know everywhere in the galaxy.

"If your foreman forces you to work a double shift, if a coworker is toadying to the Company, if your sons and daughters are being corrupted or stolen by the Company—

These evils will end. Now. If they do not, Free Vulcan will end those who commit them.

"If you have a grievance, talk about it. You may not know who is Free Vulcan. Perhaps your shiftmate, another worker down the line, the joygirl or joyboy in the Dome— even a Tech. But your words will be heard and our courts will act on them.

"We bring you justice, people of Vulcan."

COMPANY POLICY—ALL COUNSELORS AND SECURITY
EXECS—EYES ONLY

The sudden lack of participation by Mig-Unskilled workers in our grievance program has been brought to my attention. It is our opinion that concern about the tiny band of malcontents that styles itself "Free Vulcan" is excessive, since, in fact, we are now able to grasp terror by its throat.

Security Executives are evaluating the main areas reflecting such lack of involvement since the absence pinpoints areas where malcontents are located. Appropriate measures, of the severest kind, are imminent. It is strongly suggested that all Counselors make the workers for whose welfare they are responsible aware that, once these malcontents are dealt with, those who have encouraged them by participating in their kangaroo "justice" system will also be disciplined.

Thoresen.

"The thought has occurred to me," Ida drawled as she passed around glasses of alk, "that none of us are the people our parents wanted us to associate with."

"Some of us," Bet said evenly, "are the kind of people who wouldn't want to associate with our parents in the first place."

"Are we no bein' grim, lass?"

"Parents?" Frick shrilled. "Why would, colony, our colony care?" Frack squealed agreement.

"If you humans aren't creating traumas for other people," Doc said, "you can't wait to set them up for yourselves, can you?"

Sten was interested. "How do pandas get along with *their* progenitors, Doc?"

"It is not a factor. First, in the breeding process the male sheds his member after copulation and quickly— bleeds would be an analog—to death." Doc waved several tendrils. "Once the young hatches, inside the female, it exists . . . ah, as a parasite until born. Birth, naturally, occurs at the moment of female death."

Bet blinked. "That doesn't leave you with much of a sex life, does it?"

"I have wondered why the human mind isn't physiologically below the umbilicus," Doc said, "since most of its thought is concerned with that region. But, to answer your question, those of us with a proper concern for the future arrange to have ourselves neutered. The operation also extends our life span for nearly a hundred E-years."

Sten couldn't decide whether to laugh or be embarrassed.

"I can see it now," Jorgensen drawled. "Amblin' up the road. Farm spread out in front of you. You duck down behind a bush, spray the windows for snipers, then zig-zag up to the door, boot it open, heave in a grenade, roll in firin', and come to your feet, 'Ma! I'm home!'."

"Ah no ken why ye gie wha' we are so much concern," Alex finished. "Th' none a' us'll get oot'a Mantis alive." He upended his drink and went for another, not looking particularly concerned.

Sweat dripped from the Counselor's face onto his torn, filthy robes. "There was simply no truth to that story. My dealings with you Migs—"

"Mebbe we use that word," a brawny Mig said, "but that don't make it sound right comin' from you."

"Excuse me. You're quite right, of course. But . . . truthfully, I never attempted to deprive any . . . migrant worker of his rightfully earned time for personal benefit. It's a lie. A story created by my enemies."

The five cell leaders managed to look disbelieving in unison.

Sten watched closely from behind the one-way panel to one side of the "court," set up in an abandoned warehouse. He found it interesting that he didn't hate the

Counselor that actively anymore. On the other hand, he felt less than no desire to intervene.

"You can examine my record," the Counselor went on. "I've always been known for my fairness."

Bitter laughter drowned whatever else he was going to say. "We'll cut you a skate on that one," Alvor said. "Still leaves you assignin' Migs to shifts to get 'em killed 'cause they wouldn't give you whatever you wanted. I know two, maybe three people you set up for brainburns."

The Mig at the end of the table, who'd been silently staring at the Counselor, suddenly got up. "I got a question, boys. I wanna put it to his scumness personal. What'd you want from my Janice, made her cut an' run to the Delinqs?"

The Counselor licked his lips. The Mig grabbed him by the hair and lifted the Counselor out of his chair. "You ain't answered my question."

"It—there was—just a misunderstanding of my attempt to communicate."

"Communicate. 'Sat it? She was ten."

Sten got up. But the Mig holding the Counselor was keeping himself back. He looked over at the other cell leaders. "I don't need any clottin' more. Vote guilty."

And the chorus answered in agreement.

"Unanimous," Alvor put in. "What's the sentence?"

Sten kicked the screen over. "Give him to his friends. Outside."

The Counselor's eyes flared open. Who? And then he was screaming and clawing as the cell leaders had him. They jerked the double doors open and pushed. The Counselor half fell, half staggered into the arms of the workers waiting outside.

Alvor pulled the door to. But the sound of the mob outside was very clear.

That was the first.

"Just like pushin' dominoes," Sten said. He and Alex were headed back for the ship. "Three more cycles and we can stop hidin' behind bushes, start the revolution, and get the Guard in motion."

"Dinna be countin' your eggs afore they're chickened."

"What the clot does that mean?"

"Ah no ken. But ma gran used it t'mean things gang aft aglay."

"Would you speak Imperial, for clot's sakes?"

"Ah'm spikit proper, it's just your ears need recalibratin', lad."

"Bet me. But look. We're all set. A, we get a resistance set up. B, we start rightin' wrongs and killin' every Exec we can get and every Tech that can count above ten with his boots on."

"Aye. There's naught wrong so far."

"C, we build weapons and train the Migs how to use 'em. D, we set up our own alternate government, just like the conditioner taught us. Then, E, we're gonna snap our fingers in three cycles and the revolution has started."

Alex unslung his rifle—their sector was secure enough for most of the Migs to go openly armed now—and stopped.

"You no ken one thing, Sten," he said. "Man or woman, once they get their hands on th' guns, there's no callin' what'll happen next. Ah gie ye example. Mah brother, he was Mantis. Went in to some nice barbarian-class world our fearless Emp'rer decided needed a new gov'mint.

"Ye trackin' me yit? Aye, so they raises the populace, an' teaches 'em how to stand an' fight. Makes 'em proud to be what they is, 'stead of crawlin' worms."

"I am not trackin'," Sten said.

"So they runs up the blawdy red flag a' revolution, an' it starts. People slaughter a' th' nobility in th'r beds. My braw trots up wi' the gov'ment they've set up to replace the old baddies. An' the people're so in love wi' blood an' slaughter, they turns the *new* gov'ment inta cattle fodder like they done the first. My braw gets offworld wi'out an arm, an' the pro' don't take. So he's back tendin' sheep on Edinburgh, an' I goes out to keep the clan name fresh. Now, I'm takin' the long road aroun'—but best ye rec'lect.

When ye're giein' bairns the fire, ye no can tell wha'll be burnt."

He reslung his willygun, and he and Sten walked in silence to the airlock into the ship.

To be welcomed by Ida screaming, in a dull roar, "Clot! Clot! Clot!" A computer terminal sailed across the room to slam into a painting.

"What's wrong?"

"Nothing at all. But look at what your clotting Migs did!" She waved at the screens around the room. Sten noticed the other members of the team and Bet were silently staring.

"These are all the security channels. Look at those fools!"

"Dammit, Ida, tell me what happened!"

"As far as we can estimate," Doc said, "the Sociopatrol was transferring several unregenerate Migs South, to Exotic Section. One of the Migs in the shipment must've had some friends."

Sten glanced at the screens then walked to the alk container and poured himself a shot.

"So they decided to rescue him," Ida continued. "Naturally, the patrol reinforced, and so did the guy's friends. Which sucked in most of our cells in South Vulcan. Look."

Sten stared at the sweeping screens. Every now and then he recognized a face from the resistance.

" 'Pears," Jorgensen said, "like they dug all the weapons out and went huntin' for bear."

Ida sneered at Sten, then started cutting in sound from the various screens. Fascinated, Sten sat down to watch.

He saw screaming Migs charge a formation of patrolmen sheltered behind upended gravsleds. Riot guns sprayed and the Migs went down.

On another monitor a Mig woman, waving the severed head of a patrolman, lead a vee-formation of resistance fighters into a wedge of patrolmen. The camera flared and went out, but it looked like there were more patrolmen down than Migs.

A third screen showed a static scene at the entrance to

Exotic Section. The lock was barricaded, and patrolmen had blockades set around it. Migs sniped at them from corridor and vent openings.

Sten turned away and poured the drink down. "Clot. Clot. Clot."

"I already said that," Ida noted.

Sten turned to Jorgensen. "Miyitkina."

Jorgensen's eyes glazed. He went into his trance.

"Observe occurrence. Prog."

"Impossible to compute exact percentages. But, overall, unfavorable."

"Details."

"If a revolution, particularly an orchestrated one such as this, is allowed to begin before the proper moment, the following problems will occur: The most highly motivated and skilled resistance men will very likely become casualties, since they will be attacking spontaneously rather than from a given plan; underground collaborators will be blown since it becomes a matter of survival for them to come into the open; since the combat effort cannot be mounted with full effectiveness, the likelihood of the existing regime being able to defeat the revolution, militarily, is almost certain. Examples of the above are—"

"Suspend program," Sten said. "If it's blown, how long does it take to put things back together again?"

"Phraseology uncertain," Jorgensen intoned. "But understood. Repression will be intensified after such a revolution is defeated; reestablishment of revolutionary activity will take an extended period of time. A conservative estimate would be ten to twenty years."

Sten didn't even bother to swear. Just poured himself a drink.

"Sten!" Bet suddenly shouted. "Look. At that screen."

Sten turned. And gaped. The screen she was pointing at was the one fixed on the entrance to the Exotic Section.

"But," he heard Doc say, "those are none of our personnel."

They weren't. "They" were a solid wall of Migs. Unarmed or carrying clubs or improvised stakes. They were charging directly into the concentrated fire of the patrolmen grouped around the entrance. And they died, wave after wave of them.

But they kept coming, crawling over the bodies of their own dead, and, finally, rolling over the defenders. There was no sound, but Sten could well imagine. He saw a boy —no more than ten—come to his feet. He was waving . . . Sten swallowed. Hard. There were still threads of a Sociopatrol uniform clinging to it.

More Migs ran forward, teams with steel benches ripped from work areas. They slammed at the doors to the Exotic Section, and the doors went down.

Jorgensen, still in his battle-computer trance, droned on. ". . . there are, however, examples of spontaneous success. As, for example, the racially deprived citizenry of the city of Johannesburg."

"Two Miyitkina," Sten snapped.

"Ah hae a wee suggestion," Alex said. "Ah suggest we be joinin' our troopies, or yon revolution may be giein' on wi'out us."

Sten stepped through the smashed windows of the rec dome's control capsule and looked down at the faces staring up at him in their thousands. Sweaty, bloody, dirty, and growling.

It made no sense. Militarily. One rocket could take out not only the assembled Mantis team, but all the resistance workers they'd so laboriously trained and recruited over the months.

Clot sense, Sten thought, and flipped the hailer on.

"MEN AND WOMEN OF VULCAN," his voice boomed and echoed around the dome. He assumed that there were still functional security pickups, and he was being seen. He wondered if Thoresen would be able to ID him.

"Free men and women of Vulcan," he corrected himself. He waited for the roar to die. "We came to Vulcan to help you fight for your freedom. But you didn't need our

help. You charged the Company's guns with your bare
hands. And you won.

"But the Company still lives. Lives in The Eye. And
until we can celebrate that victory—in The Eye—we have
won nothing.

"Now is the time . . . Now is the time for us to help
you. Help you make Vulcan free!" Sten chopped the
hailer switch and walked back into the capsule.

Alex nodded approvingly. "Ah, ye can no dance to it,
but Ah gie yer speech a' fair. Now, if we through muckin'
aboot, ye ken we'll shoot away our signal, an' gie on wi'
our real business?"

MYOR YJHH MMUI OERT MMCV CCVX AWLO . . .

Mahoney moved aside and let the Emperor read the
decoded message:

STEP ONE COMPLETE. VULCAN NOW IN COMPLETE INTER-
NAL TURMOIL. BEGINNING STEP TWO.

The Emperor breathed deeply.

"Deploy Guard's First and Second Assault according
to Operation Bravo, colonel."

CHAPTER THIRTY-FIVE

THE BARON STARED at the figure on his screen. Frowned. It was familiar. He tapped keys, and the camera moved in on Sten. Thoresen froze a frame. Studied Sten's face. No. He didn't know him. Thoresen punched the keys ordering the computer to search its memory for a possible ID. With a little luck, it would just be some Mig with a loud mouth and tiny brain. Somehow, Thoresen didn't think it would work out that way.

Ida's model of the Bravo Project lab looked like a gray skinny balloon, half full of water at one end. There wasn't much to study; Ida had still been unable to penetrate security.

The team members and Bet eyed the model morosely. Sten, Alex, and Jorgensen wore, for the first time since they'd been on Vulcan, the Mantis Section phototropic camouflage uniforms. Ida and Bet were fitted into the coveralls of a Tech/1st and /3rd Class.

There wasn't much to say. Nobody was interested in inspirational speeches. They shouldered their packs, silently got into the gravsled, and Sten lifted it off, into the corridors of a Vulcan gone insane.

* * *

Vulcan was quickly collapsing as the Migs took to the streets. Images of pitched battles, looting, and Sociopatrol defeats floated up on the Baron's vidscreen.

The Baron turned the vid off. It was hopeless. There was nothing more he could do to put down the revolt. He would just have to let it burn itself out, then try to put his empire back together again.

A light blinked for attention. Thoresen almost ignored it. Just one more report from a hysterical guard. No, he had to answer. He flicked his computer on.

His heart turned to ice. The computer had identified the Mig leader. Sten. But he was—How?—And then the Baron knew that his world was about to end.

There was only one possibility: Sten; the Guard; Bravo Project. The Emperor knew and the Emperor was responsible for the Mig revolt. Sten was part of a Mantis Section team.

Desperately, Thoresen searched for a way out. What would happen next? How was he supposed to react? That was it— The Emperor was looking for an excuse to land troops. Thoresen was expected to call for help. He would be arrested, Bravo Project uncovered and then . . .

And then Thoresen had it. He would go to the lab. Get the most important files. Destroy the rest and flee. The Baron would still have the Emperor where he wanted him as long as he had the secret to AM_2.

He rose and started for the door. Paused. Something else. Something else. The Emperor would have ordered the lab destroyed. Sten and his team could be on the way now. He hurried to his comvid.

The frightened face of his chief security man came into view. "Sir!"

"I want as many men as you can spare. Here. Now," Thoresen snapped.

The security chief started to gobble.

"Get yourself together, man."

The chief stiffened. "Yes, sir."

He disappeared. Thoresen thought quickly. Was there anything else? Any other precautions? . . . He smiled grimly to himself, opened a desk drawer, and pulled out a small red box. He shoved it into his pocket and raced out the door.

CHAPTER THIRTY-SIX

FRICK AND FRACK arced back and forth, high above the deck of the Bravo Project lab. Hugging the ceiling, they'd gone straight down the entrance corridor, above the security teams.

They hadn't been seen by human eyes. There were, after all, no birds or even rodents on Vulcan. What the human eye doesn't understand, it doesn't see.

The security watch officer eyeballed his fingernails. He'd chewed them to the quick last shift. And he'd systematically racked every patrolman within twenty meters. There wasn't anything to do but sweat and count his problems.

And he had a lot of them. Guarding a lab whose purpose he had no idea of, for openers. Plus the clottin' Migs were going crazy—his best off-shift buddy had been found with a half-meter glass knife through his chest. And now he'd been tagged that Baron Thoresen was on his way down.

The last thing he needed was the computers being as berserk as they were, he thought. He glanced at the screen. Experimentally slammed it with one ham fist. Didn't change things. It still indicated flying objects were inside the lab proper.

The watch officer wondered why he'd taken the Company's job. He could have been very comfortable staying on as head of secret police on his homeworld. He looked up at the two Techs trundling down the corridor. 'Bout clottin' time, he decided.

The beefy first-class Tech swaggered into his office and lifted a lip. Clottin' joy, the watch officer thought. I gotta get a deesldyke. All I need now is hemorrhoids.

He smiled sympathetically at the poor third-class Tech behind Ida. Poor kid, he thought. Shows you. Bet that first-class clot tried somethin', an' her assistant didn't go for it, so the dyke makes her lug the toolboxes.

" 'Bout what I'd expect," Ida snarled. "Computer cracks up, an' all you can do is sit there puttin' your thumbs up your nose." She turned to Bet. "Men!"

The watch officer decided it was going to be a very long shift. He tried to keep it formal. "We're getting readouts," he began.

"I know what you're gettin'," Ida said. "We got terminals too." She eyed the watch officer. "I tol' you, kid, it'd turn out to be somethin' simple."

"What do you mean?" the security officer asked.

"That bracelet. You hang that much alloy near a terminal, it's gonna get crazy. Figures."

"But that's the automatic screen. We've always worn them. And nothin's happened before."

"Yah. An' those clottin' Migs haven't tied up the computers before either. You tellin' me every one a' you patrol geeks wears them?"

"Yes."

"Dumb, dumber, dumbest. Get 'em out here."

"Huh?"

"Everybody on the shift, stupid. Maybe this one'll be easy, an' the only problem is somebody's got a bracelet that's signaling wrong."

"We can't call in every patrolman," the watch officer started. Ida shrugged.

"So great. Me an' cutie here'll go on back and file that we couldn't properly evaluate the situation. Sooner or later somebody else'll come around and try to fix that computer."

The officer eyed the screen. The flying objects were still there. Looked at the third-class Tech, who slipped him a sympathetic and very warm smile. Made a decision. Turned to the com and keyed it open.

"Third shift—no emergency—all officers report immediately to central security. I repeat, all officers report immediately to central security."

Bet slipped two bester grenades from her pouch and stood up. Bravo Project's security officers were crowded inside the small office. Ida stood near the door.

"This everybody?"

The watch officer nodded.

Bet hit the timer on the grenades and dived for the door. She landed on top of Ida.

The two grenades detonated in a purple flash.

The Bravo Project patrolmen crumpled. Bet rolled off Ida and helped her up. Ida wheezed gently, muttered something in Romany, and shrilly whistled between her fingers.

Sten and the other members of the team hurried into sight, running toward them.

"We'll hold the back door. You stand by." Ida stepped inside and lifted the toolbox tray, extracted two folding-stocked willyguns, readied them, and tossed one to Bet as Sten and the others ran into the Bravo Project lab.

Meanwhile, Ida had turned the watch commander over. "What're you doing?" Bet asked curiously.

"Private revenge," Ida replied, planting one hoof firmly in the unconscious man's groin. "I suspect he thought nasty things about me."

She lifted her other foot off the ground. Bet winced and turned back to look down the long empty corridor.

"Wouldnae it be simpler," Alex suggested, "to just blow th' whole shebeen?"

"Clot, yes," Sten said. "But if we did"—he gestured

up to the ceiling—"we'd be soyasteaking all those Techs up there." He grinned. "Damfino why I'm stickin' up for 'em."

"Because," Doc said, "mission instructions were to obliterate this lab with minimum loss of life." He waggled tendrils at Alex. "Ignore him. Simple minds find simple solutions."

Alex ignored Doc. "Ah gie ye pocket-size destruction, i' ye'll tell me where Ah begin."

The lab ceiling lofted high above them. High enough, Sten decided, for the hangarlike building to have its own weather. Frick and Frack curvetted among the ceiling lights. In the middle of the lab was a small space freighter, its cargo doors agape. Mysterious apparatus sat around it on the main floor. Doors opened off the sides into rabbit warrens of minor labs.

"Set charges on any information storage file," Sten decided. "Any computer. And any piece of equipment that doesn't look familiar."

"Finest kind," Jorgensen moaned as he shouldered back into his pack. "That means he's gonna shoot anything that don't look like a sheep."

Alex wagged a finger. "Frae yon teddy bear Ah take abuse a' that nature. But no frae a man wi' his feet still i' the furrows."

And they went to work.

Thoresen, in spite of his fascination with weaponry and martial arts, had never been in combat. Nevertheless, as he entered the corridors that led to Bravo Project, he had sense enough to drop back and put two squads of the fifty-strong patrol company in front of him. Thoresen was still analytical enough to realize he was in a response situation. He might, he considered as he unobtrusively dropped back in the formation, still be running late.

Bet wiped sweaty hands on the plastic willygun stock. "Deep breaths," Ida said calmly. "Worry about them ten at a time." She suddenly realized what she'd said, and chuckled. "On the other hand, do you think a surrender flag would be a better idea? Now!"

Bet pulled the willygun's trigger all the way back. The gun spat AM$_2$ slugs out into the packed mass of oncoming patrolmen.

Screams. Chaos. Ida thumbed a grenade and overarmed it down the corridor, then crawled under the deck plating as riot guns roared.

Bet dropped the empty tube from her gun and slammed a new one home. She was mildly surprised that she wasn't as scared as she'd been watching the patrolmen come in. "Ida!"

"Go," the heavy woman said, without taking her eyes off the corridor. She squeezed the trigger.

"If I was with Delinqs," Bet managed, "I'd say the time has come to haul butt."

"But you ain't. You're with a big-time Mantis Section team. So what we're gonna do is haul butt."

Ida rolled out the door, finger locked on the trigger, then through the entrance to the labs. Bet slid after her. The two women turned, and sprayed down the corridor, then dashed toward the main lab.

Alex sang softly to himself as he unspooled the backup firing-circuit wire back toward the center of the lab.

"Ye'll set on his white hause-bane,
An I'll pike out his bonny blue een;
Wi' ae lock o' his gowden hair.
We'll theek our nest when it goes bare . . ."

Clipped the wire and fed it into the det box. Ran his firing circuitry through his mind, and glanced at Sten. Sten high-signed him, and Alex closed the det key.

"Ye ken we best be on our way. An hour an' yon labs'll be a mite loud for comfort."

Then Ida and Bet doubled into the room. Ida crouched next to the door and sprayed down the corridor.

"The patrol," Bet shouted. Slugs spattered through the lab doors, and the team members went flat, scuttling for

cover. Ida emptied her magazine and scrambled toward the
ship.

The team formed a semicircle perimeter just before the
freighter. Sten ducked behind a large machine resembling
a drill press as the first of Thoresen's troops burst into the
lab.

"Can you stop the charges?" Sten shouted.

Alex cut down the patrolmen inside the lab, then said
calmly, without turning his head, "Ah may've outsmarted
mesel' on this one, lad. Each an' every one a' those
charges I fitted a antidefuse device to."

"Sixty minutes?"

"We hae"—Alex checked his watch—"nae more'n fifty-
one now."

Tacships, darting in front of the Guard's assault transport, hammered through the drifting security satellites off
Vulcan, not knowing that Bet's massacre of the Creche
workers meant most of them were unmanned.

Monitors moved straight for Vulcan. Over the past
months, Thoresen had acquired some moderately forbidden
antimissile devices and installed them in blisters on Vulcan's outer skin. The combination of the Guard's sudden
attack and the half-trained status of their crews, however,
meant only a few went into action before the monitors'
own missiles wiped the positions out.

Obviously the normal canister-dispersing assault transports couldn't be used. Conventional freighters had been
laboriously modified for clamshell-nose loading and un-
loading. Proximity detectors clacked, braking rockets shuddered the transports down to a few kilometers per hour,
then still slower as the pilots dived out of the control positions, sealing locks behind them as the transports crashed
through Vulcan's outer skin, half burying themselves into
the world.

The noses dumped away, and suited guardsmen spilled
out. There was little resistance. None of the patrolmen
inside had realized what could happen in time to suit up.

The Guard smoothly broke down into small, self-contained attack squads and moved out. Behind them moved their semiportable maser support units and, around the ships, combat engineers went into action, closing off the vents in the outer skin.

Resistance, compared to the Guard's usual opposition, was light. The Sociopatrolmen may have thought themselves elite thugs, but, as they discovered, there was a monstrous difference between larruping unarmed workers or crudely armed resistance fighters and facing skilled, combat-experienced guardsmen.

Mercenaries make rotten heroes, Thoresen decided as he watched the Sociopatrol officer wave his squad forward. About half of them huddled even closer behind the improvised barricades Thoresen had ordered set up just inside the lab's entrance. The other half reluctantly came to their feet and moved forward.

The Mantis troopers across the room opened fire. The fastest-moving patrolman made it three meters before legs exploded and he sprawled on the bodies of previous waves.

The accountant part of Thoresen's brain shuddered at the tab. They have five men—Thoresen hadn't seen Frick and Frack, sheltered high above him on a beam—we came in with almost seventy. They've taken no casualties, and we've lost *thirty* patrolmen?

The com at his belt buzzed. Thoresen lifted it. He listened, then hastily muted the speaker. Slowly going white as anger washed over him. Mostly at himself. He had assumed the Emperor wouldn't move in without some pretext, but the panicked communications center Tech had notified him that the guardsmen were already in. Including the rebels' sectors, almost a third of Vulcan was taken.

Thoresen slithered backward to the patrol officer. "We'll need more men," he said. "I'll coordinate them from the security office." The wall above his head exploded as he snaked his way out of the lab into the corridor.

He got up and ran down the corridor toward the end. Stopped and took the tiny red control unit from his pocket, touched the fingerprint-keyed lock, and opened the unit. He tapped .15 onto the screen and closed the circuit, then forced himself to calmness as he walked away from the Bravo Project labs. A gravsled waited for him. "The Eye," he ordered, and the sled lifted.

Behind him, under the floor of the lab's main controls, the timer started on Thoresen's own Doomsday Device—a limited-yield single megaton atomic device that would obliterate the entire project lab and give Thoresen his only chance at remaining alive.

Ida raked fire across the patrolmen's barricades and grunted.

"Alex. You realize that if we stay pinned down and your charges go off, I'll never take you drinking again."

Alex wasn't paying attention. His eyes were locked on one of the instruments from his demopack. "Sten. We hae worse problems tha' the charges Ah set. Ah hae signs a' some nuclear device's running."

Sten blinked. "But where? Who set it?"

"Ah dinnae. But best we find it. Mah name's Kilgour, nae Ground Zero." He set the detector to directional, and swept its pickup around the room. "Ah, tha's so fine. Yon bomb's right across there." He waved across fifty meters of open space toward the central controls.

"Gie us some interestin' thoughts," he said. "Firs', we manage t'gae 'crost that open space wi'out gettin' dead. An' then Ah hae the sheer fun a' tryin' a' defuse it, wi'out knowin' when it's gonna go."

"Mad minute!" Sten used the aeons-old shout, and the team opened fire, spraying rounds at the barricades.

Alex grabbed his pack and rolled to his feet. Running, zig-zag. Riot shells crashed around him.

"Over there!"

Jorgensen elbowed out of cover and sprayed the patrolman shooting at Alex. Exposed for only a moment, and the patrol officer fired. The riot round armed and exploded halfway across the lab, and barbed flechettes whined out.

Jorgensen's shoulder and arm were momentary pin-cushions, then the flechettes exploded. The Mantis troopers stopped shooting momentarily, but discipline took over, and they continued mad-minute fire. Sten watched Alex as he ripped the meter-wide floorplates up and slid down belowdeck.

"Our broodmate, almost. Yes he—" and Frick and Frack launched themselves from the dome. Frack armed one of her tiny wingbombs and folded her wings.

Plummeting in a vertical dive, she and Frick made no attempt to release. They died instantly as their tiny bodies slammed into the patrol officer. Then the bombs went off. The officer became a fireball, and shrapnel sliced through the squad crouched beside him.

Sten saw Doc crawl from his hiding place near Jorgensen's body and move toward the dead man's willygun. The small panda awkwardly turned the willygun toward the barricades, then staggered up with the crushing—to him—weight. One hand pulled the trigger back and held it until the magazine went empty. More shock. *Doc* really isn't . . .

Sten swept his sights over the barricade, and blew off the arm of a momentarily exposed patrolman. As the man reared up, screaming, Bet finished him.

Alex knelt beside the nuclear device under the floor-panels. Ah ken on'y hope, he thought, the amat'oors who built this lashup hae some respect f'r betters an gie some shieldin'. Ah c'd build a better A bomb then this be wi' a crushin' hangover an' mah teeth, he thought.

The bomb was an idiot-simple device. A metal ball covered with what resembled modeling clay. Small, directional blasting charges studded the surface, hooked to a radio pickup and what Alex assumed was a timer.

He started to yank the wires off, then squinted. There were extra wires he didn't see any purpose for. Booby traps, he decided.

Thin, he thought, we'll gae the hard way. And began gently lifting each blasting charge out of its slot. Ah wonder how many ae these Ah'll yank out afore this wee bomb blows? He wiped sweat away.

The driver pushed the sled wide open, and he and Thoresen ducked behind its shield. The sled flashed down the corridor, and the Mig resistance fighters ducked. They spun, and the few with riot weapons opened up.

Far too late as the sled banked around the corridor and out of sight.

Thoresen looked up. Ahead of him was the entrance to The Eye. He sighed in relief—It was still held by a detachment of Sociopatrolmen.

"Ah hae it! Ah hae it!"

Sten saw, out of the corner of his eye, Alex's rotund form bounce out of the below-floor space and bound across the open area. He dived and skidded across the last five meters into shelter. "Yon wee beastie's safe'n mah gran," he said.

"Leaving us only one problem."

"Aye," Alex said. "Figurin' how we haul butt afore we're hoist wi' our own petard."

At least fifteen patrolmen were stubbornly holding behind the barricades. "I don't think," Ida said, "they'd be much interested in a mutual truce."

"Correct," Doc added gloomily. "Prediction: Since they've been cut up so badly, they'll assume we're bluffing." He ran another few rounds through the willygun that Sten had wedged into position for him. "Kilgour. You realize this is all your fault. Now I'll never be able to have my own practice."

"Nae tha's an advantage Ah no considered," Alex managed. "Tae many bloodybones aroun' as 'tis."

Bet shook her head in disbelief.

"Ida," Sten said suddenly. "Come on. Alex. We're going to try a superbluff. Flank 'em if they go for it."

Ida rippled to her feet, and the two dodged out, toward

the freighter's lock. Puzzled, Alex, Bet, and Doc opened up with covering fire.

Sten wedged the flare to the freighter's control room window, and shoved the portable com into his coveralls. "You think they'll believe it?"

Ida lifted her hands helplessly. "Rom don't believe in death songs. So we might as well go out trying."

Sten checked his watch. Alex's charges had only ten minutes to go. He and Ida hurried to the lock and began firing at the patrolmen. Alex, momentarily unobserved, sidled out of the Mantis Section's improvised fort toward the patrolmen's flank.

The patrolman waited. Sooner or later, one of them would show himself. Sooner or later . . . he jerked as what looked to be an explosion flared across the lab in the freighter's control room. Wild shot, he guessed. Then the freighter's external speakers blossomed out of their compartments and crackled to life. A siren warbled up and down its range and a metallic voice announced: "Two-minute blast warning, two-minute blast warning. All units clear blast area. Repeat, all units clear blast area . . ."

For the first time the patrolman realized the exhaust nozzles of the freighter were aimed almost directly at him. He didn't know what to do.

"Must've hit the computer," the man beside him muttered.

"What happens if it fires?" the patrolman managed.

"We fry," his companion said.

Sten coughed, then touched the transmit button on the portable com. Ida had linked it directly into the freighter's broadcast net. He tried to sound as much like a computer as possible.

"This is a thirty-second warning, thirty-second warning. Override. Thirty seconds from out-of-sequence computer lobe. All units, thirty-second correct transmission. Time to blast now fifteen seconds . . ."

The near-panicked patrolmen didn't see Alex break cover. Even if they had, assuming normal human reactions, they would not have had time to stop the high-gee trooper's charge.

Alex dived as he came over the barricade. The first patrolman he hit died with a crushed skull. Alex let the body cushion him while he rolled, feet lashing out, smashing through the stomach walls of two men.

He was on his feet, one-handed swinging the body of the second man like a meaty club.

Sten and Ida came up, offhanded aiming, firing. Sten gaped as Alex tore the head off another patrolman, then disappeared.

The two troopers ran for the barricades. Screams. Then silence, and two patrolmen broke, running for the exit. Alex jumped to the top of the barricade, picked up a three-meter-long steel work bench and hurled it like a spear.

It crunched into the two men, smashing their spines. Doc and Bet darted across the room. "I would suggest," the panda managed as he passed them, "we avoid the usual imbecile human congratulations. We have four minutes."

The four Mantis troopers and Bet sprinted down the corridor. Sten slammed the emergency panels as they went down the corridor. Hoping that would be enough.

The charges went just as Alex said they would. Sten, Bet, and Alex stared at the intestine-shaped lab through a port in the main passage. Ida held Doc. Light winked, winked, and again. They felt a low rumble through the plates under their feet. Then Bravo Project blew. The shaped charges blew out and down, ripping the floor and supply sections out of the lab like it was a fish being gutted.

Sten thought suddenly, "That's what The Row must've looked like."

The rumble crescendoed, and emergency alarms clanged. Debris cascaded out the bottom of the lab into space. But the top section, the Tech's housing, was still intact.

Ida and Doc looked at Alex. "Ah'm a wee bit disappointed," he said, not meaning a word of it. "I nae counted a' that sympathetic second blast. It whidny be hon'rable to say Ah done that."

And then Bet noticed Sten was gone.

CHAPTER THIRTY-SEVEN

IT WAS DONE. All traces of Bravo Project eliminated in the explosion. For the first time in hours, Thoresen felt safe.

He poured himself a celebratory drink. Odd, he thought. His dream lay in shambles, but he still felt elated. He'd beaten the Emperor after all. All he had to do was wait for Guard officers to come through his door, thank them for rescuing him from the Migs, and put himself in their hands.

What could the Emperor do? Put him on trial? For what? There was no evidence. Besides, Thoresen thought, the Emperor would be reluctant to admit publicly that an alternative to his AM2 monopoly might exist.

Thoresen would probably have to accept a lesser position in the Company's leadership. He shrugged. It would take a few years, but he would be back up on top again. And then they'd see. They'd all see.

Suddenly, Thoresen realized he was quite mad. He laughed. What a strange thing to realize about yourself. It was like being another person on the outside, watching yourself, taking note of thoughts and actions. And examining them like a Tech observing a microbe. Something crawled at the back of his brain. Was Sten really dead? That explosion? It wasn't quite what he expected. Different, somehow. Thoresen found himself wishing Sten were alive. His fingers curled, imagining them crushing into the soft Mig throat. Sten, he thought. Sten. Come to me.

There was a sound behind him. Thoresen smiled to himself and turned.

Sten was a few meters away and padding softly toward him. A knife glittering in his hand.

"Thank you," Thoresen said, "for being so prompt."

Sten hesitated. Puzzled.

"You know me?"

"Yes. Intimately. I killed your family."

Sten was on him in a rush, knife hand blurring at his throat. Thoresen dodged, gasping slightly as the knife point touched a shoulder, leaving a trail of blood. He kicked sideways and felt a crawl of pleasure as he heard the dry snap of Sten's wrist breaking. The knife went flying and disappeared in the grass.

Sten ignored the pain, twisted to avoid a blow, and struck out with his good hand. Fingers clawing Thoresen's face. And Thoresen was backing away from him. Sten went into a crouch, anticipating a charge. Then he realized that the Baron wasn't coming at him. Behind him, a few meters away, was the arms collection. Thoresen was going for a gun.

Sten sprinted for the wall, hands closing on an ancient blunderbuss as Thoresen reached his choice—Sten realized realized was a pirated willygun—and opened fiire. Sten dove to the ground, whipped the shotgun up. Fired. The charge ripped into the overhead dome lighting. Darkness. And he was rolling over and over again as the AM2 bullets stabbed through the darkness, searching for him.

He crawled behind a tree. Chunks of earth and wood exploded around him. Then silence. Sten listened. He heard a slight rustling as Thoresen moved in the darkness. Sten thought he was coming toward him. Gathered himself for a leap.

A click. A long rasp. And Thoresen opened the cages.

The tigers came out of the cage running. Two huge mutated gray Bengals. Growling softly. Lashing their tails.

Thoresen punched a control button. A tingling in their collars, and they turned, then moved swiftly away from him.

Sten moved through the brush. Where was Thoresen? Why didn't he come? A rustling behind him. Soft padding. Sten whirled as the tiger charged. Bounding. Then a huge leap, straight at him.

He dropped backward, bringing his feet together and —straight up with all his strength. They connected, and the tiger went flying over him. Landing, convulsing. Tried to get up, then went down. Dead, its throat crushed by Sten's kick.

Sten came to his feet, fighting back the pain in his useless wrist. Sickness crawled in his stomach. Then. Over there! A sound. Thoresen, he was sure.

The dome lights came on. Sten was frozen for a moment, blinded by the glare. Then he dived for cover as the willygun opened up. He was behind another tree. How many shots? He hadn't heard Thoresen reload. He had to be getting low on ammunition. Sten looked around wildly, searching for a weapon.

The tiger stood there, lashing its tail. Gathering itself for a leap. Then it screamed to freeze him in place.

Sten forced himself to laugh, a wild almost hysterical giggle.

"I got the other one, Thoresen," he shouted.

The Baron opened up with the willygun. Catching the tiger just as it jumped for Sten. It turned end over end, and crashed to the ground, dead. Thoresen kept firing. And then there was a dry clacking sound as the gun was empty. Sten charged from the brush.

Thoresen saw him, searched desperately for another magazine. Nothing. He moved back quickly—grabbing for the first weapon he could find. The saber blade rasped as he pulled it off the wall and slashed.

Sten grunted in pain as the tip of the blade grated across ribs. He dodged the backhand stroke, grabbed for a weapon. Any weapon.

The rapier flashed up as Thoresen struck. A loud

clang as the blades met. Sten twisted his wrist slightly, almost in reflex, and the saber slid off. He lunged forward, felt the tip hit the softness that was Thoresen, and then the blade was almost ripped away as Thoresen parried. Sten dropped back.

He flexed the thin foil. Trying to come up with the right hold. Then thought of a knife, loosened his grip. Thoresen took a step forward, smiling and whipping the saber blade back and forth.

Not a chance, Sten thought. The saber Thoresen held was too powerful and fully edged. Sten was fighting with just a slim piece of pointed steel. Flexible steel. Sten suddenly realized there might be an advantage. The flexibility. No matter how hard Thoresen struck, he could turn the blade away.

And Thoresen struck. The blades met. The rapier was like a snake as it twisted around the saber, using the force of the stroke to turn it away. And Sten lunged forward, felt his point find flesh, heard Thoresen moan as it slipped through.

Sten stepped back just as the saber ripped at him. Pause. Thoresen stood before him, panting and leaking blood from several wounds. But seemingly unfazed.

He charged forward, slashing hard. Sten tried to parry, but the blade foil slipped, and he felt the saber cut deep into his arm, then the limb twisted away, out of range.

Thoresen knew he had Sten now. The way the rapier point dropped, he was sure his last cut had made Sten's fighting arm useless. Like the other.

He stepped toward him, slashing down. Missing as Sten parried the blade, but still leaving an opening. And Thoresen began the backhanded swing that would decapitate Sten.

Screamed in agony as the rapier point speared into his elbow. The saber fell and Thoresen grabbed desperately, his fingers closing on steel. He ripped the foil away while feeling the flesh of his fingers turn to raw meat.

The Baron struck out with his good hand, the palm a knife edge, aiming for Sten's collarbone. He felt bone give and struck again. But Sten blocked the blow and fell back, one arm dangling. He was trying to keep his footing.

Thoresen threw another punch and Sten knew horrible agony as he caught the blow on his useless arm. He speared out hard, fingers like a blunt blade. Feeling Thoresen's ribs snap like dry wood. He stepped back quickly, to avoid a counterblow, but tripped to one knee. And Thoresen was on him, hand cracking down for Sten's neck.

Sten struck up with all his strength. Below the ribs. Bone giving again. Giving. Giving. Soft wetness.

Thoresen screamed in pain.

—Sten ripped the heart from his chest.

For an awful frozen moment Thoresen stared at Sten. And then he was falling.

Sten looked numbly at the dripping heart in his fist. Then down at the Baron's body. He turned, and threw the fibrillating organ far into the brush, where the tigers lay.

Unexpectedly, he heard a shout and peered up. A shadowy figure was rushing toward him. He tried to strike out at it.

Bet caught him in her arms. Lowered him unconscious to the ground.

CHAPTER THIRTY-EIGHT

THE EMPEROR'S FACE was stone. Cold. Mahoney stood before him, frozen to attention.

"All traces of the AM2 have been destroyed?"

"Yessir!"

"And Vulcan under a new government?"

"Yessir!"

"And Thoresen?"

"Uh . . . dead, sir."

"I see. I thought I ordered him taken alive?"

"You did, sir!"

"Then why weren't my orders obeyed?"

"No excuse, sir."

"No excuses? That's all you can say, no excuses?"

"None at all, sir."

Mahoney loomed over Sten, who was trying his best to stand at attention. Very difficult when you are head-to-toe in a hospital L5 system.

"I just came from the Emperor."

Sten waited.

"He had some rather loud comments to make. Specifically, trooper, the small matter of direct disobedience to orders. Imperial orders."

Sten imagined that he did, took a mental deep breath and prepared for the worst. Execution, probably.

"Do you have anything to say for yourself, lieutenant?"

Sten did. But thought better of it. Why waste his breath? He was already a condemned man . . .

"I'm waiting, lieutenant."

"Uh, begging your pardon, sir," Sten croaked. "But you just called me lieutenant."

Mahoney laughed, then sat on the edge of the hospital bed. "A direct commission from the Emperor himself, lad." He reached into his tunic and pulled out a pair of small silver bars. And Sten's knife. He laid them on the bed.

Sten was sure he was either dreaming or Mahoney was mad, or both. "But, I thought I, uh . . ."

"The boss man was happier than a piece of beef snuggled up to a hot cabbage," Mahoney said. "He'd had second thoughts about those orders. But there wasn't time to get to you."

"He wanted Thoresen killed?"

"In the worst way. Saved a lot of explanations."

"Yeah, but a commission," Sten said. "I'm not the officer type."

"I couldn't agree more. But the Emperor thought otherwise. And a good trooper always obeys his commander. Ain't that so, lieutenant?"

Sten grinned. "Almost always, anyway," he said.

Mahoney got up to go.

"What about Bet?"

"Unless you got any objections," Mahoney answered, "she's joining your Mantis team."

Sten had no objections at all.

The Eternal Emperor reverently dusted off the bottle, popped it open, then poured two healthy drinks. Mahoney picked up one. Looked at it suspiciously.

"Scotch again, boss?" he wanted to know.

"Yep. Except this time it's the real stuff."

"Where from?"

"I ain't saying."

Mahoney took a sip. Gagged.

"What the—?"

The Eternal Emperor beamed. Took a big slug. Rolled it around his mouth, savoring it.

"Just right," he said.

Filled up his glass again.

"You took care of everything? On the Sten matter?"

"Just like you said, boss."

The Emperor thought a minute.

"Let me know how he works out. I think that Sten is a boy to watch."

"He sure is, boss. He sure is."

Mahoney forced himself to finish his drink. And then held out his glass for more. In his job, you made sure you always kept the boss happy.

And the Eternal Emperor hated to drink alone.

About the Authors

CRIS BUNCH is a Ranger—and airborne-qualified Vietnam Vet—who's written about phenomena as varied as the Hell's Angels, The Rolling Stones, and Ronald Reagan.

ALLAN COLE grew up in the CIA in odd spots like Okinawa, Cyprus, and Taiwan. He's been a professional chef, investigative reporter, and national news editor of a major West Coast daily paper, winning half a dozen national writing awards in the process.

BUNCH AND COLE, friends since high school, have collaborated on everything from the world's worst pornographic novel to over 30 television scripts. Currently they're story executives for MGM-Television, on the GAVILAN series. This is their first novel.